D1255043

The Gaunt Woman

The Gaunt Woman

By

EDMUND GILLIGAN

NEW YORK

CHARLES SCRIBNER'S SONS

1943

To

CAPTAIN BEN PINE
of Gloucester

The Gaunt Woman

CHAPTER I

THEY TOOK thirty thousand pounds
of halibut out of the *Daniel Webster's* pens before
midnight. By daybreak she lay ready for the
Grand Banks again, stores aboard and all hands
agreed on sailing that very day, except Marty Higgins, who was sick in the belly, and a boy who was
for the Navy. Since this meant laying off a much-
needed dory, every able man in Gloucester had been
buttonholed in the streets or roused from his bed.

Nothing could be done. There wasn't a fisherman to
be had for love or money. The war was drawing men
out of the fishing fleet and taking them to the decks
of destroyers and minesweepers or into the navy
yards. There were hale men of seventy years who
were willing to go, but their wives wouldn't hear of it.
And the younger lads wouldn't think of going fishing
for halibut. Those voyages were too long for them.
Eight or nine weeks of rowing and slaving amidst the
ice and snow seemed a hard way of making a living
to them. They liked the shorter voyages in the drag-
gers, where a man could earn his pay in a week or so
and go ashore for a spell.

Twice during the night, the jolly Lutheran pastor had come down from Boston Bethel with a fine-looking squarehead in tow. They were men who knew well enough how to strike a gaff into a thrashing halibut. They knew the uses of the gob-stick. One look under the old *Daniel's* afterdeck had been enough for those seamen. She had no engine in her to back up her new suit of sails and the sea-going generation had become used to the pounding of a motor while they slept or walked the decks. No one could blame them for turning away, especially when the *Daniel's* voyage lay in waters not well known to them. A hard war was being waged on the Grand Banks and already the great bergs and the ice floes were coming in with the last of winter. So the exiled sailor-men stumped off again, looking down stolidly into the round, earnest face of Pastor Kramer as he passionately argued the unique sailing qualities of the *Daniel*. He puffed his red cheeks and declared she knew the Banks so well that she could sail there by herself. Aye! and come back with a fine stock of fish, if she could only set a trawl singlehanded.

"Are they afraid? Hey, Cap'n Bannon?" Old Mr. Dolan, owner of the *Daniel,* held his hands, pudgy now with 'longshore living, over the little stove in the schooner's neat cabin. He turned his plump, rosy face away from the blazing coals and looked angrily at his young skipper, a hard-bitten Gloucesterman, who was clumsily counting over a pile of dollar bills at his cubby-hole desk. The skipper was a sound chip off an old Gloucester block, a fatter and a taller man than his uncle, Marty Higgins, who had himself taken the *Daniel* to the Grand Banks a hundred times before he fell to ailing and, at last, had to give it up.

Mr. Dolan ran his hand through his shock of silvery hair and repeated his question: "You tell me, Patrick, are them squareheads afraid of something? Have you heard something that might make them scared of signing on for a bit of fishing?"

The skipper didn't look up from his counting.

Mr. Dolan, being a bit deaf on the port side and stone deaf on the other, cupped his left hand up and shouted: "Hey, Cap'n?"

The skipper shoved the money into a cubby-hole and stood up. He kept his red-thatched head bent a little for fear of knocking it against the smoke-blackened beam above him. "All correct," he said to himself, as if he hadn't heard the old man's words.

When he looked down into that worried moon of a face, he laughed gently. "Why, Mr. Dolan, I wouldn't say they're afraid. I never heard of a squarehead being afraid of anything." He picked up a blue reefer from the locker and added: "I know they're not afraid. It's just that the young fellows can't sleep easy on a schooner unless they can hear an engine running night and day. Why, there's sixty of them on that Norway bark near the island and they ran her out of the German Ocean. Took her through hell, I hear. But I'll bet there isn't one aboard her who'd willingly come with us today. A schooner's different."

The old man snorted in disdain. "That's not it, Patrick. Both those men that the Parson brought aboard have been torpedoed. And they won't be for it again. They've heard something bad about the Banks. I know what it is. And you don't. The whole town knows there's something queer going on in the fisheries. But you that's just come off the Banks—you don't know. That's the long and short of it, my young friend."

The skipper swung the reefer over his shoulders and slipped his arms through the sleeves. "I tell you what, Mr. Dolan. I'm going ashore to say good-bye to my mother and bring down some pies and a few loaves of bread. Then I'm sailing. Short-handed or not."

"Hem!" Mr. Dolan took an angry turn on his heel, stamped over to the cabin port and sent a long look out over the harbor. Far away, driving low through a blue, foamy horizon, he saw three destroyers steaming eastward. High above them, her balloon gleaming in the morning sun, an airship glided on her submarine patrol. The old lad groaned and faced his skipper. "Maybe you won't be going at all! Ever think of that, Patrick? Hey? Speak up now!"

Captain Bannon grinned. He knew well enough that the old veteran of the Banks was thinking fondly of his beautiful schooner, a sweet sailer and a good earner. And the next to the last of all the famous halibuters sailing out of Gloucester. For three long generations she had kept the fires burning and the cupboards well-stocked in the mansion on Strawberry Hill. And the old man himself, during the last war, had seen the enemy rise out of the sea and ravage the Gloucester fleet. He had watched schooners burned and dories gunned. The *Daniel* had shown the U-boats a clean pair of heels, but she had once lost a good man, brained by shrapnel on her deck. Twice she had come angrily home all tattered and scarred. No wonder that he could think of tying her up in a safe haven, despite the high price of halibut. So the captain let a solemn look darken his boyish face. He struck his big brown hands together and paid attention.

Mr. Dolan gave a satisfied smile. "Well, Patrick, you'll listen with all due respect?"

"Oh, aye! Sure, I'll listen, Mr. Dolan. No fear of that. I don't forget I'm working for you. But—take my word for it!—I'll bring your vessel home, gunpowder or not. With her pens full." He came nearer to the old man and touched his shoulder gently. "I know the Germans and their dirty tricks. They'll not lay their hands on her. You can trust me."

"You and your wild father before you!" shouted Mr. Dolan. "God rest his iron soul! Didn't he try to ram one of them last time with the *Mary & Martha?* Hey? Tell me that, young Bannon!"

"He did! He did! And damn their guts—he'd have stove her in if there'd been more than a capful of wind to bang him along." He struck his hands together again and gave a quick look of pride at a glassed-in photograph over his cubby-holes. The face that stared out at him was the older image of his own: a full, genial mouth, cheeks beaten in by Grand Banks weather—and all saved from too much thinness by a good-sized nose, fit to snuff out a halibut swimming a hundred fathom down. "But bear in mind, Mr. Dolan, that the *Mary* was his own ship and if he wanted to make war with her—well, 'twas his own affair. Not Gloucester's. Not the insurance company's."

Mr. Dolan held up a hand to signify that the affair of the *Mary & Martha* was past arguing. He then said: "Now, Patrick, you haven't asked me the strange thing I've heard. Why is that?"

"I hear many strange things aboard my vessel in these days, Mr. Dolan. And I see many strange things at sea and expect to see more. So I don't bother my head with every yarn that makes the rounds in Gloucester. But go on. You tell it to me. For I can see you find it important in the conduct of our business."

"I do, Patrick." The old man sat down on the locker, bent himself over to be nearer the stove, and at once cried out that it was a fine state of things he was coming to in his old age. "For I've never heard the like of it, Patrick, and you'll say the same yourself—mark my words!—when I tell it to you."

"Tell it!" said Patrick.

"Now I got this official. Mind you that, Cap'n. I know this to be gospel truth. They—meaning the Navy, of course—were knocking about off Nantucket not a week ago and—by the Lord Harry!—a lookout picks up something a mile or so off the port bow. Right smack under a full moon. Now, let's see, Patrick, when was the moon last full? Hey?"

"Why," answered Patrick, "she was filling up on Wednesday last. Or Thursday. It slips my mind now."

"Say Wednesday. Yes, let's say Wednesday, Patrick. So he—the lookout—slips down to the deck and they cut over that way and—what do you think?"

Patrick stared.

"Yes, sir!" shouted Mr. Dolan, bumping up and down on the locker in his excitement. "A damned, stinking U-boat! Lying there, bold as brass, and charging her batteries under a full moon. Ha!"

"What did they do?"

"Patrick, the destroyer gives them a taste of hell-to-come and before the damned and double-damned

Germans have a chance to say what's-his-name—
why! the game is over! Aye! before they could blow
her bottom out or say what's-his-name, the Navy boys
come down on her and clap them all in irons. Not
two hundred miles away from this very wharf, mind
you."

Patrick shook his head in wonder and admiration.
"Good for them! But what's all this got to do with my
going today to the Grand Banks? Mr. Dolan, there's
no fish I want off Nantucket."

"Ha!" cried the old man, tasting his triumph in ad-
vance. "You wait a bit and see. You'll learn what
rogues they are. What smart devils they are. Then
maybe you'll laugh on the other side of your face,
my perky cock-of-the-walk! Now, will you listen,
Patrick?"

Captain Bannon put on his sober look again. He
thrust his hands deep into his reefer pockets, straddled his long legs comfortably and nodded in a grave
fashion.

"Now, Patrick, as I was saying—the Navy gives
those rascals a clip on the side of their thick heads,
kind of to remind them they weren't in the German
Ocean, and they lay a hawser aboard her and make
up a prize crew to steer the U-boat into the Navy
Yard at Charlestown. So they put two lads at the helm
and get under way quick, it being dark now—what
with moon-set and the wind rising from the East with

rain in it. And now there's a warrant officer was put
aboard to command that boarding party and he
begins messing around in the torpedo compartment
just to make sure that there's no time-bombs all set
to go off and blow the boat to smithereens. Well, happen he kicks over a bucket of waste, left handy by
somebody who'd been polishing up the bright-work.
This warrant officer kicks over the bucket and—sure
as my name is Dolan!—he sees something in said
bucket. He thrusts his hand down and brings that
something up. Now then, my handsome Bannon, I'll
give you three guesses as to what he found therein."

Patrick turned his brightened face upward and let
loose a roar of laughter that made the old man gape.
He leaned forward and put both his hands on Mr.
Dolan's shoulders, just to keep him ballasted in his
place. "I don't need but one guess, old friend. Theatre tickets! That's what the warrant officer found."

The look of story-telling pleasure on the owner's
face changed to dismay. He struggled beneath the
skipper's hands, brushed them off, and jumped to his
feet. "Who told you? Did government tell you on
your way home? Is that what the destroyer captain
boarded you for?"

Patrick shook his head. He was sorry now that he
hadn't let the old lad have his full say. "No, Mr.
Dolan. No, government didn't tell me. And a little
bird didn't tell me, either. Just you go ahead—"

Somebody pounded the deck above their heads. The lamp shook in its brass chains. A voice sang out. Patrick said: "Who's that, do you suppose?"

" 'Tis that hard-working parson back again with another of his unfortunate countrymen. Another Dane that won't go fishing. Let him stand, Cap'n. Let him wait. I want to get to the bottom of this. I had the yarn official. Official, you see?"

A loud voice came cheerily down to them and again the pounding shook the lamp. The skipper turned his face upward and bellowed a word at the skylight. The men on deck fell to silence.

Mr. Dolan somewhat ruefully resumed his stirring tale. He sent a vexed look across the reddening lid of the stove and said: "Well, Patrick, 'tis true. The warrant officer did find theatre tickets in the waste and those tickets had been bought in Boston and used in a Boston theatre. Only three days before! Mind you, now. That's the sort of rascals they are. They come over here and bang away at our innocent seamen and then they tie up somewhere and they go ashore. Walk right up to the window and buy a pair of tickets. And they eat dinner right in front of our people and go to the theatre and sit comfortable, watching them young ladies a-kicking and prancing." He snorted and grumbled. "What in hell's name are we coming to? Bad cess to them! That's what I say. How do I know they're not lurking behind Ten Pound Island this very minute?" He hurried over to the port and took another look across the water, as if he actually believed he might spy a periscope cutting through the harbor.

Patrick said: "I tell you, Mr. Dolan, you needn't worry."

"And why not? Why not? They're up to something on the Banks, too. You're a cool customer, and a smart one, once you start thinking, but—no! They'll steal the *Daniel's* stock of fish, knock you over your rail and blow the schooner out of the water with their blasted bombs. Oh, damn them entirely! It's the same as last time. Only worse. Never thought I'd live to see the day, Patrick. Never!" He turned his ancient, sea-blue eyes up and down the length of his man and, with a little suspicion in his glance, asked, "Who told you about them theatre tickets?"

"I'll tell you, Mr. Dolan. Hear what I say. First place, I don't give a damn if the Banks are crawling with Germans, so long as they don't get snagged up in my trawls or show their bloody noses. We're going fishing!" He lifted his voice to a shout. "Fishing! Hear that, don't you?"

Mr. Dolan nodded.

"Second place," said Patrick, "the story simply isn't true. I heard it first when my father came home from the last war. He told it to me often enough when I was a kid—and he always laughed at it. Now, I'm not saying it couldn't happen, Mr. Dolan. And I'm not saying it didn't happen. It's just sort of tiresome to have an old yarn like that bob up again so soon. With the war still fresh on us. Besides, the Germans themselves started it. Last time and this time. Just to convince people they've got the guts to do something like that. Which they haven't. They're yellow! My father always told me so—and he proved it." He bent down and looked right into the old man's gloomy eyes. "What's the sense of arguing? The war must be won and a good thick halibut steak is a fine thing to win it on. So we're sailing as soon as I come down the hill again. You're going to let us go. You are, aren't you? Say you will."

Mr. Dolan growled, twisted his head this way and that, and growled again. He kept his eyes away from the frosty young ones staring down at him and he gave an odd shake with his head. "Not going to let you go. At least, not short-handed, I won't." He then faced the gaze and cried out: "Yes! Go! Go and come back, you young rogue! Oh, I know what's going on behind those innocent blue eyes of yours. You'd as soon hook off with my schooner if I didn't give you the word. All the same, I believe the story's true this time—I had it official—and I tell you they're close up on us and you've got to keep an eye peeled. That's all I'll say on the matter." He jerked

his thumb upward and added: "Tell the parson to
come below."

Patrick replied: "That's exactly what I was going
to do." He sent a shout booming upward and presently the Lutheran pastor came down into the cabin.
Two seamen followed him.

The pastor cried out in pleasure at the sight of Mr.
Dolan. He pumped the owner's hand eagerly and
said: "Look! Two fine boys I have for your skipper!
One has been on the beach six weeks because his ship
was knocked from under him. Come forward, Conrad. Here he is, Mr. Dolan. Look, Cap'n! Pretty big
boy, eh? Call him Conrad. Ah, I have him well
fed by our countrymen at their hospital and he is
ready to go again. A fine Danish sailor, he is. Shake
hands with your new captain, Conrad. That is
right."

The sailor was nearly as tall as Patrick. He was
bundled up in a hand-me-down Chesterfield coat. A
white scarf lay knotted under his formidable chin.
When he took off his cap, his hair shone like yellow
gold. He gave Mr. Dolan a shy bow and then sized
up Captain Bannon with a quick, sea-going glance.
This done, he smiled a bleak little smile, and turned
his anxious eyes where a good seaman always turns
them under such circumstances—on his cap, twisting
in his long, tough fingers.

He held out his hand when Captain Bannon took a step towards him. The skipper, keeping good hold of the hand, took his time before he returned the sailor's smile. He looked keenly into the high-boned face, marked here and there with white scars of frost. He took a deep dive into the Viking eyes and let his own eyes stay locked in the gaze. The seaman knew well enough what was going on. He stood up to the gaze and waited.

The skipper suddenly turned over the hand he held and examined it closely. "All the frost out of you, Conrad?" he asked, his face still without sign of welcome or friendliness. "Because I see you've been bitten not long ago."

"All out, Captain," answered the sailor. "Toes all right, too." He smiled over the clasped hands and added: "I steer well, Captain. Uncle Klaus—he show me long ago in his yawl."

The skipper gave his nod then and let the sailor's hand drop. "You know where we're going, Conrad? Parson told you? Know the fisheries at all?"

The sailor opened his mouth to speak, but the parson broke in. "Aye, Cap'n! Sure! Conrad knows them. He was just eight days on them in a lifeboat. Torpedoed on them he was by those—by those—oh! the Lord forgive my anger!" He put his hand fondly on the young sailor's shoulder. "Conrad's all right, I tell you, Cap'n. Not like those good-for-nothings I

brought down in the night. He is not afraid of anything. Only I don't say he's been a fisherman." He
spoke quickly in Danish to the sailor, who at once
shook his head. "That's right," said the pastor, "Conrad's never been a fisherman, but he says he can do
it all right."

"I believe he can," said the skipper, "and if he's
for it—well, he's my man. I like his looks." He turned
to Mr. Dolan. "What do you say on that score, Mr.
Dolan? Will he do on the Banks?"

The owner nodded. "A fine lad! Only one thing—
let me ask him one question—" The sailor, tugged
forward by the whispering parson, changed his cap
from one hand to the other and made another school-
boy bow. Mr. Dolan smiled and said: "A mannerly
boy!" He then cried: "Hem!" and added: "You
know, don't you, that you're signing on a sailing vessel? No damn engine down there? Hey?"

"Speak up loud, Conrad," said the pastor.

Conrad opened his big mouth and bellowed: "Aye,
sir! I know. I am glad."

Mr. Dolan settled down on the bench again, then
turned to take a look at the second candidate, a
smaller and a darker man, yet of good size and seamanlike, except that he had been poorly fed lately
and had no flesh to spare. Something had thinned
out his mouth, had given it a sharp, shrewd twist. He
wore an old navy pea-jacket, tied at the top button-

hole with a bit of yellow twine. He had a strange sort of stocking-cap on his head, rummaged out of some chest at Boston Bethel. He slowly pulled the cap off when the parson whispered to him.

"And this man," said the parson, rubbing one hand over the other in satisfaction, "this man is a fisherman. A real fisherman, Cap'n, who is also our countryman. That is right. You call him Holger. He can shake a halibut off a hook and he can drive a dory hard with those arms of his. He, too—he knows them Germans. Knows all their dirty tricks. When he was a boy he fished in German waters and sold fish to them—to their navy vessels—and he can speak their lingo better than he can English. A good man is Holger. Been two years now on the American tankers and come to my house last trip from the Gulf because the stink of oil makes his belly sick. It isn't because they're blowing up so many tankers. Holger's not afraid." He took the man by his hand. "You are a fisherman, Holger? You know what a sailing vessel is like? You are willing to sign on and work for a great captain? That is right?"

"Yes, Parson," replied the sailor. "I know. I can steer her. I will work hard. I kill halibut once—he weigh two hundred pound." He then looked, in a beseeching fashion, at the skipper, who thereupon stretched out his hand and said: "Glad to see you aboard, Holger."

"Glad to be aboard, Cap'n," said the sailor. He touched his forehead smartly.

Captain Bannon turned to the parson. "You've seen their papers? All in order there?"

The parson laughed happily. "All in order, Cap'n. No fear on that score. Conrad here—for him I had to get some new ones because he lost all—lost all when his ship went down. But he is known to me through his uncle and by other things. And Holger— Holger has his papers all O.K. Only I keep them here for them. Yes." He spread out a handful of papers on the locker, seaman's tickets and Danish certificates and their first citizenship papers.

The captain looked at them, holding each one up nearer to the light. When he nodded and put the papers down, the parson put his finishing touch to the business. "You are taking both my boys, Cap'n Bannon?"

"I am—and thank you, Parson."

"That is good. Then I will be spared the trouble of taking them to that *Golden Hind*. She's for New-foundland today, short-handed or not."

"And what's the matter with the *Golden Hind*, Parson?" cried old Dolan. "Except that she's got a stinking engine in her and tanks of oil where good fish ought to be?"

"Two things, Mr. Dolan," answered the parson promptly. He held up two fingers of his left hand and began to count off the charges. "The food is not so good as it is here—and I tell you my fine boys need beef and plenty of it just now. And I know you got it aboard. I see it and legs of lamb and crates of fresh, brown eggs. Ah!" He touched the second finger. "That is one thing, Mr. Dolan. Second thing—there's a woman aboard the *Golden Hind* this trip and that is bad luck on the fisheries. It is worse than a bucket upside down." He waved his hand at the two sailors and said: "I do not wish any more bad luck for my good boys. No, please God!"

"A woman aboard!" shouted Captain Bannon. "Aboard the *Golden Hind?* Why, you're wrong there, Parson. The skipper of the *Golden Hind* hasn't a woman to his name. No—and never will have."

"Therefore," chimed in old Dolan, "you're foundering in error, Parson, and I'm terribly sorry to find you so. Patrick is right. No woman could possibly look twice at Bart Delaney. His mug's too ugly." He rose from his place and pulled his coat about him. "I'll say good-bye now, Patrick. A quick voyage and a safe one and the blessing of God on you. Don't ram anything—unless it's a two-hundred pound halibut. And bear in mind that whites are bringing twenty cents at the Boston Fish Pier." He shook the captain's hand and gave the new men a kindly thump apiece. "Take them up forward, Parson, and have them see

the cook. The tide's about to serve and they'll be going out on it."

On his way home, Captain Bannon stopped at the
head of Ben Pine's busy wharf and looked down at
the *Golden Hind.* He searched her gear-cluttered deck
for a sign of the woman passenger, it being a curious
thing that the parson had said and hard to believe.
There wasn't even a man stirring on her, not to men-
tion a woman. He heard voices in her forecastle and
he hailed her loudly, but there was no answer, only a
noisier burst of wrangling and laughter.

He returned an hour later, on his arm a covered
basket, full of brown and white loaves and apple pies
from his mother's oven, who knew well enough how
to make a halibuter's heart bear up in the long days.
His mother had no word of a woman sailing on the
Hind; indeed, she wouldn't believe the parson's story
for a minute.

This time, however, Patrick found that it was so.
The woman passenger was standing on the deck of
the *Golden Hind.* It was no woman, indeed, but a
strapping girl, done up in sea-going style with a reefer
like his own, thick trousers of blue woolen, and a pair
of somebody's old rubber hip-boots. Her head was
bare to the wind and the long down-sweep of her red
hair shone in the cold sunlight like burnished copper.

Patrick stood and stared at her bending body. Her

back was turned to him and he had his full of staring
while she unlashed a big bundle of oilskins, good yellow stuff, fit for the Banks and Banks weather. He
turned away, shaking his head in wonder. He knew
every good-looking girl ashore—or thought he did—
and it puzzled him hard that here, before his wondering eyes, was a big Gloucester girl, so much at home
on the deck of a schooner that she moved about like
an old hand. He turned his head once more to see if
he could catch a glimpse of her face, though he was
sure enough that it was a fine-looking one.

He saw her looking after him. And a pretty scowl
she showed, as if the cut of his jib was far from her
liking. Her eyes were gray as the sky overhead, but
they were rapidly being overcast by a black anger
inside her. Her mouth might possibly have been
sweet, because the lips were good, full ones, but just
now her pout made the mouth nothing but a storm
warning.

She put her bare hands on her hips and kept looking angrily up at him. She spoke. The words came
sharply after him like the cry of gulls. "Now, say that
you don't know me! Go on! You that used to wait
outside of church for me."

Patrick put down his basket with care. He took
three long strides back towards the *Golden Hind.*

The girl stepped forward to the *Hind's* rail and
waited, her handsome face upturned. Her eyes stayed

dark, just the same, dark as the fine curve of the lashes over them.

He took in his breath sharply and did well to hide his surprise from her. He knew her well enough. Even a sailor doesn't forget a mouth like that, though it be a score of years since he saw it, not just six. Or was it only five? He caught on so quick that a deep flush ran up under his cheeks, making the sea red of them change to the hue of bricks. He touched his cap politely and said: "Oh!"

She wouldn't leave off staring. Nor would he. He made a good pretence of sizing her up. He cocked his head this way and that. He measured her, scratched his red thatch in a studying sort of way, and put on a puzzled look. "What was that you said, ma'am?"

"Ah!" she cried, making herself even more terrible with her wrath. "Ah, you villain of a Bannon! Has that owner of yours taught you how to play deaf?"

"Why, no, ma'am," replied Patrick. "No owner can teach me anything. Anybody that knows my name, knows that." He smiled in his gallantest fashion and asked: "What was that you said about a church, ma'am? And how do you happen to know my name, please? Of course," he added comfortably, "I'm well-known to all the people of Cape Ann, but to have a perfect stranger hailing me from a deck— that is, indeed, remarkable."

Her lips moved silently, no doubt in a shrewish

word. She gave him one last destructive look, drove it home with a who-are-you-anyway glance, and turned back to her pile of oil clothing. She held up a broad sou'wester and pulled it down over her head. She threw it off and took up a slicker, stiff and creased from being bundled tight. She gave it a shake and then sang out clearly: "These will do fine, Uncle Bart. They're all right."

A voice answered her briefly from below.

Patrick had decided, by this time, that perhaps he could make the required sacrifice. The mouth alone was worth it. He tenderly lifted the napkin that covered his basket. A crusty fragrance of fresh bread and an intoxicating odor of cinammon in apple juice charmed his magnificent nose. He sniffed and sighed and then, widening his nostrils, he snuffed deeply. He sighed again and drew the napkin back into place.

"No!" he whispered, "I can't do it. She's more beautiful than ever, but love—even for a strawberry blonde—must stop somewhere." He slipped his basket back onto his arm and stood up.

He strode away and began to whistle blithely. He loudly answered a hail from a Lunenberg vessel that had just tied up next to his own. It was then, above the rattle of gear and engines turning over, that he heard her sing out again. The sweetness of her voice made him infirm in purpose. His stride faltered. But his mouth watered like rain and he hugged his basket to him. Yet, without daring to look backward, he could see a fine pair of gray eyes going dark in anger and he saw a mouth that might possibly be as sweet as it once was, happen he could ever make it smile at him. He swung around, marched back to the *Golden Hind,* and jumped lightly down to her deck, basket and all.

The girl turned swiftly at the thumping sound of his boots and faced him in scornful silence. He humbly touched his cap and said: "Bannon, the baker's boy. Let's see, ma'am, what was it you ordered? One apple pie?" He pulled back the napkin. The delicious fragrance drifted by his nose and was wafted to her. "One apple pie, wasn't it, ma'am?"

"Two!" said the strawberry villain.

"Ah!" said he, "I must have come to the wrong vessel." He looked around in landlubberly speculation. "Why, of course, I've made a mistake. This is that *Golden Hind.* The men don't eat apple pies and home-made bread on this vessel." He shut up his basket. "I thought it was the *Daniel Webster.* Can you tell me, please, where she's lying?"

"No!" The girl stamped her foot on the deck. This did her no good at all because her boots were thick and no angry sound came from her stamping. "No, Patrick Bannon, but I'll tell you that you're lying.

There! And if you don't give me two apple pies and a welcome kiss home—why! I'll order you off the vessel. Put an end to your fooling now, will you?"

Patrick stopped his fooling. He didn't look up from his basket and he didn't say anything until he had laid out two of the pies and three loaves of bread. He stood up then and looked at her squarely. She was peaceful now, but remained a perfect, absolute danger.

He said: "There are the pies, Margaret MacLean, and I'm sorry about the fooling. But I won't give you a welcome home kiss." He looked judiciously at her mouth and shook his head. "No, we're grown up now and I'm not waiting for you to play in the sail-loft with me." He held out his hand. "I'll shake hands with you, if you please, and bid you welcome. Welcome, indeed!" She gave him her hand and he covered it fondly with both of his. "Many years have passed since I walked with you and now you're a woman grown. I heard you were in England."

She nodded. "And you a skipper with your own vessel. A thinner, older boy. No, a man now. Patrick, how's your mother?"

"Fine, thank God! Still dreaming at night of the old man. You knew we lost him on the Banks?"

"Patrick, I wrote to you when I read it in the Gloucester Times. When I was a nurse in Washington."

"Aye! indeed, you did, Margaret." He smiled away her reproachful look. "And so I gave up my schooling, which I liked, in a way. And I sailed with Uncle Marty on the *Daniel* until this winter he said I was to be skipper in his place. He's not well. And now he's made his last voyage and I sail without him in an hour. And you, Margaret, you're sailing to Newfoundland. Why so? I thought it was a strange thing. I never in my life have seen a woman passenger aboard our vessels."

She gave the tenth part of a smile with her answer. "It's a simple matter, Patrick."

He said quickly: "Why, then—simple or not, Margaret, 'tis none of my business. You're sailing with your uncle and, if you give me leave, I can guess why."

"You may guess, Patrick, and if you don't guess right—I'll tell you."

"The *Hind* has extra stores aboard and two frozen beeves packed in ice. That you must have bought. And you're aboard. So I put two and two together and it adds up to this: that your people in Newfoundland are in trouble and you're going back to stay with them a spell and nurse them. You MacLeans are a kindly, clannish lot."

Her face swiftly saddened. "You're right in what you say, Patrick. There's trouble enough. Worse than trouble." She tried to hide her strong emotion by a quick downfall of her lashes, but the sorrowful meaning of her look didn't escape him.

"Not death?" he asked.

She shook her head. "No, Patrick. Not yet. But my father—"

"Oh, forgive me, Margaret! I heard something in Newfoundland last trip. A queer, terrible story. I'm sorry for you." He touched her arm gently. "I know how dearly you love that good man."

"Newfoundland was a second home to him," she said. "He was born there. That's why he went with the Canadians when the war came. Went back to the minesweepers, where he served last time. Well, it happened. I suppose it had to happen. He's terribly hurt, Patrick. I won't tell you how badly." She rubbed away a tear from her cheek with the sleeve of her jacket. "That's why I'm going. I'm bringing them food and money. The only provider for them is long since gone. A prisoner in Germany. And there's much illness up and down the coast. The few doctors they've had are long since under arms. So I'm going. And when I come back, I'm to have a nurse's commission in the Army. A lieutenant I'll be. I'll see you then, Patrick, won't I?"

He took up his basket. "Not then. Before."

"How?"

"Your people still live in the village of Trabo, don't they? On the Straight Shore of Avalon?"

"Surely, Patrick, you know that. You've gone in there often enough for bait." She looked at him curiously. "Of what are you thinking, Patrick Bannon?"

"I was thinking how pleasant it would be, happen there's no herring to be bought elsewhere for our bait—how pleasant it would be if you would say: 'Well, Patrick, we'll be at Trabo before you, so do come in there this time for your bait?' "

He held out his hand. She put her hand into his once more, studied the matter—and him—briefly and then said: "Well, Patrick, the *Golden Hind* will be at Trabo before you. So do come in there this time for your bait."

CHAPTER II

THREE NIGHTS LATER, the *Daniel Webster* lay have to and sound asleep on the northwest peak of the Grand Bank itself. A thin ice was making on her rigging. Festoons of snow blew from her riding sail and fell. The black Atlantic heaved under her in a long swell. While the schooner slowly jogged about, her running lights made a dim show of emerald and ruby gleams, now glancing deep in the dark troughs of waves, then sparkling in cascades of foam. A yellow glow rose from her cabin skylight, making her seem tight and cozy, like a cottage awake at night on a dismal plain.

Conrad, the Danish hand, was standing watch alone. From time to time, he stood clear in the half-light that came twisting off the sea. He stood alert by the wheel and gazed into the East, then went forward and stopped in the waist of the vessel and peered again into the moonless night. He climbed up into the rigging once and stared again into the East. He came down, went forward and beat his mittened hands on the foremast boom. He stood clear of it and scanned the obscure horizon to the West and the whitecapped waters between. Often he beat his arms against his chest and once, when a squall came howling out of the North, he crouched in the lee of a nest of dories until the icy spray ceased to fall.

Below in the snug cabin, Patrick lay in his bunk, his face calm in sleep. He had driven his vessel hard from Gloucester, after one backward look at the old sea town, at the white smoke rising from his mother's chimney and the black smoke rolling from forges and clanging shipyards. He had waved farewell to the *Golden Hind* and to the girl gazing from her deck. Before he had waltzed past Eastern Point, he had seen the *Hind* turn from the wharf and take after him. The wind had lain in the south-west all that first night and, it being fair for the *Daniel,* the voyage to the fisheries had been put behind them in jig-time. In all that sailing, Patrick had sighted only two big vessels. The first was a navy cruiser running out to sea with a fine bone in her teeth. The second was a square-rigged ship, a craft not often seen in those waters, although rising rates had brought some sailing vessels out of harbors where they had been rotting away. This windjammer had briefly showed her staysail that day at dusk when the wind suddenly hauled into the north-east and made the *Daniel* lurch and her lee rail go under. So had the distant stranger labored heavily, while Patrick watched her through his glass. Sometimes she rolled her lee yardarms down to the waves. She had vanished just before the *Daniel* heaved to for the night.

Now the morning came. A spray of green light bubbled up in the eastern murk and the sky began to clear rapidly. Conrad, back again at the wheel, watched the green spray until it grew into a fountain and changed to a rosy hue. He then went forward, entered the forecastle, where the men lay sleeping in their deep bunks, and woke up the cook. He went on deck again. The first hard, cold light of the sun sped to the North and South. Conrad turned towards the cabin. At that moment, a swift gleam of new light stopped him where he stood. It came out of the sunrise, yet it was not part of the dawn. He knew what it was. It could only be the early part of day glancing off an icy sail. He went below.

The moment he laid his hand on Patrick's shoulder, the sleeping captain came awake. He turned toward Conrad and said calmly: "Has the wind changed?"

"No, sir."

"What woke me up?"

"I did, Captain."

Patrick rubbed his eyes and reached under his bunk for his boots. "A squall hit us hard an hour ago. Eh, Conrad?"

"Yes, Captain. A hard squall from the North."

"Cook stirring?"

U-boat campaign. Such talk doubled his natural wariness, had given him a useful habit of thinking fast and hard, instead of just barging into trouble as he used to do and trusting to a Bannon's luck to get him out of it. He had more respect than most Gloucestermen for the daring and ingenuity of the common enemy. He knew their desperate reckless-ness, knew how easy it was for them to shed innocent blood. He kept his own mouth shut when he was ashore, simply trusting in those men whose bounden duty it was to wage the war. At sea, it was a different matter. Here, on this vessel, he was President, law-giver, and, if the chance came, he was war-wager, too. He hated the invader of these fruitful pastures of the sea, hated him not only for ships shot down and dories gunned, but also—perhaps even more—for the cruel wastefulness of good men's work. Now, there she rode, a vessel that only last night had been a fellow way-farer; and now she had become, in an instant, a new burden to his mind and heart. Yes, Conrad had gaffed the thought that had been swimming deep in him ever since he had sighted the loafing stranger that first time. Had gaffed it and flung it down before him. What evidence? None, except the tried instinct of an exiled sailor, a man driven off his shores by treachery. Patrick showed his teeth in a savage grin. He ground them together in an anger that made his hands clench on his glass. And then, quite suddenly,

old Dolan's image came, blue-coated and furi-
out, before him and—"Theatre tickets!" whispered
Patrick.

A moment later, he said aloud: "By the Lord
Harry! If I didn't have to go fishing—I'd tail you,
old lady, until I found you out!"

He lifted the glass once more. The stranger had
sailed out of sight.

After breakfast, he changed his fishing plans a little. He had intended to set out a tub of trawl where
the vessel lay and keep her at anchor; for there
wasn't enough bait aboard to keep all his dories at
work very long. He figured, too, that it would be
easier for the green hands, Conrad and Holger, if the
dories took it slow for the first set and haul. Now his
wily heart shied from the thought of staying long at
anchor. Like his father before him, he wished to keep
his vessel lively, to keep a little way on her, so that
the old hen could gather up her chickens should danger or the quick nor'easter come. So he ordered the
anchor up and gave instructions for the flying set;
and the older men among the crew smiled approv-
ingly because they loved to hear him use the terms his
father and his grandfather had used. Yes, and do
things the way they used to do them in the days before
powered vessels sailed on the Banks.

The gear lay ready. Jugs of tea and bundles of
bread and meat and bigger jugs of water, flanked by

sundry bottles of rum, stood on the desk. Before they had turned in, the dorymen had sliced and chopped the frozen herring into small chunks. Now the long lines of the trawls, from which hung shorter lines carrying baited hooks, had been coiled into tubs of the old-fashioned kind, each with the name *Daniel Webster* branded on it. Buoys, buoy-lines, anchors and flags—all were ready in their places. The men began to lift the first dories from the nests.

The vessel got under way in slack water and sailed easily on a sunlit sea until she was out of the shallower water of the peak. The first dory was made ready and Patrick, breaking an old rule, said he would go in it himself with Conrad for his dory-mate. He left Caleb at the wheel. Before he went over the side, he once more repeated his orders: that at the sound of gunfire every dory was to cut trawls and get back to the vessel and the basket run to the masthead was a signal for the same action.

Patrick took up a black keg-buoy. A flag, marked with the figure 1, had been fixed on it so that the trawl could be easily found when the hauling of the hooked fish began. He threw the buoy over the side and fed out the line as the buoy fell astern. This done, he climbed into the dory, settled Conrad on a thwart, and signed to the men at the tackle to lower away. The dory splashed into the sea. Conrad took up the oars and gave way. The *Daniel* sailed on with No. 2

dory hauled up to the rail and a doryman ready to toss his buoy over the side at Caleb's signal.

Eager to learn the Yankee way of taking halibut, Conrad watched every move made by Patrick as he took up a small anchor to which the buoy and the trawl itself were made fast. Patrick tossed the anchor over. They were fishing in seventy fathoms of water and the anchor, which was to hold the buoy in its place, took some time to go down. Then Patrick began the set. He held up a short stick of peeled willow that had been thrust between the rising and the sideboards.

"Give it a name, Conrad," he said.

Conrad grinned with the pleasure of his new knowledge. "The heaving-stick, Captain?"

"Right the first time. You'll be a good dory-mate."

Patrick deftly thrust the tip of the stick into the top coils of the trawl and flipped the first ganging and hook over the side. In a quick, rhythmic motion, he heaved the uncoiling line over while Conrad rowed. The trawl went sliding into the sea and sank quickly under the pull of the big hooks and their weight of herring.

Patrick looked up from his labor. "Is it like home a little, Conrad?"

"Like home a little. Yes, Captain."

"Keep her headed so, Conrad. That's well." Deftly he uncoiled the trawl and kept it feeding into the water. "I'll set this morning, Conrad. And when we haul with the tide—for that's what we do on a day like this—I'll show you the tricks and next time we make a set you can do some hauling. You'll have time to study your lessons because we'll be on our way to-morrow. To Newfoundland for bait."

"My shipmates say so, Captain. They said English Village."

Patrick laughed. "They said wrong. It's Trabo this time, Conrad. I've got a reason." He laughed again. "That is, maybe I've got a reason. I hope I have. Maybe I'll tell you about it later." He paused a moment to take an inward look at the strawberry villain of the *Golden Hind* and said: "Trabo. It's farther up the coast. Up the Straight Shore of Avalon. A pretty name, isn't it?" He shook his head in vexation over an unbaited hook that flashed by and signed to Conrad that he should row a little faster.

Conrad lengthened his stroke. "I landed near the Straight Shore, Captain. When they blew up our ship."

"Ah, so you did. I had forgotten." He frowned at the recollection of Conrad's terrible eight days in a boat. "Can you see the schooner now?"

"Yes, Captain."

"Keep an eye on her."

Patrick, who really didn't fear the sea as much as he should, became gayer as he worked. This was money in the bank. He had no time to look up at the brilliant sky, where the gulls were already gathering over the *Daniel's* wake. The sun had brightened the Atlantic, had turned it from black to rippling green, a change that pleased him mightily and made him talk big about the halibut feeding down below. "For I feel better, Conrad, when we've got a few pounds stowed away in the pens. Last trip we were here only two weeks and then we hooked it for home with six pens full and a good lot of cod."

Conrad suddenly shipped his oars and stood up in his place. The dory fell off the line, but he looked intently over the waves, then sat down again and rowed smartly.

Patrick glanced up at him in quick anger. "You keep rowing, Conrad, my friend." He pulled a tub of trawl towards him and seized the line. "If there's any looking around to do—I'll do it for you. See a fish feeding? Sometimes the big ones chase a cod right to the surface, but never mind—"

"No, Captain. I saw one of our dories. That is all. I am sorry I stood up."

"Where?"

Conrad nodded his head towards the East.

"Hell and damnation! What's the matter with that guy?" Patrick gripped the trawl in his right hand, straddled in his tippy place, and stood up. "There! That way, Conrad?"

"That way. Aye, sir."

"You sure?"

"I saw a boat. It came up quick on a sea, Captain, and went down quick. Into trough."

"There's none of our dories there. Hold on now. Steady as you go. That's well." Patrick waited until a sea ran under the dory and lifted it high. In that instant of soaring he saw nothing, but just as the see-saw of the waves took him down again, he spied a boat dipping and turning aimlessly half a mile away. He yelled in astonishment.

"You make it out, Captain?"

"You're right I make it out. Ease up, Conrad." Patrick took up a knife, cut the trawl, made it fast to the windward buoy and flung buoy and anchor over the side. "Give way, Conrad! We'll take a look. God knows, you never can tell what you'll find in a boat these days. Row, Conrad. Put your beef into it."

Conrad, a sure master at the oars, put his beef into it. He sent the dory driving up and hurtling down the sea valleys. At each shout from Patrick, he lifted the stroke until, at last, Patrick flung up his hand and cried: "We're on it! There's no one at the oars. It's empty."

The last billow reared between them and the drifting stranger. From this high perch, Patrick looked down into the boat. There were men in it. They were huddled together on the bottom boards. One face was turned to the blue, beaming sky. One hand was held stiffly upward in a gesture of appeal. The other faces and the other hands lay hidden in a wash of darkened water.

Patrick sank down to the thwart. "Merciful God!" He covered his eyes with his salty hands.

Conrad calmly said: "Alongside, Captain?"

Patrick nodded. "There are men in it, Conrad."

"Aye, sir. Men."

"Dead men, Conrad."

"Dead men. That is right, Captain."

The dory slid up to the boat. Conrad shipped his oars and looked. Patrick laid his hands on the gunwale of the stranger craft and held the two boats together. He cried out a terrible oath and turned his furious face upward to the sky.

There were three seamen lying dead there. They had been shot to death.

CHAPTER III

C<small>APTAIN</small> <small>BANNON</small> <small>LOOKED</small> down in sorrow at the dead mariners. It was plain to him that they had been murdered in that boat, shot while they sat at the oars, which were all gone, except one. Its shattered blade lay under a body sprawled in the stern. There were many bullet holes in the boat. Patrick's fingers, clutching the gunwale, had sunk into a splintered hole, cut clear through by a bullet. He could not bear to turn his eyes towards those staring eyes of the one upturned face. Instead, he looked again, without speaking, to Conrad. Later, he remembered how his own heart had cooled when he saw his dory-mate gazing with half-shut eyes, eyes that changed from blue to the greenish light of the changing sea. The eyes were calm, seemed to have no depth, seemed to shimmer without life. This, he knew, was the Dane's rage working, his shrewd mind at a new labor. Yet no curse came from his bitter lips, not even a mournful sigh, not a shake of the yellow head. Conrad merely moved a little, quite carefully, on the thwart and, in almost childish curiosity, he examined the boat in which these men had died so mysteriously.

Conrad suddenly thrust out his right hand and laid
it on the gunwale of the other boat. It seemed to Patrick, staring from his place, that the gesture was like
a caress, a heartfelt greeting to a thing of much meaning. "Captain Bannon—this boat is a Dane. She is
made in my country."

He said this in a voice and manner almost quaint,
so formal and matter-of-fact it was. And yet Patrick,
who had learned a little of this man's heart and mind
since he came aboard at Gloucester, knew that he
was already thinking of another Danish craft lately
seen and thinking also of this ruined boat swinging
from her davits. Indeed, Conrad had already turned
his head to the East and was staring at the green-
and-white horizon, where the stranger had manœu-
vred in such outlandish fashion.

Patrick looked swiftly up and down the length of
the boat. He couldn't remember that he had ever
seen one like it before. Yet there was nothing unusual
about it. It simply wasn't a dory. It was foreign to
him.

"Conrad," he asked, "are these men Danes? Are
these poor fellows your countrymen?"

Conrad gazed coldly upon the dead. A sea curled
under the *Daniel's* dory and tipped it up, giving Conrad a high seat. Patrick saw the Dane poised an
instant against the blue space of the sky, the spray
bursting flowery white beneath him and making a

hurrah. The wave toppled and the two gunwales struck together. Conrad leaned out a little farther and Patrick watched his slow examination of boots and sodden trousers, of jackets and caps, and, at last, of the one visible face and the stiff, uplifted hand. In the end, Conrad shook his head in a way that bespoke his doubt. He said something in so low a tone that Patrick couldn't hear it above the hiss and clatter of waves.

"What do you say, Conrad?" shouted Patrick. "Danes? Are they Danes?"

He bellowed his answer through cupped hands. "Cannot tell yet."

Patrick signed to him to take up the oars and then he fished up the dragging painter of the foreign boat. He made it fast to his own, took up his oars, and together they rowed back towards the buoy of their trawl. Glancing over his shoulder after each few strokes, Patrick soon caught sight of their buoy. Before they reached it, the *Daniel* came sailing towards them, Caleb at her wheel and all the others shouting and staring from the rail.

Patrick leaped aboard and faced his crew. "You men seen anything?"

They shook their heads. Only the cook spoke. "Two sail in the West. Schooners. One painted gray."

"Run up the basket. They'll know what that means, if they're friends of ours. Perhaps the gray

one's in the Navy. Maybe we'll be needing some help
here. There are three dead seamen in that boat. Shot
to death. Help Conrad."

When the three bodies were laid side by side on the
Daniel's deck, Patrick turned again to Conrad. He
was standing next to Holger, the other Dane who had
come aboard at Gloucester. Holger's dark, cadaver-
ous face was impassive, yet a certain grayness, a sort
of pallor, was pushing up into his cheeks. He, too, had
trouble in looking at those slain. He kept his eyes
fixed on his boots.

Patrick, just as he was going to speak, saw a warning in Conrad's intense gaze. The moment Conrad
saw that his warning was understood, he jerked his
head ever so slightly towards Holger. There was no
mistaking his intention. He wished to have Patrick
ask Holger to say who and what these murdered seamen had been.

Patrick spoke clearly, subtly. His heart beat hard
and his inner excitement grew; for he now had another sign, from a man in whom he trusted completely, that the enemy was here, standing before him
with bowed head on the deck of his own vessel. Inwardly he thanked his stars that such a man as
Conrad, so hard and shrewd and imaginative, had
been with him at the discovery of the bodies. He could
not yet see what the game was going to be, but he
made his opening move adroitly. He singled out a

Cape Breton man, a sober, middle-aged hand, bent from a life in dories, and said: "Frank, these men aren't Americans. Nor Canadians. They're foreigners of some sort. Are they Frenchies? Are they St. Malo men who were with the cod fleet? Or Portuguese? You know the cod fleet. Take a look. What do you think?"

The Cape Breton man pulled off his cap and took one step forward. He was bending over to take a closer look at the dead men when Holger, faltering in his stride, passed him and knelt by the dead. He bowed his head over them. His right hand reached out in a weak, aimless gesture. His thin lips parted, but formed no word. He gasped and whispered: "Danes! They are Danes! Oh, Captain, my poor countrymen!"

His grief was hard to watch, although it was soundless, was shown only by shoulders hunched in wretchedness and red, briny hands that groped and came to rest upon a lifeless cheek. The men murmured compassionately.

The Cape Bretoner said: "I don't know, Cap'n."

A Gloucesterman cursed the murderers.

Conrad said nothing. Out of his eyes he sent Patrick a signal of alarm and then he, too, knelt and pulled off his cap. He laid his hand on Holger's bowed shoulder.

Holger cried out a word in Danish and looked in

despair at Conrad, who was praying aloud in that same language. This seemed to loose Holger's tongue. He raised his voice and began to curse. He threw up his hands in passion and lifted his face towards the sky. The crackling, swinging words, harsh and sweet in turn as an East Wind in rigging, poured from his twisted mouth in endless sentences.

The Cape Breton man, being nearest, took another step forward and laid his hand on Holger's head. Tears were in his eyes and in his hoarse voice. "Don't take on so, laddie. See now! They're at good peace, now and forever."

Patrick studied that mourning man.

Conrad opened the ripped jackets of the dead men and searched their pockets. He drew out a knife and held it up and put it back again. He opened one man's shirt and found there an oilskin packet. He opened it, took out two folded papers and looked at them. He handed them up to Patrick and, as the skipper bent to receive them, Conrad looked at him intently and said: "They are Danes. As I said. That is right, Captain. These are Danish tickets. There's his union card. Same as the ones I lose."

Holger arose wearily and returned to his place among the fishermen. They comforted him and the man who had cursed in the beginning cursed again. Caleb put the helm down and steered towards a sail that was approaching from the West. The gulls, impatient for the fishing to begin so that they might feed on the offal, wheeled down close to the deck and screamed over the dead.

Patrick spoke to his men in order to have their counsel. "All these names and the condition of the men and their boat will be written in the log for a report to the naval authorities. All their papers will be saved and turned over to the Navy. It looks to me as if the best thing to do with them"— he pointed to the bodies—"is to let them go now into the sea."

The men stood in silence. One or two nodded their heads. Holger spoke a sentence in Danish to Conrad, who pondered briefly, then shook his head.

"What does Holger say?" asked Patrick in a kindly tone.

Conrad replied: "He asks have I the Holy Book. I say no. I lose it."

"That is a good and proper question," said Patrick. "It should be done according to the customs of your country. For these are your countrymen. But if you have no Holy Book, then I can say a prayer. It will serve." He turned to the Cape Breton man and said: "Frank—and you, Jim—help Conrad and Holger sew those bodies in canvas. Weight them with sacks of coal. Since we haven't their own flag, lay our colors on their bodies for a little while."

This was done and Patrick, cap in hand, recited the Lord's Prayer over the bodies now swathed and bound in folds of sail-cloth. One by one, the murdered men then went sliding into the current, which was then setting swiftly towards the outer sea.

"Now, then," said Patrick, taking over the wheel as he spoke, "there's an end to a hard, cruel business. They are dead and may God rest their souls. We know well enough who did this thing. It was done by the same men—or their sons—who brained Eb Parker on this very deck with their shrapnel. In my father's day. Aye! and tattered the sails on that very main-mast there. We'll get on with our duty and our busi-ness. All I say is"— his voice loudened and his face grew fierce with anger—"all I say is: the curse of Christ on the forebones of those who killed the sail-ors! I've held off from war this last few months because it was required of me, but I tell you that once I lay this vessel alongside Ben Pine's wharf I'll be go-ing to another vessel—and you know the one I mean. One with guns on her. And I'll hunt them as my father did when I was a boy and I'll stuff the long drink down their swine throats. Same as he did." He struck his right hand hard against the spokes and cursed under his breath. "Now, cook, see that they eat dinner just the same. And a drink of rum for all hands. A mug for Conrad. A mug for Holger. Go on now."

After dinner, the fishing began in earnest. By this time, there were several vessels in sight. Sails gleamed in all four quarters as the schooners moved about on the wide waters of the Banks, taking up dories and dropping them off. The gray-painted vessel came slapping by to ask about the basket aloft and to pass the time of day. She was a Boston fisherman and her skipper said that he had heard that henceforth all ships must put on a gray coat before they left for the fisheries. Patrick told him of the harsh find he had made. The skipper threw up his hands in horror. In being borne away, he cried out: "There's something queer going on in these waters, Patrick. Watch yourself!"

Patrick sighted his buoy then and told Conrad to make ready for the hauling. He turned the wheel over to Caleb again and joined Conrad in the dory. The Dane sat in silence, a silence full of words, to be spoken when they were free of the vessel. Once away, Patrick left his place and sat near Conrad, waiting for him to speak. But he did not do so, only labored at the long oars.

Patrick said: "You made a mistake back there, Conrad." He nodded toward the flying *Daniel*.

"Yes, Captain."

"I mean that you pretended to make a mistake. You made believe."

"Yes, Captain. I knew."

"You knew what?"

"What the captain knows."

"I know the dead men were not Danes."

"That is right."

"I know they were not Frenchmen from the Malo fleet."

"Not Frenchmen, Captain. No."

"I know, Conrad, they were not fishermen at all."

"That is right, too, Captain."

"Conrad, I looked at their hands—"

"I saw you. I looked, too, Captain. I touched them."

"I looked carefully at their hands and at their faces. One man had soft, delicate hands. Not a hard spot on them and not a speck of dirt. Nothing but his own blood. I'll tell you, Conrad, what he was before he died. He was either a yeoman or a radio operator. Something like that."

"That is so, Captain." Conrad's face, that had been cold and lightless, became alive again and his expression changed to one of admiration. "That man, Captain, never had his hand on this." He glanced down at the sweeping oar.

"True for you. Good for you. And he never reefed a sail or stood a trick at a wheel."

The dory ran up to the buoy. Patrick reached for it and hauled it and the anchor aboard. He came back again to be near Conrad and said: "As for the other two dead men, all that we say of the first one applies to them also. Except this—that their hands were the hands of engine-room ratings. They were black with grease and oil. And their faces—why! Any lubber could see that those men had been living their lives below. Never on deck. Never in the sun. Seeing the sun only through a periscope for weeks on end. I've seen my pals in the Navy with that worn look on their faces. And that queer sort of pale color. Conrad, those three men were Germans. Hands serving on a submarine!"

"Aye!" Conrad shouted his agreement. "Men from under sea. You are right, Captain. Right in everything."

"And two things more I know!" cried Patrick in an exulting tone. "I know, first, that the men were executed. They were shot by their own officers. Either in a mutiny—"

"That is it! Mutiny!"

"—or they were caught trying to escape from something terrible. Something they couldn't stand any longer. They looked like men gone mad. Mad with more than a fear of death."

"I know! I know! Some hate the U-boat after a long cruise, Captain. Oh, I have stories of men who killed themselves before they go back." He leaned forward on his oars. "That is one thing, Captain. What is the other thing you have found?"

"The boat," answered Patrick. "The boat we found them in."

"Ah!"

"Big as they are, Conrad, no U-boat ever carried any such thing as that. And you said that it was a Danish boat. So, now we come back to something I can't forget. The Danish vessel." He struck his hands together so hard that the brine spattered off in gleaming drops. "I say that this is true: those three men were killed escaping from that square-rigger! She has been meeting the U-boats. I know somebody has been feeding them stuff. Oil and food and arms. The Navy knows. You can tell by the questions they ask. Conrad, it's a crazy, daring stunt they've tried—to use an innocent-looking vessel like that—but it's working!"

"I say so, too. I say square-rigger is the—"

"The mother-ship!"

"Aye! They have done it before, Captain Bannon, —last war and this time. I know. I know. They take windjammers out of Danish harbors and put guns on them and fool Norwegians and British, too." He laughed bitterly. "We have it! And there is one last big thing—"

"I'm thinking of it—"

"This one who calls himself also a Dane and carried good Danish papers. Papers just like papers off the dead men. This Holger aboard our vessel, I mean."

"Holger! Did you listen to him sharp? Wailing over the dead men?"

"I did."

"I knew what you were up to. Tell me, he spoke Danish well? Very well?"

"He speaks it too well. He speaks it like a gentleman. He speaks as I hear them speak in the fine streets of Copenhagen."

Patrick knew what Conrad had in his mind; and he knew also why he wouldn't take the lead in their talk. It was a cautious rule, learned by hard lessons. He knew that Conrad, a man without a country, could not risk what little he had won—this berth on the *Daniel*—by speaking freely, by saying something that might draw the vessel and her men into trouble. He said: "You were worried about him before this happened, weren't you?"

"That is right."

"Why?"

"He knows too much. For just a common hand like me. He speaks German. That's what Parson said at Gloucester and told why. Holger also speaks French. He reads French newspapers. So he did at Boston Bethel. He speaks English good, too."

"Well?"

"He knows my country well. Too much. Better than I do and I live there and sail from there all my life. But little things he don't know."

"For instance?"

"A knot. He cannot tie it. Old stories of our Danish

ships. He don't know them. Some rough words and sailor talk. He shake his head. I know it is true, as Parson said, Holger was on tankers out of the Gulf. Sure. Why did he go from them? Parson Kramer says he was sick of oil smell."

"He looked sick to me, Conrad. I'll say that much for him."

"No, Captain. Not sick. He leave tankers because so many are sunk by U-boats. And I think he help sink them. He is a German. I will risk my job on it. And my life. You are right."

Patrick said: "I think we are right. Listen now, Conrad! Do you understand what it means to run with the hounds?"

"No, Captain."

"The hunted one—the hare—he back-tracks and runs behind the pack. Why, I've gone ashore at Nantucket and watched a pack of beagles over-run a rabbit and go yapping down the hillside, so hot on the scent that they didn't use their eyes and see the rabbit hopping along with them."

"I see now, Captain."

"We are the hares. We are the hunted. But—see here, Conrad!—we are back with the hounds now. You and I. For I sum up this man Holger as a man to be watched. Be careful and smart. That is all. I know he could see the things that we saw in that boat and the signs of those men. He knew they weren't

Danes, but he made a fine, clever show to fool us. You say that he spoke your language well when he was bending over them? Better than you perhaps?"

"Much better, Captain. Better words, Fine, long words. But no good curse words. Like me. No, he cursed like a fancy gentleman with eyeglass in his head."

"He is a Nazi spy, Conrad."

"He is the hound."

"Then he will lead us to the others. Sooner or later, he must. He is going to them. Somewhere on the Newfoundland coast, perhaps. It wasn't chance or a sick belly that led him to the parson's home and then to us."

"He is cunning, Captain Bannon. Like all them. But also a fool."

"Because he despises us."

"He is sure I am a stupid one, Captain."

"No doubt, he thinks I'm a fathead, too."

"Try to make him think so. That will be good."

"We'll close our mouths on this matter for the time being, Conrad. I say this last thing: that the secret— maybe a great and important secret—lies in that square-rigger. If I see her again, I'm going to board her. I'll get a look at her and her cargo if I have to monkey up her side with a knife in my teeth."

He held his hand up. Conrad took it in a hard grasp. "I go, too, Captain. Your dory-mate."

Patrick grinned. "And now, my friend, we'll make some money for ourselves and for Mr. Dolan. Here goes!" He heaved on the trawl, passed it once around the spool-like drum of the gurdy and turned the long iron handle. He showed Conrad the trick of winding up the trawl on the gurdy and then Patrick took his place aft to slat the fish off the gangings when they came up. A good many hooks came up empty before, at last, the trawl showed the strain of a big fish, diving and tugging hard.

"Watch him, Conrad!"

The Dane gave the gurdy handle a half-turn; then, in obedience to Patrick's order, he let the trawl sweep aft until it came to Patrick's hands, which were well guarded with woolen mitts. Patrick leaned over and grasped the line. Yielding stubbornly to the pressure of hook and line, the fish ran under the dory until the strain Patrick put on the trawl brought him back.

Patrick set his boots firmly down and gave another slow, inch-by-inch haul. Eager, as always, for the first kill of the day, he glared into the bubbling green water. His mighty nose snuffed up the spray's champagne, as if, indeed, he could make sure whether he had a fat halibut on the hook or an unwanted skate. Dim and mottled under a screen of foam, the fish soon showed his heaving tail. It was a big halibut. He fought hard and thrashed his tail, striving to keep his hideous head away from the light of day.

"Here he comes!" Patrick gave one last short heave. The halibut rolled to the shimmering surface and splashed a rain of foam into Patrick's face. A curl of white water hid the fish again; then, in a sudden quiet, the round, fierce eyes gleamed in the sun, the broken mouth gaped and blew. Patrick, roaring with joy at the sight of the broad, thick sides, picked up his gaff and drove the iron into the fish's head. He bent backward, pulled the halibut up to the gunwale and hauled him into the bottom of the dory.

"Money in the bank!" shouted Patrick.

"Good work, Captain!" The fish leaped and rapped the dory with his tail. At Patrick's signal, Conrad lifted a gob-stick and battered the halibut into quietness.

The next three hooks came up bare and the following one carried only the ravaged carcass of a fine cod, torn and devoured by the ravenous halibut. More bare hooks passed up and through the gurdy. It was halibuter's luck. Twenty or so big fish like the first one would have made a fine day's work, but Patrick labored for an hour before another good fish, over a hundred pounds, came thrashing to the gob-stick.

Yet, by the time the dory reached the leeward buoy, where they had cut the trawl earlier in the day on sighting the dead men's boat, they had a fair dory-load. They got the buoy and anchor aboard and

then they started back across the empty sea, seeking
the flash of the *Daniel's* sail. Soon it showed, going at
a slow pace against the lengthening light of the afternoon. Presently, after the dory had been held high on
the top of a real comber, the *Daniel* abruptly changed
course and ran directly down upon the dory. In half
an hour, the dory lay alongside the schooner and the
fish were pitchforked aboard. Already the knives were
at work on the deck, cleaning the fish for icing-down
in the pens. The other dories were picked up, one
with a load so heavy that Patrick scolded the dorymen, gave them a dressing-down as foolhardy and
greedy fishermen. But they laughed and scorned him,
swore they'd do even worse next time, and fell to their
jobs.

Now, their fair luck having held for a day, it was
decided amongst them that they should make another
set thereabouts in the morning, but there wasn't
enough bait on board for any such fishing.

"Then," said old Caleb, who was helping Holger
in a trick at the wheel, " 'twould be best to buy some
herring from yonder vessels, if such a thing be possible. There's one among them that has come just
now out of Nova Scotia with a plenty of the best."

"Happen you see the *Golden Hind*," said Patrick,
"we'll try her. I guess old Bart is fishing over yonder."
He pointed into the West, where two or three sail
were working.

"Why for?" asked Caleb, sending half a wink to Conrad and the other half to Holger.

"Maybe she can let us have some bait," said Patrick. "At a fair price, of course."

"Cook seen you confabbing on the *Hind* with one of her crew," said Caleb. "Maybe 'twas about bait now? And how much they had to spare?"

Conrad, who had heard something in the forecastle about the *Hind's* passenger and the way she had wangled pies and loaves from the skipper, turned his head to hide his smile.

"What's that you said, Caleb?" asked Patrick.

" 'Tis nothing, Patrick, nothing." He put the helm over a little and lifted his head to scan the distant sails. "I'll run you over, but I don't think you'll be finding the *Golden Hind* tonight. There's bait aboard her, I hear. But not the kind that'll catch halibut."

"You can one and all go to hell!" cried Patrick, seeing now that the others had the gaff into him. "That's my girl old Bart has with him and I'm not to be blamed by the likes of you if I want to make sure about it."

He gave them a wicked scowl and went below to work on his log; for this was a duty old Dolan insisted on in his old-fashioned way. A full, well-written log was his standing order, because he liked to take it home when the *Daniel* came in and study it, entry by entry, so that he might make the voyage in his mind and thus live over again his young days on the Banks. Patrick laid his big thumb athwart his pen and faithfully scratched down, line upon line, all that had happened since the vessel drew away from Gloucester.

Once he rose from his place and turned up the wick of the brass lamp and then went back to his work again, his head close to the leaves of the book. Winds and clouds he put down and vessels spoken and sets made and fish taken. But when he took out from his pocket the papers of the three dead men, he stopped writing and considered how far he should go in recording his suspicions. It was a dangerous business to write this matter down before the proof of it was in his hands. There was always the chance that his log might fall into another man's hands before the game was over. And there was Holger to be kept in mind. So, in the end, he stopped writing in detail of the murders and gave a barer, factual account of the discovery of the boat, the examination of its strange cargo, and the later destruction of the boat itself, which he had ordered.

This done, he filled his pipe and began a leisurely smoke, there in the splashy music of his cabin. In a state of peace, happy that he had made a start in the filling of the *Daniel's* capacious pens, he sat there a while. He looked at his father's picture, gave it a greeting, and lay down in his bunk to take a Gloucesterman's forty winks. It was then, lying at ease in the handsome cabin, that he became conscious again that fishing would soon be over with him. He had taken his oath to go to war. The time of his departure was not far off. Once the *Daniel Webster* had a good stock of halibut aboard, he'd take her home, leave her, and might never return to her. His beautiful, swift ship! Doing her job in the old way, taking her power down from the winds, up from the tides and currents of the sea, going like a wild goose over the water. His eyes became a little misty with a tender regret, a yearning for the old peace, the seasons of hard work and hard-won ease ashore. His lids drooped slowly, then lifted again. There was a new world to be fought for, once again.

"This time," he whispered in his drowse, "they must give it to us."

He heard a voice sing out: "Ahoy, there! Is that you, Archie? Have you seen the *Golden Hind?*"

Another voice, one that he knew, roared back: "Gone to Trabo long ago!"

Patrick frowned and gave his luck a damn.

His man above shouted: "Any chance of getting some herring off you, Archie? We're out of it and have struck it good yonder."

"Sure! Sure! Come and get it, Caleb."

Patrick fell deeper into his sleep amidst the thumping of the dories and the shouts of the men scrubbing down the deck.

CHAPTER IV

LATE THAT NIGHT, while the *Daniel Webster* was sailing again on the northwest peak of the Grand Bank, a squall came ripping out of the East and struck the vessel hard. Caleb, who was on watch with Conrad, became uneasy and sent him to take another look at the dories, which had to be double-lashed in case a real blow came on. While Conrad was gone, the wind backed a bit into the North and then began to pipe in earnest. Almost at once, there came a whirl of hail, followed by sleety snow. This soon ceased.

The night turned pitch-black. An enormous black cloud, in the shape of a whale, swam up swiftly and shut out the dimming stars. This darkness stayed for a time and increased, until a mass of white clouds came driving up from a little South of East. From this mass, which rolled close to the sea, a stream of light fell. The light stayed long enough for Conrad to make out another schooner, apparently hove to a mile away, but he had hardly pointed her out to Caleb before she swung around, showed her port light in a stumble, and sailed off. When her lights vanished, the radiance from the sky also vanished.

A second squall came and hit the *Daniel* so hard that she took a heavy lurch to leeward. Her rail went so far down that when she found herself again her deck was full. This was bad business, because the *Daniel* was not the sort that would do well with a burden of water. Once she had run four hundred miles, laboring all the time, because the water got into her and they couldn't free her. Now she shed it quickly and kept herself up. The weather became colder, the wind set up a howl over the ocean and made a wild racket in her rigging.

Caleb, shouting above the noises of the rising storm, told Conrad to call the skipper, but he had hardly reached the companionway before Patrick came up, already in his oil clothing. He sent Conrad forward to call the other men and went himself to stand by the wheel, which was becoming too much of a job for one man to handle easily.

"We're in for it, Patrick!" shouted Caleb. "Never see it come so quick."

Patrick took a look around, tasted the wind and replied: "It looks bad. Keep her so."

He laid his hands on the wheel and sent Caleb forward with orders to shorten sail. The snow set in harder and in no time at all the wind had risen to a gale. Patrick was somewhat anxious for the green hands, it being their first blow aboard the vessel. He peered through the flying spray. At times the dark forms of the men, bending at their work, showed clear when the mainmast ranged high against a rift in the clouds. Rift and all then vanished in the gloom and stayed hidden until a wall of water, rushing upon the schooner, turned into a wall of flashing foam. Again he saw his men, straining in new postures. Soon they had taken in the mainsail. This helped the vessel mightily, but the squalls kept ramming in, one after another, and she once labored so hard to pick up her rail from the pressing tons of water that Patrick shouted angrily at her and gave her a kick. She tried hard and put her best foot forward, but soon she shipped another sea and it swept the deck with such force that he was afraid it might knock the masts out of her.

Caleb and Conrad, knee-deep in the water that she could not quickly shed, came aft. Close after them came Holger, crouching for shelter, then running aft when the force of the water abated. He lurched towards Patrick and shouted: "Running light to port, Captain!"

Patrick, straining at the wheel, looked for the light. He couldn't make it out in that swirling mass of water. His vessel was sailing at a tremendous speed and the merest touch against another hull would have meant her death. He brought the helm over a

little, but the *Daniel* went so slow that another sea
sprang down upon her, hammered at her dories and
rushed upon him with a roar. He clung to the wheel.
The sea struck at his knees and swept him off his feet.
It passed over and he regained his footing. He kept
the vessel off. Once more she darted forward and, at
last, shook herself free of the water that was now
carrying her down deep.

The *Daniel* sped forward like a racehorse. Her
shuddering ceased and she more nimbly shook off the
seas as they came aboard. Patrick seemed to feel a
lessening in the strength of the blow, but in the next
minute the schooner ran into a worse spot, one where
the water was being whipped up in spouts. A thick
stream of snowflakes, caught in an odd down-draft,
whirled about in the shape of a waterspout. This was
freakish weather and he didn't care for it. He turned
to speak to Caleb, but he was gone forward on some
business of the vessel, being an overly cautious seaman, forever making sure of the work of others. Conrad and Holger stood straddled there, bending forward in their yellow oil clothing, staring and watching for a signal from his hand.

In the next instant, Patrick thanked his lucky star
that he had come on deck. A new squall suddenly
split the spray and whirling snow on the port bow
and made an opening, wide as a church door, in the
murk. A queer saffron color had been mixed among

the clouds and it lay beyond this opening, like an enormous silken curtain stretched between sea and sky.

Patrick gazed spellbound through that opening. It was almost dead ahead now and he let the *Daniel* drive right up to it before he shouted a warning and put her helm hard over. A vessel had suddenly appeared in front of that glittering expanse of vapor. It was a square-rigged ship, hove to and laboring in a dead fashion. White seas were leaping over her bows and running onto her decks.

"Conrad!" Patrick summoned the waiting seaman to the wheel. "Holger!" Both of them plunged through a frothy brook and stood to the wheel.

Patrick raised his arm. "Look there!"

A sea lifted the ship high. The expanse of saffron vapor held itself unbroken behind the pitching hull. Indeed, the phosphorescent quality of that light grew until it became fiery, as if a harvest moon was glowing beyond it. Patrick saw a lantern gleam on the ship's quarterdeck and then, as another sea drove her up, he saw a huge and tattered sail fly away and into the wall of light like an enormous bat. The ship reeled down, vanished for a long breath, and then emerged in a bursting welter of foam. Another savage blow swung her broadside on and Patrick knew her for what she was—the Dane.

Once again she sank and rose again. This time she

showed herself even clearer against the glare beyond. He saw that she was badly iced up and that her mainmast had already gone by the board. The strain on her stays had dragged her foremast down. It was plain that she had been caught asleep or had been tardily handled during one of her mysterious sea tasks. Patrick could see a yardarm dangling over her weather rail. As the *Daniel*, now well in hand, sailed on at unslackened speed, he caught a glimpse of a tangled mass of gear tossing in the waist of the vessel. Lanterns gleamed there, too, and he knew that the seamen were clearing away the fallen masts with axes.

He felt Conrad's hand on his shoulder. He gave a quick glance backward and saw his dory-mate's face gleaming under the brim of his sou'wester.

"It's that one, Captain!" shouted Conrad.

Holger stared like a man in a trance. He cried out: "She goes deep! Heavy laden."

"Coal probably!" Patrick's words were snatched off his lips by the wind. He twisted his head around and away from the wind to lend life to his words. He shouted again, meaning that Holger should plainly hear. "Coal, I guess! Keeps her down. Hard to stow."

The *Daniel* drew up rapidly, then plunged smoothly into the darkness and at once struck water that she liked—a long, descending swell. Down she raced, dashing her bowsprit against the seas in the

prettiest manner possible, happy as a girl in a twilight meadow. Patrick laughed at her antics and
cried: "Act your age, will you?" And he lifted up his
voice, making it ring like a bugle; and Caleb laughed
to hear it because the keen sound of it was like hearing again the Bannon that was lost long ago.

"All hands!" shouted Patrick. "All hands! Make it
lively now! Come, boys, come! Bear a hand on that
foresail! Get it on her, will you?"

A little later, the *Daniel* hauled to on the starboard
tack. When the dawn came, a gush of bottle-green in
the darkness, she again lay over in her fancy pace and
headed back to the waters from which she had been
driven. Patrick lay asleep below, having given orders
that he should not be called unless the wind changed
or a sailing vessel, a Dane with a mast or two knocked
out of her, was sighted.

The new watch was turned up in time to sail the
Daniel into the sort of fog that Grand Bankers expect
and fear after such storms. A light breeze, directly
from aft, bore the vapor onward in a swirling ad-
vance. It piled up with such speed that soon the
helmsman could see little of the schooner's wake.
They shortened sail, keeping as little way on her as
they could, for they had company in the wilderness,
phantom vessels that slipped slowly by and vanished
in a breath. Once they heard a horn blowing a low
warning note. Now and then the sun pierced the gray

ceiling with a feeble show of light that dwindled fast
and faded quite away.

The schooner sailed in a silence so perfect that
when the water slapped her the sound struck like a
pistol shot. There was need of silence. This was a time
when a man's shout might well save the *Daniel*
trouble. The Cape Bretoner, who was at the helm,
spoke in a low tone to Holger when, once more, a
shaft of light came down from the sky in a gleaming
passage. "Sun will soon scoff her up, Holger. 'Twon't
be lasting long."

A little later, the sunlight did some good. The fog
didn't lift, yet here and there the warmer air shattered its solidity. Openings and channels formed in
the flowing vapor, some so wide and clear that a man
could see a cable's length on one hand or the other.
Those empty vistas soon closed again and the fog
crowded the lanes of pearl-hued water. The wind began to blow a little harder. When the schooner answered to this increase, one of the men, on watch
near the wheel, began cranking the fog-horn.

Patrick, awakened by the alarm, sent up word that
the lead should be heaved and kept for him. When
this was done, he came on deck and touched his
finger-tips to the grains of bottom gravel that had
come up stuck to the grease smeared on the concave
tip of the lead. Caleb also rolled some of the grains
between his thumb and forefinger. He cocked his wise

old head and half-shut his eyes so that he could the easier rack his full memory for that same delicate feeling of texture and size. He said: "We're sailing on the peak again, Patrick. Where we was when the blow came last night." He then shut his eyes completely, laid a few of the grains on his tongue and judged them again. He spat and declared: "My reckoning's correct. So it is."

Patrick rolled the grains in his fingers. "How much of water was there, Holger?"

"Thirty fathom, Captain."

Patrick nodded. "Near enough, Caleb. We're back where we sighted that square-rigger last night. And since there's no fishing yet a while, I don't mind being hereabouts. If that vessel hasn't foundered, she may be near at hand. Maybe we can help her out."

He said no more on that point then. He knew that the men hadn't forgotten his sworn promise to get aboard that mysterious stranger, if fair chance came. Now he intended to make that chance. He was actually searching for her, compelled to do so by seaman-like instinct. It was so strong in him that when his vessel had been driven off by the storm, he had clearly kept the stranger's position in mind, had swung around again to be near it. The Danish ship, now lying somewhere in that outer obscurity or rolling on the bottom, had become to him a symbol of evil, a thing to be coldly hated, a conundrum to be solved.

Indeed, his hatred of her had become so violent, since the finding of the dead men, that it had invaded his sleep. In a dream of the night past, he had seen her black hull proudly dashing the waves aside. From her mizzen the flag of all evil flaunted its bloody cross and her scuppers ran with blood.

The repassage of that vision jerked a harsh word out of his mouth. He came to in lively fashion and looked at his men. They stood there, waiting for a signal from him, waiting for something to happen.

Patrick relieved the helmsman, who went forward with others in his gang. Conrad and Holger stayed near the wheel, peering into the fog and listening. The vapor ahead piled up thicker than ever and the fog-horn renewed its clamor. Just as the horn began, Patrick saw a glint to starboard, a glint of water pouring off a shape of metal, half-seen in the gloom. He said nothing, only stared. His vessel moved on slowly. He brought the helm up a little and kept his eyes fixed on the hedge of vapor from which the glint had come.

He struck Holger on the arm and said in a low, angry tone: "All hands! Lively now. Stop that horn!"

"Aye, sir!" Holger ran forward.

Patrick called Conrad. "Turn them out below there!" He jerked his head towards the cabin. "Easy now! No noise!"

Conrad turned from the wheel. In that instant,

Patrick saw a burst of yellow flame above the glinting shape beyond. And, in the next instant, an explosion shattered the silence of the sea. The peal came hurtling across the water and struck so hard that Patrick shrank against the spokes. He bowed under that blast of sound and shook his head. His deafened ears rang, but he could hear the echo of the shot rolling.

The silence then returned. He lifted his voice and roared: "All hands! All hands! Lively now!"

Conrad returned. Patrick lifted an arm and pointed. An opening came in the vapor. They saw a U-boat lying there. It was so clear to them that they could make out the crew serving a gun forward of her tower. One gunner turned his face up towards the sky. In the tower itself, an electric torch burned with an orange-colored light. Once its beam lay briefly on the aft gun platform and revealed a tall man standing there alone.

The gun fired again.

Patrick saw the gunners stand away, bend and straighten. Their action was quick and forceful, like the movements of automatons. A billow of fog then heaved up between the *Daniel* and the U-boat.

The schooner glided away. The cannonading continued. Each round burned the vapor and sent a peal rattling against the *Daniel's* hull. The peal rolled close to the surface and echoed loudly in the upper sea of vapor. Twelve rounds were fired and the gun ceased.

"Now then!" Patrick gave the wheel to Conrad and spoke loudly to the crew, all standing nigh, except one or two kept forward to watch her going. "That was close enough of a call. Know what it was? A U-boat shelling a vessel. Who else saw her?"

"I did, Captain."

"Yes, Conrad, I know. Who else?"

Nobody answered. As before, they looked silently at him, not knowing what to expect, all having had some experience of his violent temper. He singled out one of the older hands, a thin shaft of a masthead-man, who stood next to old Caleb. "Darby, you've served a hitch or two. Would you say it was a five-inch gun we were hearing?"

"I would, Patrick. Though I must say I didn't hear much after the first crack. We was that close on it."

"You, Conrad," said Patrick. "You've heard this sort of gunnery before now."

"Why, Captain," answered Conrad, "I never hear it so loud. No. But I do hear. I see. Yes, five-inch gun shelling a ship beyond."

At this point, Caleb came among them again and the men gave way before him, he having served longest in the vessel and by tradition held high place in the schooner's councils. Patrick, knowing there was always some good to be gained from the old man's words, waited until he was nigh. "Well, Caleb? All secure, eh?"

Caleb nodded. "All secure, Patrick. We was near enough to that devil to gaff him, wasn't we?"

"Aye! Might have spit in his bloody eye, happen I didn't chance to make him out."

"You've eyes in your head like your father's, Patrick. You have, indeed."

"My father!" Patrick laughed in the joy that always came to him at the naming of that man. He cracked his hands together and then he laughed again, this time in a harsher fashion. He looked from man to man, but said no word.

Caleb's voice took on a forbidding tone. "None of your Bannon tricks now, Patrick. Your thinking-cap is on, ain't it? Don't be for trying to ram that one down."

"Not for a minute! This is Mr. Dolan's ship and it has your earnings in the hold and more to go in. No, I wasn't thinking of that." He took another look around and said: "It's lifting ahead. Keep her so, Conrad, and maybe we'll find a little room to prance in. Case of need."

It was true that the light showed a good increase and soon a square of beaming sky appeared in the West. The wind hauled to southward and came a little brisker, so that the *Daniel* quickly swam into a

fair, clear space. Nevertheless, the fog that she left
behind her did not lift. Indeed, it seemed thicker than
ever, as if it were rolling back upon itself.

Patrick was seeking the judgment of his men. He
watched their faces turn more frequently down the
sparkling wake. He knew where their kindly thoughts
were speeding; for they were all good men aboard
a vessel and understood their duties as seamen. But he
didn't wish to speak of that matter. He wished to
leave it to another.

He hadn't long to wait. Darby, whose backward
look showed much anxiety, finally said: "I wonder
now. What was that German shooting at?"

The others piped up at this question. Patrick, still
holding off, said: "I was wondering that myself,
Darby. There was no torpedo fired. Only the gun."
He spoke to Conrad then. "You that knows—wouldn't
that rat swim off quick enough, once he'd done firing?"

"At once he would go."

"If he knows anything," said Caleb, "and I think
he does, he'll find himself deep water and lay low in
it." He considered his speech carefully and added:
"No doubt there's boatloads of seamen back there.
No doubt at all."

"Are you thinking, Caleb," asked Patrick, "that we
should run back and take a look?"

Caleb looked at the nodding heads about him and, in a most judicious tone, answered: "I am that."

Patrick grinned and waved his hand at the mainmast. The men hoisted the sail briskly and the *Daniel,* staying on the same course, sailed into the sunlit area, which was swiftly widening. The first gang, of which Patrick was a member, went to dinner, for there was no use beginning their search until the fog had gone off entirely. Once rid of it, the schooner could accomplish in an hour what might take a day of stealing about in the dangers of the vapor.

After dinner, the *Daniel* sailed in a long swing to be westward and then came legging it back along the old course. The fog had receded farther and was much brightened by the sunlight. The vessel followed after the fog, keeping a sharp watch on all quarters because there was no telling where the U-boat's victims might have gone. Whenever the schooner ran into a straggling bank of vapor, her horn blew loudly until she came into the clear again. In mid-afternoon, a sail was sighted so far down that it couldn't be made out clearly. The *Daniel* swung over to take a closer look, there being some chance that the lost men had set up a sail. That vessel was soon near enough for them to see that she was a fisherman, bound about her business. An hour later, there came down from the sky a strum of engines, pulsing strong over the calm surface of the sea. For a while, the planes couldn't be seen because of the clouds. A few minutes later, they came into sight. There were three bombers headed towards a Newfoundland base.

"Now," said Patrick, "by the Lord Harry! If one of them should peel off we might see some fancy hunting." The formation slid out of sight before he was done speaking.

At dusk, the *Daniel* tacked again and sailed on a new course which, Patrick figured, should carry them a little to the northeast of the place where the bombardment had been seen, thus completing a second circling of the area in which the lifeboats were likely to be. Night was coming on fast. Patrick, treading anxiously up and down the deck, passed the word along that they should keep an eye peeled for lights, since it was now dark enough for lanterns to be used as signals.

It was then that a rocket curved up into the air and burst against the dark blue of the western sky. Four or five of the crew saw it and sang out. Caleb swung the vessel over and, the wind being fair for her, she stepped along like a good one. By the time the second rocket leaped into the sky and burst in molten bits among the stars, the *Daniel* had run half the distance.

Now the signalling craft began to bulk up in the twilight. It was not a boat. That was soon clear. It was a big vessel.

Patrick didn't like the looks of things. He wanted to

help and he could do so only by answering the rockets, as he was duty-bound to do. Yet he was warier than ever. Even more than that, he was suspicious. He didn't know why, yet he could feel his blood begin to tingle and his heart rouse up. A ringing came in his ears. He opened his mouth because his nose, big as it was, couldn't give him enough air. The inner excitement was stifling him. He sucked in his thin cheeks and tried to be calm and reasonable and thus play up to this thing, whatever it was, in open fashion. There had been a time when he couldn't think and be himself at the same time. He loved and respected his own emotions and the play of his instinct, even when all signs ran against them. Now, sharpened by the perils of the new war, he kept his head in command of his angry heart.

He suddenly whispered: "To hell with it!" and then he shouted: "No lights! Pass the word along!"

The word passed along the waist and into the galley. "Lights out! Lights out!"

Conrad went below and put out the big lamp in the cabin and the glow in the skylight faded. Others did the same for the running lights. Thus, dark and sealed and purposeful, the schooner bore straight down on the stranger and kept ready to bear swiftly off at a sign from Patrick's tense, lifted hand.

Ten minutes later, the sun, which was itself out of sight, sent up its last long rays. Those red swaths

struck a mass of clouds far up and glanced down
again in a flood of crimson, down into the sea beyond
the black hull. Patrick saw then what he had come
to see. A cry of pain and anger came from his lips.
It was the Dane. It was the mysterious square-rigger
lying there. And she had been shelled. All his
profound suspicions of her vanished. All his dreams
of a wild exploit against her became foolish in his
sight.

The men, stricken into silence by that desolate
image, stared open-eyed. Only Conrad called out
and all he said was: "Ah, Captain, Captain!" Holger
leaped up into the shrouds and gazed eagerly from
that high place. He cried out a muffled word when
the schooner rose in her sailing and gave him a better
look at the ship beyond.

Patrick, sick at heart, stared at the Danish ship.
She was a floating ruin. She rode deep and heavy and
a little by the head, as if she was taking water. The
stump of her mizzenmast stood. The others had been
cut away or lay broken in a tangle of gear. Part of a
tattered sail had fallen over her poop-deck. It flapped
in the wind and gave out a cracking sound, loud as a
rifle shot. A smell of smoke came down when the
Daniel sailed to leeward of her. Patrick saw a light
gleam in her cabin skylight when the torn canvas
blew aside. He couldn't tell whether this was a lantern burning or the embers of a fire. The brilliant

spread of sunset went out then and the night swarmed over the square-rigger.

Patrick couldn't keep his eyes off her. For a time, his thoughts changed to those natural to a seaman. He pitied her. He could imagine how beautiful she would be with all her sails set and a fair breeze bowling her along. Never in his life had he set foot on a ship like that, but he had heard much good talk from his father of their massive timbers, vast holds, and the comfort and spaciousness of their quarters.

Conrad spoke to him, said something about that ship being the one they sought, the one they had suspected of evil traffic with the Germans. Patrick hardly listened. He looked at Conrad in silence and he saw again that the Dane's face had taken on that cold, icy look, that same lofty expression which had stiffened it when they found the three dead men lying murdered in the boat. Patrick nodded grimly.

Conrad spoke again. "Keep off her, Captain."

Patrick stared at him in astonishment. Keep away from this pitiful shambles? Something within him answered: *Yes!* At once his tender sorrow over a ruined vessel left him and he put the helm down. Once more that dark, waiting hulk took on her first sinister meaning. She again became the enemy, daring, resourceful, murderous.

"I'll keep off her." Yet he couldn't help seeking

some reason to bolster their wariness. He asked: "Why do you say that?"

Conrad whispered: "Who can tell? You said: always watch out."

"Yes, I did."

"Why did they fire guns at her? I know they do not use guns that way. They board a vessel and put a time-bomb in her hold. Set it for an hour away. Then go back to U-boat." He groaned deep at some memory and added: "So they do in the North Sea. So everywhere. Time-bombs all the time."

"They have ruined her on purpose." Patrick, staring at the shadowy outline of the receding ship, whispered his conjecture.

"Yes, Captain. Maybe."

"There may be Germans on her right now."

"That is right."

Patrick called out to Caleb: "Top dory. Port side. I'm going to board that vessel. Alone."

"Alone? To hell you are!" said Caleb.

"Conrad," said Patrick, "go below and get my gun. It's in the left-hand cubbyhole at the bottom. Tell cook to put extra stores into that dory. I may have to stay a while."

"I go with you, Captain, please?" Conrad waited. At Patrick's nod, he went below and came up with the *Daniel's* old navy revolver in his hand. He had also picked up an electric torch. He tried it on the palm of his hand, which gave off a reddish glow, and then he thrust the torch into Patrick's pocket.

Patrick sang out again. "Pass the word along. I'm going to board that vessel. In the line of duty. I'm not answering her rockets just now. For reasons of my own. Good and sufficient ones. I want one other man to go along with Conrad and me. But no man in the first gang can go. That includes you, Caleb, so quit your jawing and get that dory over." He then said to Conrad: "It's fit and proper you should come with me because she's a Danish vessel and it may be we can help your countrymen. Therefore, 'tis fit and proper that Holger should be asked to go, too. He'll want to, I suppose."

Holger, who was helping the cook put the stores into the dory, heard his name spoken. He came running towards Patrick and cried eagerly: "I go, Captain. Please take me along!"

"Good! That's all then." Patrick turned the wheel over to Caleb and said: "We're going now, Caleb. Mind you keep this vessel lively. Sail around that ship and be on the look-out. Don't let any boat come nigh you. I'll signal you plain A-B-C if I want you to come alongside. And I'll use your last name in the message. O.K.?"

"Blink her slow. That's all I say, Patrick."

The dory ran at a fast pace under the stranger's

bow. Conrad and Holger sat at the oars and laid into it smartly, while Patrick looked and listened. Once he flashed the light against her side. He saw nothing strange, nothing out of the way, except what he ex- pected: a mass of cordage and twisted yardarms and folds of sodden sail, all hanging in an unsightly man- ner from her bulwarks. He stopped the rowers there and let the light dart into the wreckage. He saw a yard that had been newly painted gray. Another spar, which might have been a masthead, had a coat of white paint. The vessel was not anchored, but the mess of dragging gear served as a sort of sea-anchor and held her fairly steady where she lay.

When the dory ran under the stranger's stern, Pat- rick sent the silver circle of his torch in a dipping flicker up and down her stem. The sternpost had been hit in two places. Her rudder had apparently escaped harm. Above the gashes, where the outer rim of his light wavered, he saw an arc of golden letters across her stern. He raised the torch and swept its bull's-eye along the fancy scroll. It said: *Den Magre Kvinde.*

"Can you see that, Conrad?"

Conrad leaned forward on his oars. "I see it. Yes." He read the name aloud. "She is a Dane all right. I don't know her, just the same."

Holger then repeated the name aloud. Patrick, straddled in the stern-sheets, took the time to look at him. A shower of light, reflected from the ship's hull, touched up the seaman's face. Patrick saw that his gaze was intense, that he was alert and seemed full of an extraordinary expectation. It was a sort of hidden, disciplined excitement, with no mark of sorrow or anger in it. In that brief inspection of a man to whom he had given the name of secret enemy, Patrick discerned that houndlike eagerness which he had seen when the square-rigger was first sighted that evening. His suspicions of Holger grew alarmingly in that moment. He couldn't fix the evidence to his own satisfaction. He was sure of himself. Holger's pretension of grief over the dead men had been enough. But Patrick wanted more. And there was a way, right now, of being surer.

He took it. He suddenly switched the light away from the ship's stern and flashed it directly against Holger's face and then out over the water. The beam darted a full cable's length over the waves. Patrick turned it off and whispered: "You men hear anything out there? Oars?"

They made no answer. Patrick had gotten an answer to his inner question. He had seen Holger's face. It was gleaming with sweat, although the night blew cold.

Patrick's hackle rose and his heart roused up again. The vessel towering above him had some special meaning to Holger. There was no question of it. Patrick said: "We'll lie here a minute. Keep her so. Then off

a bit and one of you—you, Holger—give her a hail
in her own lingo. Easy now. Easy does it. Maybe it
was a boat. Answer no hail from that quarter, boys.
I feel in my bones there's something stirring out
there."

This was a lie. Patrick felt no such thing in his
bones. He had an ague in them, a fever, and it was
new to him as the act of telling a lie was new. This
fever was an almost intolerable desire to kill Holger,
there and then. To blast him between the shining
eyeballs with a bullet and heave him over the side.
Or to step forward and smash his skull with the butt
of his revolver. Patrick knew the meaning of killing
in hot blood. He had heard of it in open warfare when
his father had slain the enemies of the Republic.
Here, in these very waters. But murder in cold blood,
with the blood calmly feeding the impulse of his
brain—this was a new thought to him. New and en-
ervating. New and sickening. So much so that, at the
sound of Holger's voice, Patrick moved backward
abruptly and sank into his seat. Nevertheless, the vio-
lence of that urge forced his hand into his pocket. He
took out the pistol.

Holger had asked: "Pull away now, Captain?"

Patrick replied: "Pull away. Pull away a little."

They gave way. As the distance between the dory
and the ship increased, Patrick twisted around to take
a look at her deck. He began to note this and that

about her. He saw the Jacob's-ladder dangling on the starboard side. He saw a red star marching up the sky and another clambering through the imperfect shrouds of her mizzen. In order that he might calm the murderous impulse in his heart, he counted the stars in a whisper. He sought others beyond in the West. Yet this child's game failed to soothe him. The steel of the revolver warmed under his fingers. He permitted his forefinger to unbend and gently embrace the trigger. And then he remembered what he had said to Conrad—that they, the hares, were running with the hounds. More strongly than ever, he felt this to be true. He put the gun away and let the game go on.

"Now, Holger!" he cried, "give her a hail."

Holger cried out: "Ahoy! Ahoy, *Den Magre Kvinde!*" His shout rang loud. He spoke again in Danish. "Ahoy, ahoy the ship! Is there anybody aboard?"

They waited. A livelier ripple ran under the dory, tossed it, then slapped hard against the shadowy hull above them.

"You, Conrad," said Patrick. "Give her a cheery hail and say that there are Americans here."

"Ahoy! Ahoy, *Den Magre Kvinde!* Americans here!"

"No answer, Captain," said Holger.

"What!" whispered Patrick. "Was it a dying man then that sent up the rockets?"

"It is a dead ship, Captain," replied Holger.

Patrick stood up. "I'll give her a hail. What would you say that name meant? A woman, eh? Some kind of woman?"

"Aye, Captain, that is right," said Conrad. "Thin woman—no, woman starved. I have not the English word." He spoke to Holger in Danish and Patrick, getting the hang of it, cried out: "Gaunt? Gaunt? Is that it?"

"That is right," said Conrad. "You got it."

"The *Gaunt Woman?*"

"The *Gaunt Woman*," said Holger. "That's the word for it."

"A damned odd name for a vessel, boys. Though God knows she's gaunt enough this minute to be called that. And more." He made a horn of his hands and shouted: "Ahoy! Ahoy the *Gaunt Woman!* Ahoy there! A Gloucesterman standing by! Anybody aboard?"

No voice replied from the lonely deck. Patrick called for oars and the dory once more aproached the ship.

Patrick tried the hail again. "Answer the hail, will you? Ahoy, the ship! What are the rockets for?"

The vessel sighed and yielded a little to the wind

A spar clattered. The sail over her poop-deck bellied up and flapped with the same loud cracking sound. The wind found a whistling place in the stump of a mast and blew a shrill note.

Patrick said: "Get aboard her, boys. Make fast to the ladder, Conrad. Don't you come on deck until I tell you to. Holger, you follow Conrad. But don't come up until he tells you to. Now watch yourselves. It may be that they've abandoned ship since they signalled. But I don't think so. She's taking water, but not much."

He swung onto the ladder and climbed swiftly. He crouched a moment behind the bulwarks and lifted his head slowly until he could look out over the wide, cluttered deck. He leaped inboard, alighted on both feet, then shrank down into the scanty shelter of the bulwarks.

A dead man lay an oar's length away, staring at the night sky. His right knee was drawn up at a sharp angle. His other leg lay stretched out. His right arm lay gracefully across his breast, as if death had rapped him in the act of bowing. The other arm was flung out and upward. The curled fingers of that hand clutched a sailor's cap.

Patrick shouted: "Now is there anybody aboard this vessel who will speak to a man?"

He took out his revolver and cocked it. He then bided his time, listening to the multitudinous small noises of the ship and ocean—the clack of blocks, clank of chains, and a curious moaning from her forecastle, as if the sea was striking a hollow part of her. Her longboat lay crushed under a spar. A smaller boat swung in the davits. The carcass of an enormous white pig was stretched out near the splintered boards of some kind of wooden case. The pig-pen had been knocked about by a heavy sea, but it was whole. The smell of smoke had gone off entirely. In its stead, his nose found another fragrance, spicy and heavy. He couldn't name it and his able snuffing helped him not at all.

The moon was rising. It was a newish one and would lend but little light to the scene. Yet Patrick longed for that light and determined to wait until he had it. The moment he had accepted this necessity, he spoiled it by switching on his electric torch. The reason was plain. He was too frightened to stay hidden and cornered. He wished to invite his fate.

He let the torchlight stop upon the dead man's face. He saw a growth of beard, smears of grease or coal dust, and a bullet wound in the center of his forehead. There was blood on all sides of the wound. Patrick took note of these matters in order that he might serve his wariness, gather up the clues for which he longed. He then saw something—or the lack of something—that made him suck in his breath and shoot it out quickly between his clenched teeth.

It was this: there was no blood on the deck directly under the dead man's head. The deck itself was spotlessly clean, yet the cheeks were smeared with blood and dirt. Patrick knew then that the body had been placed there for a reason he could not fathom. The man had bled and died elsewhere.

He turned the torch off and crouched against the bulwarks again. He cursed savagely under his breath. "In a damned Hun trap! What are they up to?"

He leaned out over the bulwarks and cried: "Come up, Conrad!"

Conrad slid over and stood by his side. In the dark, Patrick whispered all that he had seen. The Dane listened and nodded. He made no answer. He took the torch from Patrick's hand. He then went swiftly up to the dead man, bent over him and turned the light full onto the face. Patrick watched him touch the dead hands and search the man's clothing with a fumbling, slow sweep of his fingers up and down. Conrad came back and whispered: "He is shipmate of the three dead we find. No seaman of this vessel. Could not earn his keep aboard her."

"I thought as much. Keep on your toes now. I don't like it here. What we figured out was true. The U-boat wanted somebody to board this vessel. And I'll find out why right now." He shifted the torch until it lighted the main hatch. Some shreds of canvas and bits of spars were strewn on the hatch, but he could

see that it was well battened down and that the tarpaulin over it was secured with strips of metal. He
pointed to it. "Down that hatch is where we'll find
the proof of our pudding, Conrad. One look below
would be enough for me. 'Twould make a fool of me
or a wiser guy than ever I thought I was. But not
now. Not yet." He gave a little groan and shut off
the light. "I can damn near smell gunpowder from
here."

Conrad said: "Something stinks damn bad, Captain."

"I know. But I can't tell what it is. Call up that
guy in the dory. He's part of this game and must be
kept at hand."

The first thing Holger said was: "Schooner just
sailed by, Captain. No signal."

"Good!" Patrick flashed a beam out over the sea.
Presently the *Daniel* acknowledged the signal. He
gave his message slowly. "Caleb Pond. All O.K. so far.
One of crew dead by bullet. No answer to hail. Going
into cabin now. Keep off and stand by." And then,
for the devil of it, he added: "Tell cook fat pig here."

The distant beam blinked and went dark.

Patrick led the way down into the forecastle. The
bunks were empty and unmade. Considerable oil
clothing hung on the hooks, but the lockers had been
cleaned out. Conrad went into the apprentices' quarters and called Patrick after him. Leaving Holger be-

hind, Patrick joined the other Dane and flashed the light up and down the rows of bunks. The quarters had been extended far down into the deck. Two steel ladders led to rows of bunks below. There was room enough there to sleep thirty men and more. Conrad whispered: "Too much room for one ship's boys."

They went on deck again and Patrick led the way towards the cabin under the poop-deck. He kept Conrad five or six paces behind him and Holger that much behind Conrad. He whispered to them: "They'll not jump us all at once this way."

Patrick walked quickly down the littered deck. The moon had now cleared the horizon and its light made their going easy. When they came to the dead seaman, Patrick turned to Holger and said: "What do you make of that? Killed by shrapnel?"

Holger, who had said nothing when he first saw the body, stared at it in silence now, then slowly nodded. "Perhaps the crew put up a fight, Captain."

A rooster flapped down from his perch in a cascade of tackle between the mainmast and the mizzen. Again the moaning sound came up from the forecastle and the ship pitched heavily.

Patrick went slowly down the companionway that led to the cabin. He crept forward until he stood close to a port. He looked through it. The moon sent irregular flashes of light through the skylight and through another port that lay open beyond. Patrick stepped backward, stretched out his hand and turned the torch ray through the port.

A man inside the cabin cried out and fired a shot. The bullet ripped through the glass and sent fragments tinkling at Patrick's feet.

"There he is!" Patrick grasped Conrad by the arm and whispered: "Hail him friendly like. Tell him in Danish we are friends."

Conrad shouted: "Friends here. Lay off there! Lay off on that gun! We are friends."

A deep groan within answered him.

Patrick said: "Here goes!" He walked into the cabin, his light playing before him. It struck on a large and neatly made bunk, then moved onto an open desk. Nothing stirred. No other sound came.

Speaking in an ordinary tone, Patrick said: "You are all right now, friend. I am the master of a Gloucester schooner, answering your rockets. Are you wounded?"

He then let the torch play into the far corner of the cabin. This time he found a man, one of the best looking he had ever laid eyes on. He was a bearded man and a big one. His beard was red and square-shaped. It came down to the lapels of his brass-buttoned coat. The beam picked out a few white hairs in the red. The man's eyes were fierce. Some trick of the mixing lights gave them a reddish hue. He wore a merchant captain's visored cap. Despite his circumstances, this cap lay at a jaunty angle. But this might have been an accident.

The man stared unblinking at the light. He then tried to look beyond it. Patrick saw that the eyes were bloodshot.

Conrad and Holger entered the cabin, took their places behind Patrick, and stared over his shoulders.

At that moment, the bearded man said: "Skalder!" His voice was a fine bass one and made that emphatic word sound beautiful.

Patrick asked: "Captain Skalder?"

No answer came.

"I am Patrick Bannon, master of the *Daniel Webster,* a Gloucester fisherman. I have with me two of my crew. If this is a Danish vessel, then these men"— he turned the light first on Conrad's face, then on Holger's —"these men are your countrymen." Holger's face streamed with sweat; his eyes burned. Conrad's face retained its calm and frigid expression.

Words came out of the magnificent beard in a mutter. "I am crazy! Crazy!"

Patrick, having much faith in the uses of formality, said rather stiffly: "We observed distress rockets fired from this vessel early in the evening. We made sail and proceeded to your position with all possible speed. Our hails not being answered, I boarded this vessel to give aid, as required by law."

"Crazy! Crazy!" The bearded man spoke without

stirring, without shifting his reddened eyes. This time
he spoke more distinctly and his teeth shone yellow.

"Sir?" said Patrick.

"I shot at you." The great head waggled ponder-
ously. "At you!"

"Think nothing of it, Captain. We can stand a shot
or two." He turned his torch upward. There were
two iron lamps hanging from a cross-beam. "Can we
have a light now, Captain?"

"Sure! Sure! A lamp?" He lifted both his hands,
held them momentarily about six inches above the
table, then brought them down with a thump. "I
apologize, Captain Bannon. I thought—I said to
myself: 'They have come back for me. I will kill!
Kill! Shoot and kill!'" His voice ran up into a
scream. His eyes widened with fury. He ground his
teeth so hard that their gnashing sounded clear above
the sighs and groans of his vessel. He began to curse
in Danish. The words came clanging out of his beard
like bars of iron falling.

Conrad said to Patrick: "The captain curses the
U-boat and its commander. He has been boarded.
Also robbed and shelled. Also other things. Some one
is killed."

Patrick's heart sank. Once again, his doubt assailed
him. The ruin and destruction aboard the vessel could
not help but convince him that the *Gaunt Woman*
had been waylaid and shelled. Now the fury and woe

of the man before him made it even harder for him to cling to his belief that this vessel was the murderer of many others. Nevertheless, as he stood there, burdened by his doubts, an inner warning rang loud again and the image of the dead man on the *Gaunt Woman's* deck rose in his mind to make that warning logical and real. He kept his silence.

Holger lighted the lamps. One wick failed to draw. It flickered and went out, leaving an embered ring within the fouled glass chimney. The other lamp welled up and cast a glow over the cabin. Now, in this fresh light, Patrick saw that Captain Skalder had been hit. At least, there was a smear of blood on his white shirt front and on his right cuff. He was about to speak of this matter when he spied a redder gleam, the shine of a drop oozing in the beard. He took a step nearer. The big teeth were pressing down upon the lower lip. "Captain Skalder! Be at ease, sir! We'll save your vessel. Your men will be picked up in the morning. Or they'll reach Newfoundland."

At this, the captain began to rise from his armchair. His shoulders bent forward. Patrick involuntarily recoiled half a step as he watched the majestic head rise and rise and the true bulk of him come into plain sight. This was a whale of a man! Taller even than himself, twice as old, and yet a hefty man, one who could handle himself.

Patrick asked: "Are there any of your men left aboard, Captain?"

The captain seemed not to have heard. He kept his eyes fixed on the shattered port beyond. A powerful emotion held him in a trance. He began to draw his hands from the table. A dragging, clinging quality to this movement fascinated Patrick.

Suddenly the captain jerked his hands all the way to his hips and placed them there, the fingers extended in the akimbo pose. At once a new manner, a loftier and a sadder one, came upon him. He opened his mouth and cried out in a voice that was again almost a scream. "My son! My son! They shot him on my own deck!" He left off his roughly accented English and roared in Danish, sentence after sentence bursting with pell-mell curses.

When he had done, Holger said to Patrick: "The Germans stopped him. Told him to clear off with his men. He is the owner, too. He and his son would not abandon ship. He told men and son to go. The son fired at the boarding party which came with time-bombs to sink her. Then they shoot him on the deck. Then they are frightened off and try to sink her by shell fire. Fog made shooting bad. So!"

He seemed to slur over the word "frightened." This didn't escape Patrick. He asked: "What frightened them off? A war vessel?"

The captain lifted his hand, showed its pinkish palm in a dreary gesture. "I do not know, Captain Bannon. It was a signal from the submarine itself. It was that—a flag signal—that made them go. They killed our pig. But they didn't stop to take him. They ran." He looked down at the table and whispered: "He was foolish! Foolish to shoot! My poor boy."

Patrick said: "You lost some of your gear in that nor'easter, Captain Skalder."

"True! True! But we could have handled her. If only"—he groaned piteously—"if only I had not bad luck to be seen by those monsters."

"What is your cargo, sir, if you please?"

"Rum, Captain Bannon. Barrels of rum from the West Indies. My papers." He bent down and picked up a bundle from the floor. He unlashed it, undid two folds of sail-cloth, and pushed a number of documents along the table towards Patrick. He gave them a brief, perfunctory glance, knowing perfectly well that the forging of ship's papers was an easy job.

Patrick asked: "Where were you bound, Captain?"

"To Port Halifax. I am blown far off my course. I have sold this rum—it is my own speculation—I have sold every barrel of it to the military. To our English protectors. I must go to Halifax."

The great game—if it was a game—now opened

in earnest for Patrick. He determined to play it with
a free, hard hand. He inwardly resolved that nothing
on earth would stop him from getting down into the
hold of the *Gaunt Woman*. So he said: "We will
gladly help you, Captain. But I advise you strongly
to refit elsewhere. Port Halifax is no place for a
merchantman in these days. You can't get things
done there. It would take a month—two months—
to get new spars for your vessel there. If you could
get them at all."

"I tell you I must go to Halifax, Captain Bannon!"
Skalder then made a gesture of the utmost politeness
to soften the harshness of his voice. He sat down
heavily. "My whole life, my money, all—it is in this
vessel. This cargo. I cannot go on without her. But
you have come! I am helpless without you. I signalled for you to come. Then—ah! I went crazy!
Crazy! I said: 'Surely they have seen the rockets—
those monsters—and they know I am still afloat.' "
He stared at his clasped hands a while, then turned
to Holger. "And you—where are you from, my boy?"

"Skanderborg."

"And you?" he asked of Conrad.

"Ringkjobing, Captain."

"Skanderborg and Ringkjobing." He muttered the
names over and over. "She has been in those waters
—the poor *Woman*. Yes, in the good times of peace.
Now, ever since the war, she has worked hard and

never at home. In South America. Coal, wool, drums of oil. Anything. Now rum. I must go to Port Halifax."

Patrick spoke up again. "You are still master here, Captain Skalder. This is not a salvage for us. We are here to help you. As you would help us. I have a plan. If you like it—well and good. If not, I will do exactly what you say."

"You are a good seaman, Captain Bannon. You talk well. To the point." Skalder stroked his magnificent beard. His fingers touched the wet strand. He looked at his own blood and growled. He reached into an inner pocket, drew out a handkerchief and dabbed at his lips and at his beard.

He then asked: "What is your plan, Captain?"

"Let these men, who were trained on ships like this —let Holger and Conrad get a jury-rig on her. We can sail her to Newfoundland. That's going to be hard, but not dangerous, if the weather holds. You can't run the risk of taking her back to Halifax under such a rig. And you can easily refit her in a good little harbor I know there. You can buy—"

"What harbor is that, Captain Bannon?"

"Trabo!"

"Ah! I've read that name on my charts."

"You can buy what spars you need. There's a small shipyard up the river. It's busy now. Building a corvette. But there's men to be had. Shipwrights and

sailmakers. Good ones, too. Do you have a new suit of
sails for her?"

"Yes, Captain. A good locker full."

"Then there's an old rope-walk farther up the coast.
Why, you'll have no trouble, Captain Skalder. No
red tape. No talk, but damned good men willing to
work hard for an honest dollar. It would be a good
thing for Trabo and it's all right for me because I'm
on my way there now to buy bait. And besides, if
your men reach shore we'll hear of them there and
get your crew together again."

For the first time since Patrick had entered the
cabin, Captain Skalder's expression of hatred and sorrow changed to a gentler cast. Although he was still
brimful of the strongest sort of emotion, it was tem-
pered now with resignation and hope. Repeatedly he
sighed while he ran his long forefinger up and down
the chart. At last, the finger stopped and he said:
"Trabo!" He looked up, gave Patrick a grave smile
and added: "On one condition, Captain Bannon."

"Willingly, sir."

Captain Skalder lifted another fold of his sail-cloth
bundle and revealed some packages of American cur-
rency, banknotes of large and small denominations.
"I know your vessel fishes on shares. So much for the
owner. So much for the master and so much for each
man. That is so?"

"Yes, Captain."

"You are the owner of the schooner?"

"Mr. Dolan of Gloucester is the owner."

"My condition is that you accept from me a sum to pay each man his share of last trip's earnings. Pay the same amount to each one. I cannot deprive honest seamen of their livelihood."

"That's a thoughtful thing to say, Captain. I don't think Mr. Dolan would like it, but it's a matter we can talk over later. At Trabo—if we get there."

"Then Trabo it is!" The giant stepped lightly to a locker of mahogany wood, flung up the cover and took out a bottle wrapped in straw. He set metal mugs down on the table and poured dark rum into them. He handed them around, held his own up, and faced Patrick.

Patrick was thinking clearly in a chaos of emotions —doubt, fear, and a desperate desire not to make a fool of himself, especially in Trabo. He could not rid himself of the conviction that he was right, that this vessel and the man standing before him had something to do with the dead men he had found and with the U-boats that had killed so many more. He decided then and there to gaff the giant, to find out whether his brain had the strength and agility of his extraordinary body. The uplifted drinks offered a chance. Patrick waited, gazing solemnly the while at the rim of his mug.

"Skoal!" cried Skalder in his nor'easter accent.

"Skoal! Skoal!" Conrad and Holger moved their mugs to the right and left in a rhythmic motion.

"Skoal!" cried Patrick, his eyes half-shut. And then he added: "God rest the soul of the hero, your dear son!"

He bent his head back and tossed the rum against the roof of his mouth and, at the same moment, he risked a split-second glance at Skalder. The captain had been caught off guard. Patrick saw the mug, tiny in his enormous fingers, stop short of the wounded lips. He saw the eyes open wide and quickly close again. He had seen enough. The eyes, in less than a breath of time, had revealed one of two things: terror or suspicion. Whichever it was, Patrick saw that Skalder, pleased with the plan to go into out-of-the-way Trabo, had missed his cue.

The captain drank and gently put his mug down. He bowed his head and whispered: "Eric! Eric!"

Patrick knew he had been lying. He knew then that the young man lying dead on the *Gaunt Woman's* deck was no son of Skalder. He knew that the dead man could only be another U-boat hand, executed for a breach of discipline and flung down on that deck as a sort of stage property for a well-wrought play.

Encasing his triumph in a mock look of sadness, Patrick said: "Let us bury your poor boy, Captain. Let us give him a sailor's burial." He sighed heavily and added: "Only a little while ago, we did the same thing for three of your countrymen—"

"Ah!" Skalder, startled by the swift and cunning introduction of this story, flung up his head. This time he had skill enough to make his attitude a natural one of distressed concern.

"Yes, Captain," said Patrick. "We found three dead Danes in a boat. They had been killed by a shrapnel burst. It must have caught them when they abandoned ship."

"Ah, good God!" Skalder flung his arms upward and groaned in his beard. "That such things must be!"

He led them out then and, standing inflexible and proud by his shattered bulwarks, he prayed in Danish while they wrapped and weighted the body and mournfully slid it into the sea. This done, they made a survey of the *Gaunt Woman* and agreed that the jury-rig should be set up around the stump of the mainmast. All else was beyond saving. The mizzen, which had seemed to be in better shape, was cracked in several places. Patrick called the *Daniel* alongside. All night long the axes hewed and knives slashed and Holger and Conrad sewed and bent on the new canvas. Soon after dawn, the captain, who had worked tirelessly and with great skill, took the helm and both vessels got under way with a fine rain falling on a calm sea.

The *Gaunt Woman* moved sluggishly, but she had kept her buoyancy and answered as well as could be expected. In the afternoon, a breeze came up that was fair for her and Conrad bent on a queer triangular spread to the ruin of her foremast. This improved her sailing because her cargo seemed to have shifted and had the effect of keeping her head down. The added sail, small as it was, helped this fault and the *Gaunt Woman* began to make four or five knots. On Sunday morning, Patrick sighted the cliffs and forests of Newfoundland. At dawn of the next day, he saw the somber and snow-streaked hills that hid the harbor of Trabo.

CHAPTER V.

AMBLING ALONG under jib and foresail, the *Daniel Webster* led the way into the long tickle that ran from the sea into Trabo Harbor. The *Gaunt Woman* followed, helped by a flooding tide that filled the passage with a surfy roar. On both sides of the channel, there were cliffs of blackish rock which ran up a hundred fathoms and more. These cliffs held jagged and somber crests against the sky and shut out much of the sunlight, but the passage was clear enough, deep water all the way. Half a mile from the sea, the tickle abruptly widened into a well-carved stone bowl, big enough to berth a squadron. The sun beamed there on a bay that was green and calm, except at the eastern shore where the Trabo River rolled a swath of black, fresh water into the salt.

Patrick stood at the helm of the *Gaunt Woman* while she made the passage. Captain Skalder walked anxiously back and forth on the poop-deck, fearful lest some trick of the strong tide drive his vessel onto the rocks at the last moment.

"Sixty fathom here, Captain!" shouted Patrick.

"And a bottom of gravel from the hills. Are they ready forward?"

"Aye! Ready to let go!"

"In ten minutes then."

Skalder went forward and joined Conrad and Holger at the anchor.

Patrick looked ahead and saw the *Daniel* already at her anchorage. Her sails were down, her anchor going, and a dory over the side. He saw a masthead-man slide along the stay from main to fore. A few small craft were moored off the village wharf and on the wharf stood a score of men, a few women with their black skirts flying, and children staring.

He let the ship sail onward until she felt the rough push of the river current. He then lifted his hand and the men let go the anchor with a rattle and splash that drove the gulls screeching away.

Patrick let himself go a little, too. He was all in, all tuckered out. He was dirty and the red bristles of his face stuck out in an unsightly fashion. He was thinner, too, for he had eaten poorly in the *Gaunt Woman's* galley during the hard passage up the coast, had kept going on coffee laced with rum. He laid his tired arms upon the wheel and rested his head upon his arms. He felt miserable. Nevertheless, he was jubilant within. He had conquered. He had tricked the hated shark into a weir from which there was no escape, unless to a doom worse than the terrible one he had

in mind. He lifted his head and laughed. There were
three things he wanted now and could have in Trabo
—a shave, a thick beefsteak, and a walk with Margaret. He looked for her among the black skirts and
the shawled heads of the women staring under their
uplifted hands. He saw her standing in the lane at the
head of the wharf, not thickly togged out like a doryman, but dressed in a jacket and skirt of green woolen
cloth, bright as daybreak on the ocean. She was looking at the dory rowing away from the *Daniel.*

He heard a man's voice sing out: "Ahoy! Hey!
What ship is that?"

Patrick waved his hand.

Skalder came to his side. He, too, had changed
during the sleepless nights of the passage and the
anxious days of handling the ship under her jury-rig.
His eyes seemed deeper in his head and his cheeks
hollow. His hands still trembled with the exertion of
getting the anchor over. But he was glad to be at
anchor and spoke with feeling of the good work done
by Conrad and Holger. "And you, Captain Bannon
—the high qualities of your seamanship have saved
my vessel and my cargo. I thank you and congratu-
late you. For a man so young, you have great skill and
knowledge. You will not be the loser by it. It is not in
vain—your magnificent struggle." His accent turned
"vain" into "wain" and he smiled a little ruefully at
it.

Despite his suspicions, this speech pleased Patrick, who hadn't been a skipper long enough to do without the praise of other captains. He grinned and said: "We're here, Captain. That's the big thing. And now the job is to get you ship-shape and out again. That's the next thing and there"—he swung his arm towards the wharf—"there they are. The lads that will do the job in jig-time and do it well." He looked again at the group ashore. The ship was swinging in a little and he could see the men clearly. "I see the head boatbuilder, old MacDonald. He's the man for you, Captain. Couldn't lift a maul now to save his soul, but he knows all there is to know. He's made vessels like this in his time and there are men in that town who have sailed them for him. So we're all right now."

They went ashore together, leaving Conrad and Holger as an anchor-watch until another could be recruited ashore. When the two captains climbed onto the wharf, the villagers crowded forward with their greetings to Patrick and their questions about the *Gaunt Woman*. Patrick told them how he had found the ship dismasted on the Grand Bank and a lone man on her. "This is the man," he said, putting his hand on Skalder's arm. "Her master and owner. He stayed with her, even when the U-boat shelled her. No! he wouldn't leave her. Not for the death of him!"

The Newfoundlanders murmured that this was a good skipper and they gazed in admiration at his bulky figure and his handsome beard. Skalder bowed and shook the outstretched hands and Patrick again praised him to the skies for a keen sailor. And then, hushing his voice, he told of the dead men he had found in the boat and how he had later found another man shot to death on the *Gaunt Woman's* deck. "This man's dear son."

A cry that was almost a wail rose amongst the women. One of them crossed herself and whispered the words: "His dear son!"

An old man, bent over a crooked walking-stick, listened with sorrowing eyes to the tale. He kept one parchment of a hand held to his ear, kept his mouth an empty circle. He cried out shrilly against murder and chiefly against murder on the innocent, high seas, a deed which seemed most foul to him. "Ah, Skipper Patrick," said he in a windy voice, "sad it is, b'y, that such things must be."

These were the very words, Patrick remembered, that Skalder had uttered when first they met in the cabin of the *Gaunt Woman;* only then the words had been a mocking lie.

Patrick greeted the old man. "Skipper Ben, I'll have you shake hands, if you please, with the master of that vessel. I've brought him all the way up the Straight Shore to put his fine ship into your care."

Skalder courteously took the old man's hand.

"I seen yon craft," said the head-builder, "I seen her come about off the tickle and I seen she was a square-rigged vessel, Skipper, and I says to Jonathan here: 'Jonathan, b'y, she's clean swept from sprit to post, she is!' And I knowed there was work to be done on her and we be the lads to do it. Aye! and will do it."

"That's the way to talk, Skipper Ben!" said Patrick. "Sure, there's work to be done aboard that vessel. Plenty of it and good pay. There's not a whole stick left standing in her. Her deck has been swept and her rigging gone to smithereens. So I'll leave you to talk with Captain Skalder when you've told me one more thing. Is there herring to be had for my own vessel? We need to be about our business."

"Not one, Skipper Patrick!"

"What?"

" 'Tis what I say. The *Golden Hind* took all our loads and lucky she was to get them. No, Skipper Patrick, there'll be no bait here or anywhere for a time to come. Wednesday, maybe. Or longer. Not until the herring say so. And they don't like the ice knocking around over their heads." The old man looked at the others and won their nods.

"I won't mind a few days ashore," said Patrick. "So there's no harm done. Unless the price of halibut goes down—and I don't think it will."

"You look poorly, Skipper Patrick," said the old man. "You do well to stay ashore, for there's a plenty of good beef in Trabo now, thanks to that girl there"—he pointed his stick towards Margaret, who was slowly walking towards them—"and Mrs. Mac-Lean has been expecting you. So I hear. So a little bird tells me, Skipper Patrick." He winked happily because he well remembered the Gloucester boy and girl together in Trabo in years gone by. He waited then until Margaret came and stood by his side and he narrowly watched their greeting, even clucked his tongue in surprise at the grave air of children grown up. Captain Skalder bowed over Margaret's hand and, like Patrick himself, showed an almost reckless interest in the lively, glintful face under the fall of red hair.

Old Ben fidgeted a bit during their greetings. His wrinkled cheeks twisted in the excitement of what he had to say. He tapped impatiently with his stick and cried out: "But I've some good news for ye! Fine, good news." He hitched his ancient frame about until he faced Skalder square. "For you it is."

"For me?" Skalder, plainly astonished, looked quickly at Patrick in a way that asked: Is the old one daft? Patrick perceived that Skalder's astonishment gave way at once to uneasiness. He muttered some word in his long, untidy beard, glanced at Patrick almost in alarm, and then stroked the beard nervously.

"News for Captain Skalder?" asked Patrick.

"'Tis for he, b'y. 'Tis about his crew."

"My crew!" Skalder blew the words out in a trumpet blast. Quick relief brightened his eyes; and the change in him warned Patrick that he was dealing with a man full of the wariness that his strange circumstances demanded.

Old Ben cackled in pleasure. "One and all, Skipper, is safe and sound. In English Village. Not a man-jack among them bitten or wetted." The fresh look of joy that came into Skalder's eyes put a stop to the old man. He laid his fingers on his mouth in a gesture of doubt and said: "If it's the same vessel. And I hope it be. What be her worthy name?" He thrust his stick out towards the mastless hull.

"The *Gaunt Woman*!" cried Patrick.

"Then I be bogged in error, b'y!" said old Ben sadly. "It was a square-rigged vessel they left on the Bank, but no such name they give in English Village. 'Twas a queer one, tho' God knows that's queer enough what you say."

Skalder took a step forward. He was terribly agitated. "Please!" he said, "was the name *Den Magre Kvinde?*"

"Eh, Skipper? Say over."

"*Den Magre Kvinde?*"

" 'Twas!" Old Ben rapped the planks with his stick. " 'Twas that very blather of words, Skipper. 'Twas that old Paul tied his tongue around and haggled over on this very spot."

"Then, sir," said Skalder, "they are my poor men. Thank God for this news." He turned away from them, much affected, and Patrick heard him whisper a phrase in Danish and then: "My poor men! Safe, thank God!" And the Trabo men and women, watching in delight the captain's joy, were proud that one of their number had given the news and they said: " 'Tis fine, good news. Ah, his poor men. Thank God for that news!"

Patrick struck his hands together and shouted with pleasure. "Skipper Ben, the names are one and the same. Those Danish words mean *The Gaunt Woman.* Or something near it. I was dumb to use that name. But never mind! Now, tell me, how did the good news get to Trabo? Has Paul been in?"

"Why, Skipper Patrick, 'tis easy. Yes, old Paul was by in his trading shop yesterday. He and his old woman. With white flour—the best—to sell and a ration of tea all around. And he was there in English Village when in came the two boats of them, after hanging off the shore half the night, poor things, not knowing where they were. We'll send a word to them, eh? Poor, dear men!"

Skalder cried: "Good! Who will go? Is there a vessel to carry them here? I will pay such a vessel well."

Patrick struck in forcefully at this point; for it was clear that the sudden arrival of the *Gaunt Woman's* crew would be a trouble to him. It wouldn't be well to have those seamen back in their quarters aboard the vessel. He said: "The *Daniel* and no other will do the job, Captain Skalder. She's the only one big enough to do it and we should let her finish what she has well begun. The first thing in the morning after my men have had a turn ashore."

They all walked then up the rocky, winding lane that led into Trabo, a sort of Mother Goose hamlet, tucked into the steep bank above the river. There were a score of cottages, blue and white and brown. In the midst of them stood the little tavern—not much more than a boarding-house—that Margaret's people kept. Its first story was of brick, its second of stained logs. Next to it, and connected with a covered passageway, was another cottage, where Margaret lived with her aunt. Wood smoke streamed up from the stone chimneys of the tavern and a good smell of baking filled the air.

Leaving the shipwrights to talk with Skalder in the tavern, Patrick led Margaret away and back into the lane. Above the village, the lane dwindled into a path and this presently split into two. Pacing together in silence, they took the one that turned towards the sea. They passed through a grove of stunted evergreens and stopped at the brink, under which the sunlit sea roared in long combers over the reefs and the narrow beaches. This was the Straight Shore of Avalon, called Avalon because Trabo lay in the province of that name, and called Straight because the shore ran westward in an undeviating bulwark of cliffs.

Patrick was much moved by their silent walk together in the scenes where they had walked before. He had no mind just then to begin their grave business. It was grave because he had determined to tell her all that had happened. He had made that decision the moment he had seen her looking for him in the *Daniel's* dory. Why he made it, he couldn't tell. He had a desperate desire to confide in somebody, to find some support until he had clearer proof of his suspicions in hand. Conrad was not enough. And there was a practical reason, too, for seeking her help. She had spent much of her girlhood here. She knew the people much better than he did, despite their friendliness to him. And she knew the beaches and the cliffs and caverns as well as he knew the stones of Gloucester, a knowledge that would be useful if he found in the hold of the *Gaunt Woman* the things he expected to find. Besides, there had never been a secret between them in the old days and he wanted none now, wanted to make a swift return to their youthful courtship.

She looked, in an unbroken silence, over the sea. Two sails gleamed in the sunlight. Far beyond, on the reefs of the Mull, the bones of a schooner shone white; and directly below, in the outer channel that led to the sea, a black and rotten hull reared upward on Widow's Rock.

Patrick took that chance to look at her face more intently. It seemed to have changed, even in the few days since they had parted in Gloucester. Her cheeks were still well-colored and good to see, but there was a hint of pallor in them, a hint of anxiety in the half-pout of her handsome mouth and her downcast eyes.

"Your father, Margaret?"

She nodded. "It was the first time I had seen him since it happened. As I told you, it was bad."

"But you are glad you came?"

"Oh, yes! He should never have left St. John's. He had good care there. If I hadn't come—" she looked directly at him then and said: "He lost an arm, you know."

"An arm!" And then he whispered: "A fisherman!"

"He'll never go fishing again, Patrick. That's the thing that hurts him most. Not the pain so much. Although he suffers. I took the room next to his and I hear him at night."

"What happened to him, Margaret? I knew he left Gloucester when Canada went to war. But I never could get the straight of it since."

"He went into the Canadian Navy. Took command of a mine-sweeper. The very one he had in the last war when he fought alongside your father. He won't speak of it now, but Aunt Julia says he went aboard a vessel that a U-boat had stopped off Cape Race. They'd put time-bombs in her hold to sink her. He went down into the hold alone—it was a big vessel and much needed—and he took the bombs out of her. But something happened, some trick they had, and a bomb went off. A booby trap. That's what they call it overseas. I've seen some results of that work in England while I was nursing there. But my own father! Well, I'll say no more about it." She gave him a grave smile. "You, too—you look as if you had come through something hard. Was it bad—on that vessel? You did well. I was proud of you when they said: 'By gorry! 'Tis Skipper Patrick himself has saved yon vessel!'" She laughed at her droll imitation of Trabo's speech. She repeated her question: "It was hard work for you, Patrick?"

He replied: "It wasn't the sailing that was so bad."

"What then?"

"I mean that before I found the *Gaunt Woman,* I picked up a boat with three dead men in it."

"Patrick! How awful! They weren't from home?"

"No, they weren't. It was a foreign boat."

"Danes?"

"They had Danish papers on them."

"Danish papers?" she repeated. "You say that in a way that shows you doubt that they were Danes." She smiled again and added: "You see, I've not forgotten much about you in these years, Patrick."

"I'm glad of that, Margaret." He didn't smile. He reached forward and took her hand, then let it go. "I'm going to tell you something pretty terrible, Margaret. I want you to know it. No one else knows, except Conrad, the Danish hand I took on at Gloucester. I tell you because—because I must. Because I'll need your help, if what I suspect is true. I'm going to tell you something, Margaret, that may be the means of saving thousands of men, hundreds of ships—"

"Patrick!" Her face went white. She looked away from him and down at the *Gaunt Woman*, lying below in the hidden harbor.

He took her hand again and bent forward so that she could not escape the intensity of his gaze. "It is war! Those men in the boat were dead—dead by murder!"

"Murder!" she exclaimed.

"Aye, Margaret, murder! Now listen—those men had Danish papers. Yes. But they were Germans."

She repeated his last word in a thoughtful whisper, like a child doing a sum. She then asked her first even, calm question. "Had they been shot?"

"Shot by an automatic gun. In their own boat. It was shot to pieces." He then told her the story. He described the first mysterious appearance of the *Gaunt Woman* on the voyage from Gloucester and he told her how he and Conrad came to suspect Holger when he mourned over the bodies of the dead men. He told her of the dead man he had found on the *Gaunt Woman's* deck and how he was sure Skalder had lied to him in saying that the man was his own son. He left nothing out. He talked to her earnestly, almost wildly at times because—to his dismay—his story began to seem hollow and unsound, even to himself. What had he to go on? Nothing except a few sharp observations, a tenuous, vague working of an instinct he didn't rightly understand. And, as he watched the color come and go in her face, he saw that she, too, found the story incredible. He finished it and waited for her response.

For a little while, she kept her gloomy gray eyes fixed on the *Gaunt Woman* there below, and then she said: "Do you mean to tell me, Patrick, that the captain of the *Gaunt Woman* would come into this harbor and lie there, with a corvette apt to run in at any hour? Unless he is what he says he is? No, Patrick, he's a Dane. Not a German. And his men are all honest Danes."

"You forget something. You've forgotten what I told you."

"What is that?"

"Skalder had to come into Trabo."

"Had to?"

"Yes. He suffered so much in that storm that he couldn't handle his ship easily. I know he lied to me about what happened to him in that blow. He said he was caught napping. But he's much too good a seaman to be caught by weather, even a nor'easter. No, Margaret! He was tied up to a U-boat when it hit him. That's why he couldn't get clear and run before it."

She said: "You've been doing some thinking, Patrick. I can see that."

Patrick went on: "He suffered so much in that storm that he couldn't handle his ship easily. He couldn't do the dirty job he's been doing—"

"And what is that job, Patrick, in your opinion? Exactly?"

"He's been supplying the German pack with torpedoes and men and mines. Maybe dropping the mines himself or giving them to a mine-laying U-boat. That's the long and short of it."

"Torpedoes, Patrick? And men?"

"That's what I said. He has torpedoes in his hold. Not rum, as he says and his papers testify. He has extra quarters for trained U-boat men. To replace crews that are worn out. I know that he's been meeting U-boats in these waters, that he has taken off their crews and has filled their torpedo compartments. What does he think I am? A fool? Well, maybe he does. I've tried to make him think so. He's suspicious. He suspects everything and everybody. But I'm such a young innocent that he is sure I believe him. For example—what was he doing so far off his course? He told me he was going to Halifax and I find him sneaking about on the Grand Bank itself. He told me he was blown off his course. He's a liar. In short, the *Gaunt Woman* is a floating base for those German rats. Why not? He could get away with it. Conrad tells me they've done it many times overseas. It's a smart trick to be tried here. There's a few square-riggers carrying freight these days." He scowled at her. "Now laugh at me!"

She had listened intently, her head bent a little, her eyes gazing at nothing. A hundred images of her listening long ago, in just that posture and in that very place, came to him while he waited.

She said: "You know this is a hanging matter for Captain Skalder, Patrick? And all his crew? If what you say is true."

"I didn't think of that."

"Why didn't you?"

"Because I intend to kill them myself."

She cried out and took a step away from him and looked at him in amazement, as if he had suddenly changed into another man.

He understood her meaning. He said: "You're not looking at a boy, Margaret. You're looking at a man. I told you—we've grown up. I've told you that this is war. And that—" he pointed down to the *Gaunt Woman*—"that is a vessel of war." He paused a moment, then began again. "Hanging, you say? It's too good for them! I want you to listen carefully, Margaret, because I'm going to take a chance tonight on something that will go hard with me if I'm wrong—"

"What are you going to do, Patrick?"

"I'm going aboard the *Gaunt Woman* and go down into her hold."

"I will listen. I'm ready to believe you, Patrick. Only I don't want you to make a mistake. There's enough sorrow in the world—"

He interrupted her. "If you see anything absolutely wrong with what I say—why! you can help me by speaking out. Now, I figure that despite the damage the storm did to him, he could have turned about and made Port Halifax. But he didn't want to go there. It would have been much too risky. At Halifax there would certainly be a man who'd got hold of a list of Danish vessels that were caught by the Germans. Certainly Skalder would be kept outside until his ship had been gone over from stem to stern. They'd find out then what he carries. And it isn't rum. They're careful at Halifax. The port was blown up during the last war and they won't even let a canoe in unless it's been O.K.'d. No! Halifax was out, Margaret. The last port on earth for the *Gaunt Woman*. She had to refit in some place like this. No railroad. No telegraph. Nobody nosing around.

"Now you can see, Margaret, that the only safe way for him to get into a place like this was to do even more damage to his ship than the storm had done. He had to put her into such bad shape that a sail under a jury-rig to some such port as this would be a logical thing. He had to get rid of his crew and he also had to make sure that help would be at hand out there. That some vessel would come along to answer his distress signals. His rockets."

She stopped his talk with a weary shake of her head. "I can see that, Patrick. How it might be possible. But it doesn't hold—"

"Wait! I swear it's true. He had that U-boat send a few shells over his vessel. But not hit her. Perhaps they were blanks. I don't know. But he knew the sound of shellfire would bring somebody like me along."

"You are telling me something now that it is impossible to believe. Perhaps you can prove it, but you haven't done so yet, Patrick."

"What's so impossible about it? Don't you realize the kind of war we're fighting? Haven't you heard a thousand things like this in England? Tricks the Nazis have played?"

"Yes, I have! Hundreds of terrible things. The wounded men and the dying men told me. Time and time again. But you're telling me that Skalder stayed aboard the *Gaunt Woman* while it was being bombarded under such circumstances. No. He might have been killed. And the U-boat fired over a vessel full of mines and torpedoes? Never, Patrick!"

He laughed at her. "You're a child! He didn't stay aboard the vessel. He left it, stayed aboard the U-boat while the shelling was going on, and then he came back alone. Left his crew to get ashore. As it has."

"How do you know he left the vessel?"

He pointed down to the wharf. "Do you see that boat? That one painted green and white?"

She nodded.

"Well, my girl, that's where the great schemer made a mistake, although I didn't figure it out until just a little while ago. He and I came ashore in that boat. It was on his deck when I first boarded the vessel. The deck was nicely scarred up here and there and splintered by axes. A good imitation of what shells were supposed to do. They had even burned a heap of kindling and bits of canvas in the waist of the vessel to make the attack seem real. But that boat was never even touched! Not a scar on it. Why? Because that wonderful blockhead slipped up. He had to make one little mistake in all the fancy business. And he made it. He didn't think of slashing the boat up a bit so that it would match the rest of the vessel. He smashed up one boat, but he forgot that one. And he forgot it for the simple reason that he was using it—to go back and forth from the U-boat."

He stared in silence at the deck of the *Gaunt Woman*. Four or five men were taking down the jury-rig. The odd sail forward had already come down. In Patrick's own mind, the events he was describing so exactly seemed not extraordinary. Neither were they commonplace, everyday happenings. That is, when he spliced them neatly in his mind, fitted this to that and, aided by his instinct, finished the deadly pattern. The fact was that Patrick had become extremely smart. A new war and the sight of murdered men had stirred up a faculty for which, like many other Americans, he had no daily use. That faculty was his imagination. But the cruel, vicious waging of the U-boat warfare, in his own sea and in others, had taught him the great lesson. This was that the enemy's U-boats, his bombers, his legions and his crafty agents, were not to be compared in importance to another enemy possession: imagination. Ever since Patrick had found the three dead men, he had determined to imagine every damned thing he could. So he now said promptly: "Listen, my girl, I'm imagining all this! See? But there are some real, solid links in the chain. And I'll complete it tonight. Right down there!"

Margaret, without speaking, then did a thing that surprised him. She looked up at him in a tender way and slowly nodded her head. She put her right hand on his shoulder and came closer to him. She whispered: "Don't move or look around, Patrick! Do you understand?"

He put his arm around her waist and bowed his head. "What has happened, Margaret?"

She spent a leisurely moment in a glance into his eyes and then whispered: "I think, perhaps, your case has been proved by somebody else. I believe you, Patrick. Now." She drew his bristly cheek down and lightly touched it with her lips. "The captain of the *Gaunt Woman* is watching us!"

Patrick touched her glinting hair with his lips. "Alone?"

"Yes."

"Where?"

"In the woods behind us. I happened to glance that way and saw his hand move on a tree. He is quite near."

Patrick held her close. "I've slipped up somewhere. He suspects me!"

She made no answer, only came closer to him. He could feel her body grow tense and wary. Then it shuddered. "Or even me! His eyes seemed full of distrust when he looked at me on the wharf. That is why they are successful at work like this. They hate everything, suspect everything and everybody. Even themselves. One watches over the other." She stayed in his embrace. "Promise me one thing, Patrick!"

"Yes! Willingly."

"Guard yourself! Don't go anywhere or do anything without telling me or Conrad beforehand. Don't try to do things singlehanded. He suspects you, Patrick. He'll set a trap for you. I'm afraid of that temper of yours—"

"I'll watch it. I'll do my best, Margaret." He let his right arm fall from her waist and whispered: "Risk another look now. Is he going away?"

She tossed her head back and smoothed her hair. In that act, she glanced briefly backward, then turned to Patrick again and said: "He is going down the path. Smoking a cigarette. Looking innocently about."

Patrick let her go and they remained there, looking out over the sea. He was shaken by emotion, not only by the suddenness of his embrace, which stirred a memory full of such tenderness from their past, but also by the appearance of Skalder. It had been like a physical attack, a blow in the face. He dismissed the obvious thought that Skalder might have come up the path to take a look about. Patrick was certain now that the contest had opened, that he must go even more carefully towards that moment which he now considered inevitable: the moment when he would take Skalder's life and take the life of his vessel.

She spoke to him softly. "One more thing I must ask of you, Patrick."

"Ask it."

"I will do everything you ask me. I will even go aboard the *Gaunt Woman* for you. In your place. I promise you!—I would even shoot Skalder dead in my aunt's house, if you tell me to. I am capable of it! I am hard. And I can tell you in one sentence what made me so. What changed me in one awful instant."

"England?"

"No! That was bad enough. It wasn't war, but, at least, they could say it was war—what they did to London and to the little towns. And the wounded men—machine-gunned from the air while they lay in ambulances and on Red Cross ships. No, the thing that changed me was what I saw at sea. When the ship I came home on stopped and the men brought something alongside. Something I had to see and touch and work on." She tightened her grasp on his arm. "A boatload of dead children." She said this the first

time in a whisper so low that he could hardly hear it.
She then cried it out: "A boatload of dead children,
Patrick! Little English kids!"

"That they had killed."

"That Skalder and his kind had killed." She shuddered at the image her furious words had recalled.
"That is why you must understand that you can de-
pend on me. As well as on any man. Besides, we are
old, dear friends, Patrick, and I—I don't want anything to happen to you."

"It's wonderful to hear you talk again, Maggie!"
At his use of her childhood name, they laughed a little, but he, remembering what she had said of a
promise he must make, grew solemn quickly and
asked her what it was.

She replied: "You must not tell my father. Let us
keep our fears from him. Even if you find that the
Gaunt Woman is what you suppose her to be—let's
not tell him, Patrick. He's had enough of war. He
must have peace now, if he is to live at all. We can
keep it from him, can't we?"

"I promise that, Maggie. This is my show."

CHAPTER VI

A FEW MINUTES before midnight, Patrick awoke in his room at the tavern. He was in better shape now. He had rid himself of his bristles, had bathed and dined and had gone to bed early. Skalder had followed him in all these welcome changes, except for the beard business. He had stroked his own fondly when Patrick got ready to turn in and had spoken of it in melancholy humor. "I am very glad we saved this, too, Captain Bannon. It is the work of years."

Now Skalder lay asleep amidst the special comforts of the big chamber at the far end of the tavern. He had a fire to himself and the best and biggest bed in the house. By putting his head out of his own window, Patrick could see a window of that chamber. He did this. Embers in the hearth sent out a rosy ray. The house lay quiet. The night was overcast. Patrick shut his eyes and listened to the sea, loud in the narrow tickle, louder off-shore. He knew the Avalon music well. When things were bad, the jagged walls of the tickle gave out a warning, a repeated thundering, bass notes of the Atlantic organ. Now he heard nothing, only the pleasant pour of calm water.

This was his time. Two of the villagers had gone aboard the *Gaunt Woman* to relieve Conrad and Holger, who were sleeping in the tavern. Patrick had nothing to fear from the new anchor-watch, even if they did catch him stealing aboard. And he intended that they should not. He took his navy revolver and slipped it into his pocket. By the light of a candle, he wrote a note to Skalder: "Wind rising. Sky overcast. Going out to take a look at her anchor. Don't worry." He folded the note and took up his boots. He opened the door, inch by inch, waiting between inches for a spell of listening.

He stepped out into the hallway and peered into its darkness. He paused by the door to think again. Every move had to be pondered. He had put Skalder down in his books as a skillful antagonist, who was well aware that a hangman or, at best, a rifle squad, would be his fate if he made a false move. Skalder had been sedate at dinner, so full of stately guile that it was hardly possible he had dared to spy on him and Margaret. He had been intensely, but discreetly, interested in Margaret's talk of her nursing overseas; and, watching the two converse, Patrick had struck on the notion that perhaps it was her residence in wartime England that had excited Skalder's suspi-

cions. It was not beyond English skill at warfare to
send her to do other work in this very place.

Patrick stole down the hallway until he came to
Conrad's room. He scratched his fingers against the
door and waited. He heard a stir within, then a
scratching signal on the other side. The door opened
and Conrad came out. He slipped into Patrick's
room.

Patrick walked to Skalder's room and thrust the
note under his door. He took good care to lay it in
such a way that he could pick it up later, if he wished.
He listened and, after a while, made out the sound of
deep breathing. He trembled at his nearness to his
quarry. The weight of his revolver against his hip
gave him the impulse to walk in and end the matter
there and then. Skalder was alone now, except for
that other false Dane, Holger. But soon he would not
be alone. The *Daniel* would bring him twenty men in
a day or two. Twenty Germans! Patrick frowned.
That was more manpower than all Trabo could call
up. But there was no help for it. And Skalder must
live yet a while.

He went back to his room. Conrad, impassive and
cold as always when danger came, stood in the middle of the room. Patrick whispered to him: "I want
you to stay here, Conrad. I'm going now, as I told
you. I'm going aboard the *Gaunt Woman* and down

into her hold. Step here." He showed him the fire-light flowing against Skalder's window. "You can see him this way if he stirs. If he comes out, follow him. If he takes one of the boats and goes aboard the *Gaunt Woman*—you do the same. Just say to him calmly—no fuss at all—just say! 'Hello, Captain. Thought I would take a look at her anchor. The wind woke me up.' Understand?"

"Yes, Captain."

"If you have to talk with him or with Holger—watch them carefully. Skalder is suspicious. And if they make a bad move—give it to them. The knife in the ribs. And remember this, Conrad. No fair play. Don't give them a chance. The stab in the back is their game and we have to play it, too."

"Yes, Captain."

Patrick looked at his watch. "It's twelve now. Give me two hours. At two o'clock, unless I come to your door before, come down and pull me out of that hold. I'll be in it or back here."

"Yes, Captain."

Patrick went down the stairs and pulled his boots on there. He then went out of the tavern and walked up and down in plain view, gazing at the sky and snuffing the wind. In one of his turns, he came close to the cottage where Margaret lay asleep. He walked slowly past, his head bent in thought. He stretched his arms and yawned.

Something had moved near the cottage. He had heard nothing, but his eyes had caught a shape moving, a form standing among the bare trees in the garden. This discovery got his dander up. His leg muscles stiffened and his hackle rose with hate. He then took himself in hand. It wasn't Margaret that the secret man was watching. It was the tavern. His anger waned and a fierce exultation came into his heart. This had meaning to him. The game was afoot. It meant that he was right. He remembered what he had said to Conrad the day they had found the dead men. The parable of the hare running with the hounds. Now that he saw the hound again, he was glad.

He waited a moment to let his excitement abate; then he yawned again and rubbed his eyes. He took a step nearer to the cottage and gave a low whistle. He saw the man jerk around at the whistle.

Patrick took out his pipe and lighted it. He blew a bit of smoke about, then thrust the pipe into his pocket and went over the fence into the garden under her window. He moved slowly so that he might be easily observed. He put his hands on the window sill, thrust his head inside and whispered: "Are you awake, Margaret? It's Patrick."

He could see her face. She was sound asleep. He took off his boots, placed them carefully against the wall and entered her room.

"Are you awake, Margaret?"

He watched her calm breathing. He went on tip-toe to the bed and looked fondly down at her. He sighed, mortal man. Her red hair showed its gloss on the pillow. There was an alarm clock on a table near her outstretched hand. There was a tray on the table and vials of medicine and a thermometer case. There was also a scrap of paper on which she had written a sentence and two rows of figures.

He watched her face for a little time. Once her lips moved ever so slightly and a dim smile came.

"Dreaming of the Bannon boy, no doubt," he whispered.

He went back to the window, lifted the inner edge of the curtain and looked out into the murky lane. The watcher was approaching, step after cautious step. He came to the wall and stared at the window. Patrick saw the face clearly. It was Holger. Holger with his dark head straining forward. Holger, a hound for eagerness. Patrick hated him at that moment more than he ever had. Yet his joy at this confirmation of his suspicions was greater than his hate.

His exultation over the wild exploit before him grew until his heart-beat frightened him. He knew he had caught the German fools napping again. Their necks were in the noose. He had no desire to kill Holger this time. He was ready to do it, there and then.

But he preferred to keep such a blockhead alive and active. He would be useful.

Patrick took out his revolver and waited. Holger put one leg over the wall, then thought better of it and drew it back. He watched and listened. Patrick grinned and made a kissing sound with his lips. Holger turned and went into the tavern.

Patrick let him go. If he had needed anything to make him firm in his resolution, this appearance of Holger was it. They were together, Skalder and Holger. They were Germans, part and parcel of a system of secret agents that wove a vast web for ships all the way from the Gulf to the Straight Shore. But they were not so smart. Smart up one alley, dumb down the other. This was the third time that Holger had spilled the beans. First when he had mourned too eloquently on the *Daniel's* deck over the dead men and wept over them for Danes, knowing well that they were hands of a U-boat that had been on the *Gaunt Woman*. He had played the same game on the *Gaunt Woman* when Skalder had prayed in Danish over his pretended son. And now the damned fool was off to bed, thinking Patrick was set for the night in a girl's room.

Patrick gave them both a gentle cursing and slipped out the other window. He crawled through the back garden, rolled over the wall and went down the lane in his stocking feet, going like a cat on frost. Ten minutes later, he slid across the deserted deck of the *Gaunt Woman,* crowded with the shipwrights' benches and tools. He went down to the cabin and looked through the port, still gaping where the bullet fired by Skalder had passed. He heard the voices of the Newfoundlanders on watch. They were at ease. He hurried to the main hatch and began his work. The mystery of the *Gaunt Woman* was about to be settled, one way or another.

His beginning was good. He was concerned lest Skalder or Holger might come aboard and find the hatch open after he had gone below. Fortunately, the shipwrights—or perhaps Skalder himself—had flung a great square of discarded canvas over the hatch. Patrick lifted it up and crawled under it. There he laid out his tools, left his electric torch burning, and began to pry off the tarpaulin. He wasn't surprised to learn that he had a hard job before him. The hatch was battened down in a way that he hadn't seen before. The strips over the tarpaulin were made of metal and these were held in place by a large number of brass screws, whose slots were fully half an inch long. He fixed his screwdriver into the first one and turned. The screw didn't bulge. He tried again and this time the screw gave way. He spent the better part of an hour at this work. Twice in that time he crawled out from under the canvas and looked up and down the deck.

The moment he forced the hatch open and thrust his head out over the coamings, his heart filled with quick despair. An unmistakable odor of rum came up with the force of a hot breeze. He remembered, as he snuffed the odor and stared down into the dark hold, how Skalder had shoved the ship's papers before him and said: "Cargo? Rum!" There it was. He turned the light downward. It struck against the steel crossbeam. He shifted it to the right. Its circle fell into an empty space directly beneath him. He saw the heads of barrels. He swung onto the ladder and went down, halting at each step to feel his way. The deeper he went, the stronger the smell of rum became.

"I'll be plastered before I get there," he said.

He reached the 'tween-decks. Here he turned on the light again and let it play. All about him were the barrels, hundreds of them. It was a sight that hit him hard, hit him where it hurt most. There was no question about it now. The hold of the *Gaunt Woman* was full of rum. His eyes followed the creeping beam of light. He saw tier after tier, some supported by stout scaffoldings across the top to keep off the pressure of the tiers above. The spaces between the barrels were stuffed with yellow straw that gave out grassy gleams.

"Hell!" said Patrick. "Hell and damnation! I'm a born fool."

Nevertheless, he let his torch search on. The cargo was so well and fully stowed that he had hardly room to stretch out his arm from the ladder. It was like being in a well. Long afterwards, he said that maybe it was the narrowness of this space that started him thinking again. Because he had stopped thinking. It was too painful. He felt more like broaching a barrel and getting tight.

He did that handy bit of thinking half-way down the ladder. He went all the way down and stood on the very bottom before the question actually framed itself in his mind. "How in hell do they handle this stuff? What do they do if the cargo shifts on them?" His seamanship failed him, because he knew little about such vessels, but his instinct said quite clearly: "This is a fake, Bannon, like everything else about them."

In the space where he stood, the bottom tier consisted of ten barrels. He began a close examination of each barrel-head. He read the legends charred into them. He laid his hand outstretched upon the heads and tested them. He ran his finger-tips inside the rims and marked the moisture, sometimes in whole drops, that had gathered. There was no good evidence in these actions. They simply proved that there was rum in the barrels, not gunpowder. But he was impelled to do everything he could think of. He couldn't be satisfied otherwise. In this way, he painstakingly crossed the empty space. He finished the bottom row and stopped.

By this time, being a good man aboard any vessel, if given a little time, he asked himself a very seaman-like question: "Why isn't this space full? Why didn't they stow here?" And again he gave himself his own answer: "I'm on the track of it." He methodically began his testing of the second tier. This time he added a trick to his stock. He took out his hammer and, after each flash, he gave the barrel-heads a sound knock. Each one replied in a deep voice: "Rum!"

All except the fifth. It was marked the same; it had collected some moisture. But the blow of the hammer brought out a hollow sound.

"I'm a son-of-a-gun if it isn't empty!"

He had a tremendous desire to let out a whoop. Instead, he cannily stepped away and spent a short time in listening. To this and to that. To the wash of the Trabo current against the hull and to the topside murmur that came down to him faintly through the tarpaulin that he had drawn over the hatchway. All seemed well. He stepped forward and gave the same head another rap. The blow reverberated in the barrel's emptiness. He then struck the next barrel to the right. It was full and said: "Rum here!" He struck the barrel directly above the empty one. It was empty, too.

"Skalder," he said, "you're in the bucket!"

He got down on his knees and examined the trestle

on which the first row of barrels rested, clear of the
deck. He saw that this beam came to an end at the
left side of the empty barrel, that there was a tiny
space, less than a quarter of an inch, before the next
beam began. This smaller beam supported the empty
barrel. At the right side of the barrel, he saw another
such space. He knew then that the empty barrel was
resting on a specially made support.

There could be only one purpose for this odd piece
of carpentry. It was a contraption. A machine. Something to be worked, to be hauled out of its place or to
be pushed in.

Patrick put his right hand on the lower barrel, his
left on the upper, and pushed. Quite easily, without
groan or squeak, the barrels gave way before him and
slid back. He stepped onto the steel tracks that carried the secret door, and entered the hold, well-
lighted now by electric lamps that had been switched
on by the movement of the barrels.

He groaned in horror. The horror of his own suc-
cess that held him transfixed. He was frightened by
the enormous, evil secret that he had discovered. He
moaned and whispered: "My God! My God!"

And then the realization that he had been right,
that he had made no mistake in all his wild imagin-
ings, came upon him with an impact so acute that it
was like a pain. He pressed his hand on his stomach

and coughed. His mouth dried up. He ran his tongue over his lips. Moving in a trance, he stepped to one side and pushed the barrels back until the secret entrance closed behind him.

He stood in an enormous storeroom. Like a child staring in a nightmare, he took one weak step forward and opened his eyes wide. The 'tween-decks had been taken out. The upper deck and all the ship's timbers had been buttressed with girders of light metal. The entire space on his right hand was filled with racks made of those same girders. These racks were filled with torpedoes. There were scores of them, at least a hundred, all eighteen feet long. Each one was double-lashed into a metal cradle. An electric lamp burned at the head of each section. There was a passageway down the center. It ended in a bulkhead made of rum barrels. On his left hand there were other racks that held rows of mines, each in its wooden cradle and each made secure with soldered strips of metal. There were hundreds of them and of various sizes. Some were painted green; others were black and streaked with blue and green.

For a moment, his legs refused to make another step forward. He felt the blood run out of his cheeks, heard his heart bang away to pump it up again. He took his time. He waited until he was on even keel. He crammed down the burst of his exultation, kept saying to himself: *"Gaunt Woman!* I've got you, old lady!" and "Now you're done for, you murderous bitch!"

He then pushed himself forward at a quick trot, looking to the left and to the right. The whole starboard side was filled with the torpedoes, but the racks of mines took up only half the space on the port side. The rest of it was crowded with opened boxes of bombs, wooden cases, and tools in burlap bags. There, too, lay a long cylindrical object wrapped in thicknesses of canvas and bolted to the bottom. It was a five-inch gun. The wooden cases were full of shells; other boxes contained automatic guns and bullets for them. And beyond these cases were coils of electric wire and cables and tiers of unopened boxes.

Farther forward on the port side he came to a sort of cage, made of steel mesh. Its door swung open. He did not enter. There was a work-bench inside, a long steel platform placed on steel legs. On it were a number of blueprints and other papers, all carefully weighted down. A jar of blue ink had fallen over. Its spatter had dried on the steel. On the false bulkhead that formed the far side of the cage there was a large blackboard. Two charts of the Grand Banks and the Atlantic coast were fixed on it; and between them there was a large sheet of white paper, marked with ruled columns and symbols. There were also German words printed on it. He couldn't read them, but he could see the numbers. He knew these were the designations of a U-boat fleet with cruising areas, positions, and meeting dates all marked out. He looked on the nearest chart for the peak of the Grand Bank, where he had first seen the *Gaunt Woman*. It was marked with a jagged symbol in red ink and with the letter and numerals of a Code:R—184.

He ran back towards the secret door. Sweat rambled down his cheeks and the small of his back turned cold. Once he stumbled over nothing. When he regained his feet, a frenzy made him shake, a furious desire to escape from the hold before its air choked him. A fear came over him that he would be caught there, shot out of hand, and that the *Gaunt Woman* would escape to send her cargo against the ships he loved. Torpedoes to knock them down into the sea bottom. Mines to blow them up as they left the Yankee harbors. This fear almost maddened him. At the secret door, he stopped and looked once more at the arsenal. He suddenly swore that he would blow up the *Gaunt Woman* there and then. The *Woman,* himself, and all Trabo.

The wildness of that impulse forced him to pull his wits together. He turned again and jumped towards the barrels. He laid both his hands on an iron handle that was obviously used to pull the sliding barrels back. He put a gentle strain on it. Nothing happened. He jerked hard and still the door did not open. He put his back into it and hauled steadily, his teeth set on his lip. Nothing stirred.

He carefully examined the steel tracks on which the barrels had moved. He searched for a locking device of some sort that he might release. There was none. His anxiety increased to a new desperation. Once more he jerked at the iron handle. The door didn't budge. Frantically he searched the girders and beams that made up the inner part of the false bulkhead. He found only an electric switch. When he turned it, the lights went out.

"Better so!" he whispered.

He was locked in Skalder's trap.

Patrick stood stock still in the darkness and sized things up. He was caught. There was no doubt of it now. For a while, he was furious at his own stupidity in closing the secret entrance behind him, but he soon gave up that style of thinking because there was no good in it. He switched on the lights again and searched eagerly among the tiers of barrels in the hope of finding a way out. In the after part of the hold, where the rows of torpedoes ended, he saw a small hatch above him, a sort of manhole. He knew that such vessels usually had small hatches, sometimes two or three, so that one man could get into the cargo without all the work of opening a big hatch. But this small hatch was tightly closed; besides, it was far out of his reach.

He went back to the main bulkhead. He understood now that his only chance of escape was to waylay Skalder when he came down into the hold. To shoot him in his big belly the moment he came through the opening and then seize the ship. This thought angered Patrick again. He wanted more than Skalder and his ship. He wanted to let the *Gaunt Woman* sail out of Trabo, wanted to let Skalder think he had won the game. Then the *Daniel* would come down on him when he kept his first rendezvous with a submarine. Come down on him and blow him up, one way or another.

He shook his head grimly over that satisfying thought. Instantly another knocked him over on his heels. How did he know that Skalder would come down at all? It might be days before he had business to do below decks; and he certainly would avoid all unnecessary visits to the hold. He would be a fool to spend any time in such dangerous quarters, where he might be followed by a workman, innocently enough.

Patrick felt a strong need of the dark. So he turned off the lights, took out his revolver and waited. He listened for the sound of the barrels moving. He passed a hard half hour, waiting for the approach of the first man. It was now nearly two o'clock. He studied his watch and calculated the hours before sunrise. There wasn't much time.

The first new thing he heard was the muffled exhaust of a gasoline motor somewhere in the vessel. Its slight vibration, coming through the ship's timbers, ran into his bones as he leaned, tense to the knuckles, against the barrels. He thought at first that the sound might be coming from a vessel sailing up the tickle, but the vibrations remained constant, did not change as they would if a vessel were passing. He knew then that the ship's power plant—a plant for lights and radio and other gear—had started automatically.

The next thing he heard was an even vaguer sound, a sort of thumping. Once, when the vessel became unusually quiet, he was sure he had detected a dragging noise on the other side of the false bulkhead. He pressed his ear against an empty barrel and listened. No clear sound came to him. He was drawing away when something struck a hard blow against the head of that very barrel. He waited. Again the blow came and he heard the hollow sound that had led him into the hidden entrance.

Somebody was at work on the other side. Patrick cocked his revolver and stood away from the tracks. The usual noises in the hull shut out all other sounds for a minute or two; then the groping began again. He heard a man speak in a tone hardly audible above the continual sighing in the hold. It did not seem like a man talking to another near by. It seemed more like a man calling, perhaps to somebody on deck.

Patrick suddenly said aloud: "The crew!"

He damned himself again for a Gloucester thick-head. There was no reason why another vessel—even the *Golden Hind*—might not have gone into English Village for bait and have taken the *Gaunt Woman's* men up the coast as an act of charity. He sweated again at the thought of that gang of pirates coming aboard while he lay there, caught in a hold that contained their secret.

The silence returned in full. The sweat dried on him and he shivered with the cold of it. He began to tramp up and down to keep warm. The chill from the clammy deck came sharp through his stocking-feet. In that twilight, he padded up and down, taking counsel of his thoughts, waiting and longing for a helpful one to rise out of the inner chaos. He often halted and stared into the darkness, which gave out glints and tiny points of light where the mines, bristling with horns, lay in their racks. He was glad now that he had confided in Margaret. She was experienced, resourceful, and had been to the wars. She had her father there, a wounded, maimed man, but a skilled wager of war, who would know what to do when she told him that something had gone wrong. At once, against this comfort, came the counterbalance of Skalder's skill and his cruelty. He would not hesitate to murder. He would kill her and her father and all Trabo—aye! and burn the village to ashes!— in order to keep his vessel free for the work that must now be pressing.

Thus yawing in his thoughts, he was standing, with his face turned towards the after part of the hold, when he seemed to make out a barely perceptible increase in the light. At first, he thought that it might be the opening sign of the new day. But it was too early yet. He stole forward a few paces and fixed his eyes on the girders overhead.

The sound of a man's voice came down to him. It was one word, not spoken loud enough for Patrick to hear it clearly. He stepped into the working-space between two of the torpedo racks. A wave of cold, fresh air flowed by him. He sought its source. He could tell that it was blowing down from an opening in the deck. He came out from his shelter and jumped into the next space. He could now make out the source of the new light and air. It was the small hatch. Some one had opened it.

The man above then showed his face. The darkness was so intense that Patrick could see only the dimmest outline of a cheek and a gleam of an eye. The head then vanished and at once a coil of rope fell down with a thud. In the next instant, the man himself came sliding down and stood there, unseen

in the gloom. Patrick heard his boots strike. He heard
the man mutter.

Patrick lifted the revolver and made ready to
switch on his torch.

At that moment, a voice said calmly: "You there,
Captain Bannon?"

It was Conrad.

Patrick waited a moment. He was so glad to see
the Dane that he could hardly speak. He said at last:
"I am right here, Conrad. You come on time, my
friend."

"That is good."

"You are alone?"

"Yes, Captain."

"Anything stirring?"

"No. All asleep."

"Was that you nosing about in the main hatchway?"

"Yes, Captain. I could find no way through. I
opened a little hatch. I know these vessels."

"Step forward, Conrad. I have something to show
you."

Conrad came slowly forward until Patrick could
see him. Patrick took him by the arm and led him
forward to the false bulkhead. "I'm going to turn on
some lights, Conrad."

"Yes, Captain."

The expressions that came over Conrad's frost-scarred face when he saw the torpedoes and the mines were new lessons to Patrick. First a lesson in hate and then a lesson in fierce joy. Conrad said nothing, only clenched and unclenched his big hands. Once he lifted them in a gesture that was almost pleading, a sign that he did not wish to speak or be spoken to. In that electric glare, his eyes shone with a clear green light. They glittered with that Northern anger which Patrick had first seen on the day they found the dead men in the boat.

At last, Conrad took a step forward. His eyes stopped on the torpedoes. His teeth lifted off his lip and he spoke. It was a Danish word, one that Patrick couldn't understand, but he knew well enough that it was a curse on Skalder, a curse on the *Gaunt Woman* and on her cargo. He then turned to Patrick, touched his cap and said: "Yes, Captain."

"This opens," said Patrick, laying his hand on the top barrel of the secret door. "From the outside. You missed it."

"I knew something was wrong, Captain. The way they stowed the cargo. Bad. I waited until two o'clock. As you said, I came and found the main hatch open. I knew you were down here." He paused and then said: "Blow her up now, Captain."

"What!"

"Slip her anchor, steer her down channel and blow her up. It will be easy, Captain."

"No! Never! I won't blow her up. Not in Trabo. But I'll blow her up at sea. I'll finish her off and one of her lousy U-boats and I'll do it by the meanest, dirtiest trick a seaman ever thought of!"

"How, Captain?"

"Do you know what these things are?" Patrick waved his head at the racks of torpedoes and mines. "Come this way."

"I know them, Captain."

"I want some of this stuff. Look here!" He led him to the racks closely packed with iron cylinders about two feet high. "Do you know what those are?"

"Time-bombs. I have seen them used, Captain. By Germans."

"And these?"

"Depth charges."

"Yes—and why depth charges?"

"It is strange, Captain. To destroy our own submarines?"

"Right, Conrad. If Skalder happened to see one submerge in his course, he might do a pretty stroke of business. Or, for all we know, they may have surface craft operating with them. The way the Navy chases after every damned thing afloat—you'd think something of the sort was going on." He led Conrad to the mine racks. "Know this stuff, do you?"

"Yes, I do, Captain. Mines. Contact mines."

"So do I. I know a little something about them.

Not much. My father knew more." He laid his finger on the lead tip of a horn. "When a keel hits this horn, this tip bends. There's a container of acid—I don't know what kind—inside the tip. When the lead tip bends, the acid spills on some sort of explosive and touches off the whole damn thing. TNT inside."

"Keep off it, Captain."

"To hell with it! All you have to do is screw off the horns and you can handle this stuff easy. I've got to have it. Know why?"

"Yes, Captain."

"My father did it in the last war. And I'll do it in this one."

"The English did it, Captain. In Norway. Blew up a German base. All this—they put it on a cutter and sent it sailing in at night. With time-bombs set."

"I won't be aiming at a base."

"No, Captain."

"At an anchored ship. This one. In a place I know as well as my backyard. I can't miss."

Conrad said: "Tomorrow night, Captain."

"Yes. We'll take it off tomorrow night. It's too late now."

"You will not blow her up?" Conrad put his hand on Patrick's arm and pleaded with him. "Let us go ashore, Captain. Kill Skalder in his bed. And that spy Holger. Then take her out and blow her up. Make sure of her, Captain."

"No!" Patrick angrily shook the hand off his arm. "I tell you I want more. More! What's the *Gaunt Woman* to me? Now that I've got her? No, I want the pack. I want the boats that shoot this stuff. I want all of them. She's nothing to me without her U-boats. I knew before where they were going to meet. Now I find a chart over there—" he pointed to the steel cage "—that tells the whole story. The peak of the Grand Bank. Where we first saw her. That's where the *Gaunt Woman* must die. There and nowhere else. This is my show, Conrad."

"Yes, Captain."

"Are you afraid they'll slip out on us when her masts are in?"

"That is so."

"She can't do it. The *Daniel* will outsail her by five knots and more. She can't escape me—never!" He roughly swung Conrad around. "Up we go! By the time we've battened that hatch down, it'll be day-break."

When this job was carefully done, Patrick sent Conrad down the side-ladder to row ashore and wait for him there. He then flung the canvas over the hatch and, whistling loudly, walked aft to the cabin and greeted the two men of the anchor-watch, elderly sailmakers from the valley above Trabo. He told them he had been a little worried over the *Gaunt Woman's* anchor, but they assured him that it hadn't dragged its length. He chatted a while, poured a round of drinks from Skalder's bottle, and said good-night.

A light rain, mixed with snow, was falling when he rowed back to the wharf. Conrad gave him a hand up and they turned into the lane. The village lay serene in its sleep. The only light they saw, as they came up the path, shone in Margaret's house. They stayed a while in the lane to watch the tavern, where Skalder and Holger were sleeping. Nothing moved, except a mist that came down the hillside with the pattering rain. The sound of falling and blowing rain made a gentle music, a tinkling like bells among the cliffs. From the sea, however, a harsher music poured, a roaring that set up echoes in the deep tickle, echoes that sounded like salvos far away.

"Ice!" whispered Patrick. "A storm is driving it down from Belle Isle. The *Daniel* will do some skipping about to get those men from English Village."

"Time now for bergs," said Conrad.

"Aye! they'll be coming down to the Banks soon. They come with the spring. Like the bluebirds to Gloucester."

Patrick gave Conrad time to reach his room. He then turned and slipped into the woods behind Margaret's house. He found his boots and pulled them on. He went back into the lane and looked up at the lighted window. That, he knew, was her father's room. While he stared through the mist and rain, the light moved out of that room and soon reappeared in her chamber. He saw her put the lamp down on the table, write a few words more on the sheet of paper there, and study some object she held in her hand. She then flung herself down on the bed in an attitude of grief.

He returned to the tavern, making no attempt to go softly. He stamped on the stairs, even called out: "Anybody in the galley?" and then went whistling to Captain Skalder's door. The note lay where he had placed it before he boarded the *Gaunt Woman*. He couldn't tell whether it had been touched or not. He rather thought it had been moved. He turned on his torch and scrawled another message on the folded paper: "All O.K. aboard. Very little drag. Emptied your bottle with anchor-watch. See you at breakfast."

CHAPTER VII

PATRICK PUT ON a good show when he sat down to breakfast with Skalder in the dining room of the tavern. He received the German's courteous thanks for his care of the *Gaunt Woman* during the night. Patrick, just as politely, said: "Think nothing of it, Captain. I was worried about her anchor dragging. I've never put down a hook that big in Trabo—or anywhere else. Well, she was all right. Of course, I missed a little sleep. I—er—I had a little business to do elsewhere." He grinned mischievously at Skalder, who blandly smiled, as one sea captain should when another discreetly hints at affairs of the heart.

Patrick said: "I've ordered the *Daniel* to go down for your men today, Captain. Perhaps she's gone already." He rose and went to the window. "No, but they're getting under way. My men were damned glad to hear that yours were safe. It's a job they like —bringing them back."

Skalder joined him at the window. "It will be a pleasure to see my crew again. What good luck that they came ashore so near."

"Fifty miles or so," said Patrick. "They'll be here tomorrow. Or next day, at the latest. I've got to pick up some bait somewhere. I've told Caleb to drop in at some of the villages. So the run won't be as direct as I could wish it. For your sake."

Skalder lifted up his hand politely. "Think nothing of it." He laughed genially. "Your phrase, Captain. I like it very much."

They remained at the window, watching the *Daniel* weigh anchor. Margaret's aunt, an amiable woman, who had been long enough a widow to be taken a bit by Skalder's charming manner, filled their coffee cups again and brought them to the window sill. Skalder thanked her gracefully and the two captains continued their inspection of the busy scene below. At that very moment, the first of the *Gaunt Woman's* new masts was stepped in and another spar came riding up over the bulwarks.

Patrick, cold as a berg within, stared in a new fascination at the German vessel. Now, in the fresh light of a fair day, his knowledge of her fearful cargo hurt him, pressed him down, like a burden too heavy for one man. He knew that it was his fate to be the death of the man standing next to him, and that he must also be the death of the other German, Holger, who was walking up and down the deck of the *Gaunt Woman,* staring at her mock wounds and lending a hand to the workmen. It was natural that Patrick should sigh and, half-forgetting in whose presence he stood, let a sad look come over his face. The *Gaunt Woman* was beautiful, especially when seen from above. And the glint of sunlight on the fresh spars and the new suit of sails was so pretty that he could not deny a keen regret that all must perish.

In that sunny stillness by the window, he suddenly felt the peculiar force of Skalder's eyes. Almost reluctantly, Patrick parted from his dream of peace and looked frankly into those German eyes. They were unfathomable, their expression unreadable. Skalder had behaved well all the morning, had given no new hint of a suspicion that he was being watched by an enemy. He had obviously been told by Holger that Patrick had been in Margaret's room all that night. Yet none of this assurance showed in this intense look of his. He was again alert, again the capable commander in a desperate enterprise. Patrick felt that to be true. But he could not tell why, unless it was because of the profound searching power of the German's glance.

Skalder said: "Tuppence for your thoughts, Captain Bannon."

Patrick replied with quick, convincing candor. "I was putting the curse of the world on the Germans, Captain. For I love the looks of your ship—look at the line of that bow there!—and I was wishing that these were times of peace and I could go on her for a long voyage. To China maybe." He sighed. "I've never been to China."

Skalder became gentler at once. He enjoyed this outpouring of a characteristic meditation. He touched the square ends of his beard lightly and shook his head in a sorrowful way. "You are Irish, Captain. Very Irish. I am a Dane. My people have suffered, but we must not hate the Germans or curse any people. Hate blinds—"

Patrick interrupted him. "I am Irish. Yes. But our hate does not blind. No, Captain. It sharpens. My father hunted the Germans in these very waters when I was a child and his hate for their cruelty kept him on deck twenty hours a day. So that he died before his time. But he gave it to them. More than once. He gave them the long drink. And I will, too. And yet, Captain, I can't help but pity them, too. I pity them for what is going to happen to them. This time there won't be one stick left upon a stone in their naval yards. No! Nor one gun unspiked." His voice grew fierce and loud and it trembled with the knowledge that every passionate word was drawing Skalder closer into the frightful net. He paused, drank his coffee, and added: "This is my last voyage, Captain. As soon as I can get enough bait to catch a stock of fish, I'm going home to Gloucester. Then—off to the wars."

"You are a Reserve officer?"

"Yes. I'm a Lieutenant. The Navy told me to fish a little longer. Food is needed as much as anything else. And we've had some trouble at Gloucester that's kept the fleet at home part of the winter. But now I'm through. And I may have my own command. A sub chaser. In these waters." He then thrust it home with a boyish grin. "I'll take care of your ship, Captain Skalder. If she lives that long."

"She will live." He smiled solemnly. "There goes your schooner, Captain. I must go aboard my vessel and see how things go."

As soon as Skalder had gone down to the wharf, Patrick hurried out of the tavern. He ran down the stone steps and turned toward Margaret's house. He stopped short in his tracks. A man was standing there, bareheaded in the sun light. He had been pacing up and down, had turned at the sound of the closing door. The man wore a long naval officer's overcoat, the dark blue of the Canadians. The left sleeve was empty. He held that shoulder lower than the other. A World War service bar lay askew above his heart.

Patrick knew the man must be Margaret's father. Had it not been for the empty sleeve, he never would have recognized him. The genial, red-cheeked Gloucester captain had gone. The hale man who had drunk many a fine glass under his father's roof had vanished quite away. His hair had been red as Patrick's; now it was white as a breaker's crest; and his face was colorless and hatchet-thin. There seemed to be no life in him at all, except where it had always been strongest, liveliest. In his eyes. He was a patriot and his deep-set eyes said so.

He smiled at Patrick, without moving from his place, and said: "Captain Bannon, I believe?"

Patrick came up slowly and took the outheld hand. He could say nothing.

The other was first to break the silence. He saw the unwilling turn of Patrick's eyes toward the empty sleeve. He said: "It feeds the salt—my arm." A black anger swiftly drowned the clear gray eyes, made them vanish in a shadow under his temples. His mouth changed into a wan smile. "Yes, Patrick, I got it. I was lucky last time. Sitting in a radio shack and fooling around with listening gadgets. This time— mines and depth charges. The works." He sighed heavily. "I'll say no more about it." The kindly light returned to his eyes and he said warmly: "Patrick, it does me good to see you. Margaret tells me that your Uncle Marty has given up the fishing. Is that so now?"

"It is, Captain."

"And how is your dear mother?"

"She is well."

"Thank God for that. Margaret tells me that she dreams of your father still—God rest his soul!"

"She does at times."

" 'Tis well." He mused a little space over some image of the Gloucester widow and then said: "And you are skipper of the *Daniel Webster*? Good! You're over-young to be a skipper, Patrick. And of a hali-buter, too. That's fishing few men will go to in our time. Won't old Dolan put an engine in her for you?"

"I wouldn't have one Captain MacLean. I hate them."

"You and your father before you!" He laughed and said: "A jib is more dependable. That's what your father used to say." He at once grew grave, held up his hand and looked at a silver strapwatch. "I've not much time, Patrick. She is a good daughter and a better nurse. But I want to tell you that you did a fine job in taking that big ship up the coast. Is he much of a seaman, that Skalder? Or does his wit run to beard-growing alone?"

"He's the best." Patrick, mindful of his promise to Margaret that he must not speak of war to this vet-eran, made a short answer, much against his will.

"Eh?"

"The best, sir."

"Then how did it happen that a blow laid her over on her beam-ends and knocked the sticks out of her?"

"It came quick, Captain MacLean."

"But not quick enough to catch you napping, Pat-rick."

"No, sir. Not that quick."

"Well, you're your father's son. He could smell a blow making before the weatherglass did."

"Aye! he could."

Captain MacLean took another step or two in the sun. "Your own ship's gone off without you this morning. After his crew, I hear."

"Yes, they turned up at English Village."

"Caleb Pond is a good man." His tone began to show a little anxiety. "He sailed with me long ago on the *Purchaser*. A good man aboard a vessel, Patrick. But your father would never have let his vessel out of his sight, Caleb or not. Especially in war time. What's holding you here, Patrick?" He gentled his question with a kindly look. "Is that it?" He nodded his head toward the window of his room, where Margaret stood, looking down at them. "I hope it is, Patrick."

"As far as I'm concerned, Captain," said Patrick quickly when he had returned the wave of her hand, "it's the same between us as it always was." He was frantic now to have the talk ended; for he could see plain enough that the old warrior was being led to some alarming speculation by his fine seamanship. Patrick lamely added: "I don't know about Margaret."

The father replied: "It would please your mother and me. Mightily, Patrick. I was against Margaret's

going away and you were the chief reason, I may tell
you now. But she had just lost her own mother and
her heart was breaking." He held out his hand.
"Good-bye for the present. I must lie down again or
stand a scolding." He took a step away, turned his
head once more and said: "Watch yourself, Patrick.
And remember—remember what I've been. In case
of need, that is."

Patrick waited until he had gone into the house.
He looked up to Margaret and said: "I must see you,
Margaret. Soon!"

"It must be tonight then."

"I'll come for you."

She nodded and drew back into the room.

He rowed out to the *Gaunt Woman* and climbed
her ladder. Skalder was perched on the main cross-
trees with Holger and a workman. He shouted a
cheerful greeting down to Patrick and went on with
the job. The refitting of the vessel was going ahead
with a drive that might have astonished Patrick, if
he hadn't known the reason for it: that the U-boat
pack was calling anxiously for the *Gaunt Woman*
and seeking her at the Grand Bank rendezvous. Skalder had laid out money generously. He lifted the
wages of the Trabo men to almost double the usual
rate. Nor did he spare himself. He didn't act like a
merchant captain. He put his hands into the tar

bucket and labored like a Gloucester skipper, who has to turn in his hours like every man aboard.

After a time aloft, Captain Skalder came down to the deck and sent Holger and Conrad to open the forward hatch. He made no fuss about the men going below, merely said, quite casually, that he hoped to avoid opening the other hatches until he reached Halifax. He said it was a lot of work. But he told Patrick that he feared the cargo had shifted a little in the forward part of the ship and that he must take a look at it. He even went so far as to tell some of the younger Trabo men, who were naturally curious about the vessel, that they should go below, lend a hand with the rum, and break out a barrel for themselves.

Patrick, knowing that a little such curiosity on his part would be a natural thing, also went below. He came up and expressed surprise at the size of her below. Skalder said that such ships were always surprising to men who didn't know them. Patrick stayed with Skalder all that day, learned a good deal about the vessel and the ways of handling her. At sundown, he went ashore with Skalder, leaving the same anchor-watch aboard.

Skalder was so tired at supper that he could hardly keep awake. Both Holger and Conrad had put in a hard day, too, and they all went to bed early. Patrick

smoked his pipe in front of the tavern for a few minutes and then went up to his own room.

Conrad was there, waiting for him in the dark.
And he was plainly in a nervous state of mind.

Patrick asked in a whisper: "What's the matter,
Conrad? Are they wise to us? Do they know we were
in the hold last night?"

"No, Captain. I am sure not. I saw Holger lift up
the canvas over the main hatch. When we went
aboard today. He look at the hatch, then cover it
again. When Skalder come aboard, he wait a while
and do same thing. No, they do not think we did it.
They are very happy. Very glad crew is coming. Very
glad they sail soon. They talk of two days more. Then
off to Halifax with rum."

"We'll go aboard tonight and turn the trick."

Conrad whispered pleadingly. "I beg you, Captain,
kill the *Gaunt Woman* while you can. Give me your
gun. I myself will kill Skalder now. And then Holger. It will be a good pleasure for me to kill two
Germans. I have never killed one." He fumbled help-
lessly with his cap. "I say it is a great danger to touch
that stuff in her hold. I know you are not afraid, Captain. I am not. But I have seen some bad things
happen. Mines are terrible things to handle. All right
—if you have your own mines. But these on the *Gaunt
Woman*—they are German mines. Maybe more to
do than just screw off horns."

Patrick kept his silence; for, like most stubborn and headstrong men, he hated to appear so. He knew there was much in what Conrad said. Several times that day he had grown cold within when he remembered that, come darkness, he must go down and begin that fateful tinkering. Everything in that secret hold seemed to him loathsome and evil, physically repulsive. His heart shied from the endless images of torpedoes, mines, and bombs. He hated and feared them. Yet he hated something else infinitely more.

Conrad's eyes shone in the increasing darkness of the room. He whispered: "Besides, Captain, they— the U-boats are no good without her. They have nothing. They must go back to Germany."

"Not a damned one of them goes back!" Patrick bent his hand forward so that his whisper could be plainly heard. "Go back, eh? And load up again for a new cruise? No! I'm going to kill them—if it's the last thing I do in this world." He flung off his jacket. "You go to bed. Sleep a couple of hours. Then go down to the wharf and wait for me."

Conrad slipped out the door and Patrick lay down. He rested an hour, then got up and went to Margaret's window. Her light was out. But she was there, waiting for him.

"Come to the door," she said.

"I'll come in the window."

"Why must you?"

"I've my reasons, Maggie." He slid over the window sill and stood before her. He could see her laughing in the dusk.

She whispered: "You do that well, Patrick!"

"Do what well?"

"Climb through windows."

"Eh? What's this?" He came closer to her and took her by the hand. "Why are you laughing at me, Maggie MacLean?"

"I'm not laughing."

"You are, indeed. I can see you. Now, my girl, let me tell you I'm not in the habit of climbing through windows—girls' windows or any other kind."

"Not unless the girl's asleep?"

"Hey!" She tried to escape him, but he caught her by the arm. "What are you up to? Are you hinting that I've been in this room before?"

"How do I know? Has there been a Trabo girl in it?"

"Maggie MacLean! I'll—"

"And I'm not hinting, Patrick Bannon. I'm telling you—"

He stared at her. "Telling me what?"

"—that I wasn't asleep!"

"Last night?"

"Last night."

He groaned.

She said: "Think of what you missed, Patrick."

"I'll do no such thing! I know better than that, my girl."

"And I'll tell you something else—I wasn't dreaming of the Bannon boy. As you said in your pride." She struck at his fingers. "Let me go, if you please. You're hurting me."

He shook his head sadly. "Maggie, you deceived me."

"I?"

"Yes. Pretending to be asleep—and there I was! I never thought you could do a thing like that. Not to me, Maggie." He sighed for the wickedness of the world. "It's just like telling a lie. To deceive me like that. And now, to make matters worse, you insist that you weren't dreaming of me?"

"I was not. At least—why! how could I! I was awake."

"And you let me go without ever a 'how-do-you-do, Captain Bannon'?"

"I did, indeed."

"Why?"

"Must you know?"

"Yes."

"I was dying with curiosity."

"Is that all?"

"All I'll admit to."

"And why did you let me go?"

She stretched out her hand and lifted a night-gown from the bedpost.

"Cotton," she said.

"Cotton? What's that got to do with your wretched behavior? Such bad manners?"

She touched his cheek fondly. "Patrick, you're very sweet. Don't you know that a real lady never receives a gentleman—or even a sea captain—unless she's wearing silk?" She tossed the gown onto the bed. "You might let me know next time."

"I did tonight, didn't I? And now look at you! Is that silk?"

"I've enough of your talk, Captain Bannon." She left off laughing and let a solemn look come over her face. "Why did you come in here last night, Patrick? Tell me."

He told her how Holger had been on guard.

At once she asked: "Did you board the *Gaunt Woman* then?"

"Yes!"

"What did you find? Rum?"

"Some rum. But—Margaret! I was right!"

"Patrick!" He saw her shudder in the gloom.

He whispered: "Yes! Her hold is full of torpedoes and mines. And time-bombs. There's even a five-inch gun. And cases of ammunition and small arms." Quickly he told her of his invasion of the hold. When he spoke of the secret door locking behind him, she stretched out her hand and touched him.

"And now, Patrick?"

"Now Conrad and I are going aboard again. In two hours. Skalder and that other German rat are safe in their beds this time. Unless I miss my guess. Wait!" He went to the window and drew back the curtain. The night was so thick that he could see nothing, not even the trees, where Holger had lurked the night before.

"Why are you going aboard again? Why must you, Patrick?"

"This is my show, Maggie." His voice grew forbidding and sullen.

"Tell me, Patrick Bannon! What are you going to do?"

"I'm going to do what my father did before me. Kill U-boats. I want U-boats! If it costs me my life —I'll have them. One. Maybe two. Or three. Who knows? I saw their numbers on a chart, Maggie. I saw the position where they have been meeting and will meet again as soon as the *Gaunt Woman* can sail. It's a cinch!"

"What are you going to do? Tell me!"

"We're going to take two dory-loads of stuff out of that hold tonight and hide it up the river. When the *Gaunt Woman* sails, we're going after her. I can keep her topsails in sight and she can't see me. I'm going to wait until she's anchored, until the U-boats come alongside. And then I'll send those dories down on them. Floating mines! On the Grand Bank current. I know it cold. It flows like a millstream. Then—they're done!"

She was speechless. She sat there in a stricken silence. Then she said: "This is a wild and terrible thing to think of, Patrick Bannon. You will kill yourself and—who is going to help you? You can't do it singlehanded."

"Conrad. He'll go through with it. He hates it, but he'll stand by."

"Did you speak of this to my father?"

"Your father! Maggie, how could I? I wanted to, I must admit. He knows so much. Just the things I don't know. Radio and explosives. But how could I speak of it?"

"Why not?"

"I promised you. I know you. You would never forgive me if I broke a promise."

"You are right, Patrick. He must be left out of this. I know him. If he ever got wind of this—of this madness—he'd never rest until he had his hand in it. His hand!" Her firm speech quavered on that last word. He saw her face turn from him.

"I respect my promise, Maggie. But let me tell you

this—he thinks something is wrong. He's too good a seaman to be fooled by my account of things."

"What do you mean by that?"

"He wanted to know how Skalder came to be caught in that nor'easter. Why he wasn't on the job to run before it or heave to in a decent condition. You know the real reason, Maggie. It was because he was tied up to a U-boat when it hit him. Well, I did the best I could with your father. Then he asked me why I let my vessel go out without me. That was when you saw us."

"And what did you say?"

"I told him—I told him, Maggie, that it was you. You that kept me here."

She turned sharply and, by a play of the little light in the room, he saw her smile. "And did that please my father?"

"He said so."

"It doesn't please me—because it was a lie!"

He took a step away. He answered her calmly. "I had my choice between breaking a promise to you and telling the lie. I told the lie—as you call it. But it is no lie, Maggie. I told him that, as far as I was concerned, matters were the same as the day we parted. I loved you then. You knew it. You loved me. I love you now as I always have." His voice grew louder. "I'll have you understand this, Maggie MacLean.

That it is true. I am staying here for you. What I am
doing tonight I am doing for you. And for all women
like you. Why did your father fight so bravely? Why
do they all go out against this old enemy of ours? Because of love! You saw the English fight and die.
Don't you understand what they are fighting for? To
be free! And so—with God's help—shall I! Tonight."
He came closer to her. "Shake hands, my girl."

She took his hand and would not let it go. "Patrick, I beg you—not for my sake!—but for the sake
of the war—please, do the wise thing. You have him
and his ship. You can reach the naval men. It will be
easy to do it before the *Gaunt Woman* can sail. I'll
do it for you. I'll go overland. Let them take her. Let
them arrest Skalder and seize his crew when they
come in on the *Daniel*."

"Arrest Skalder!" He spoke so loud that she laid a
finger on his lips. "No, Maggie. I myself shall kill
Skalder. With these very hands! I've sworn it by my
father and the early grave they drove him to! This is
my show, I tell you. I picked the *Gaunt Woman* up at
sea. I knew there was something wrong about her. I
opened the game against her and I'm going to finish
it!" He held her gently by the shoulders. "I'll have
to go now. Darling Maggie, I fooled too much when
I saw you on the *Golden Hind*. But I wasn't fooling
inside. I was so happy to see you! I couldn't bear to
kiss you lightly. Did you know that? Tell me!"

He felt her tremble under his hands. "Yes, Patrick, I knew."

"You will kiss me now, Maggie? There's no reason why you shouldn't, is there?"

"None, Patrick."

She moaned in his embrace and held her mouth up to his. "Patrick! Once more I beg you—"

At that moment, a knock came at the door. A voice said: "Margaret!"

She did not leave his embrace. She said: "Yes, Father!"

"Is it you talking?"

"Come in, Father. It is Patrick."

Her father opened the door and stood there, without speaking. Patrick could see his pale face flaring in the darkness.

"Wait, Father." She closed the window, drew the shade there and at the other window, and then lighted the lamp on her table.

Captain MacLean looked at them in anxious concern. He said nothing for a moment, then: "Margaret, Patrick should not be in your room like this. Patrick, you should not be here."

She said to Patrick: "Now you may tell him, Patrick. The promise doesn't hold."

At the end of the story, the old Captain let his breath out in a sigh. "And now, Patrick, are you asking my opinion?"

"I am not, sir."

"I thought you'd say that. Are you asking my help?"

"I've told you, Captain—this is my show."

"I have a pistol in my room. You say it is your show. I can spoil your show by doing what I've a mind to do—go over and shoot that German slave before he can open his eyes."

"You can. But you will not."

"Who says I will not?"

"I do, Captain MacLean."

"Why?"

"I know you too well."

"Don't be too sure of that, Patrick."

"I am sure."

"Why?"

"You're not the man to make an easy job of it. To kill one German when we might kill a hundred. To destroy one foul, rotten vessel, when we might get two. Or three."

"We?"

"You and I."

A slow, sobbing breath escaped Margaret's lips. "You're not strong enough, Father. I—"

"As long as I can stand on my two feet, I'm strong enough." The furious, black look shadowed his eyes again, made their inner gleam strong as embers. His voice shook with rage. "Little did I think that I'd have my revenge. Or strike another blow for my country. The tricksters! A fair fight—"

Patrick broke in. "Captain MacLean, let me hear nothing of a fair fight or fair play this night! I'll trust no man who treats these animals as if they were good soldiers or good seamen. They are foul! Foul! Gunners of women and children. Brave, sure bombers from empty skies! Your own daughter knows them. A boatload of dead children. That's what she saw. And touched with her own hands. English children that Skalder killed! My God! how I hate them! I hate and despise them. I won't do them the honor of facing them in fair fight. I'll murder them in their sleep. Stab them in the back. Blow them up with their own mines. Anything!" He took up his cap. "Goodbye! The only thing I wish is that you and she were safe out of Trabo! And that all Trabo was in the hills. For if anything goes wrong in that hold tonight, the cliffs will fall and the end of Trabo will come. But it must be done!"

Captain MacLean held up his hand. "Nothing will go wrong, Patrick."

"I pray to God not."

"That's right. You have done that before, Patrick?"

"Many times. Yes, I have prayed since I saw what was in her hold."

"Then you have His answer. I'm your man. I can

make porridge out of that stuff and never bat an eye."

Margaret moaned. She held out her hands to her father. "Let me speak. I've asked this of Patrick and he refused me. I'll ask it of you, Father—and if you refuse, you two will not be the only ones in danger."

Her father interrupted her brusquely. "What does this mean, Margaret?"

"It means that if you go—if you join him in his crazy venture—then I will go, too. I cannot leave you. You are a sick man. A wounded man—"

Her father stopped her again. "This is no time to speak of that. I may not go anywhere. This is Patrick's show—"

"Then listen, Father." She turned to Patrick and said: "You, too, Patrick, you listen to me again. Why shouldn't you take Skalder and his spy now? Take them prisoner! And blow up the *Gaunt Woman*? Take her outside and blow her up? The job will be done then. Her crew—they'll give up when they see that she's gone. Why take the chance of losing her altogether? She might—"

"I won't!" Patrick took up his cap. "Captain Mac-Lean, I've told Maggie and I've told Conrad—who said the same thing—that I don't care a rap about the *Gaunt Woman,* now that we've got her. I'm going to blow her up—yes! But it's only through her and her radio that I can get the U-boats. I intend to get them and that's all there is to it. An end to the talk!"

The Captain said: "You've thought it out, Patrick? It isn't just that Bannon temper? Your father—he was a wild-hearted man against them—"

"To the last second and the last push of the tide—I've thought it out. My temper's got nothing to do with it. Didn't the English slip one of our old ships into St. Nazaire a while ago and bang them up? I'm going to do the same thing. And for the same reason—to kill U-boats!" He flung his cap down on the bed and whispered angrily to the captain. "If we take the *Gaunt Woman* outside and blow her up—what have we done? A great stroke. Right! But she'll be silent. She'll be sending no message to the boats and they'll hook out of here. But I know I can trick them into meeting her on the Grand Bank. And when they do meet—the works! U-boats are the thing to destroy, Captain. You know that! Not just torpedoes and mines and spies."

Captain MacLean said: "You're right. I'll take your orders. You've got the brain and heart to do it." He turned to Margaret and said: "Get my coat. My pistol is in the trunk. And my big flashlight. Go! Do as I bid you!"

She returned and held his coat for him and put the pistol into the empty pocket. She handed the light to Patrick and stood, pale and impassive, before them.

Her father said: "Make your peace with Patrick, Margaret. I know what should be between you two children. See to it."

She kissed Patrick and touched his cheek. She then spoke calmly and with no trace of fear. "There is something that I can do. Other than wait."

"There is," said Patrick. "After we have gone, stand in the garden. If anybody moves in the tavern —Skalder or Holger—go down before them, take one of the village boats and come out to the *Gaunt Woman*. Our job will be done in three hours. Goodbye now."

The two captains went down the lane. Conrad joined them at the wharf. On the way out to the *Gaunt Woman*, Patrick told him how Captain Mac-Lean had learned of their plan and why he had come to help them with his tried skill.

"That is good news to me," said Conrad as he pulled at the oars. "Now we will do it sure."

Although Captain MacLean had been well prepared by his companions' talk, he groaned in amazement when, at last, he stood in the *Gaunt Woman's* arsenal. It took very little time for him to get the blink out of his eyes and size things up. He followed Patrick into the space between two racks of smaller mines. He put out his hand when Patrick touched one of them. He kept him back until he himself had made a thorough examination of the rack. He thrust his fingers under the cradles in his search for hidden wires. "They're tough enough to rig a booby-trap right here, Patrick. Right on their own ship. He'd do it to kill the man who learns his secret—even if it costs him the vessel."

"Because he knows," said Patrick, "that such a man will be the death of him. And his ship, too."

"They'll do anything. Anything. They killed a warrant officer and four men off my ship this winter by just such a trick. They left wounded seamen on a torpedoed hulk and a mine in the skipper's quarters." He straightened up and said: "Go ahead with it. What is it you want?"

"I figure four of the time-bombs." He showed the captain a half-empty case. "These have a plain alarm-clock gadget on them."

Captain MacLean looked into the case. "Yes, I've seen them. I know that kind. They've been putting them into the holds of small vessels. I found a Lunenberg schooner that they blew up by hanging one of these over the side. These are good bombs. Run to the split second—like an alarm clock. Better take five. I'll try one of them out in the back country to make sure. What else, Patrick?"

"The dory can take two of the small mines?"

"Easy!"

"And one of the depth charges. Or two. Two would be better."

Captain MacLean nodded. "Two for each boat. Easy enough." He ran his hand over the curve of a charge. "I've never seen quite this thing before. But it's the same can. They're damned heavy. Can you two get them into a sling?"

"Yes, we can, Captain."

"Well, go to work on them. I'll take care of the mines. Don't worry, Patrick. Nor you, Conrad. We'll be out of this in an hour's time."

Patrick said: "Tell me what the trick is."

The captain laid his finger on one of the horns of a mine. "There are lightly set now. Or should be." He gave the horn a twist. It began to turn on its thread and, after eight or nine turns, came off. "Say you want to bang off this layout in a dory. All you have to do is take this horn and mount it on a piece of pipe—as long a piece as you need. You stuff the pipe with TNT from a charge and then lead the pipes back into the depth charges. You know you can bore a hole right into a charge and it won't go. As long as it isn't shocked. Know that, did you?"

"I knew that. Yes, sir."

"Well, you could put all this stuff into a dory. Rig up your horns again with the lead tips sticking out and set a time-bomb near them. Then you've got a tool that will knock off the *Gaunt Woman* and everything else within half a mile."

"That's what I want."

"Then that's what you'll get." Captain MacLean took a step forward and stopped at the steel cage. He whistled when Patrick showed him the charts of the Grand Bank. "You can't miss, Patrick. That's where you picked her up and that's where they're waiting for her in the shoal water where she can anchor." He took another step forward and peered into the far corner of the cage. "The radio shack is behind there, I'll bet a dollar. See that line in the bulkhead? It's a sliding door. Don't touch it." He swung around. "You and Conrad get the charges on deck. And the time-bombs. I'll dehorn these babies in no time."

"Everything we take," said Patrick, "comes out of the inside racks. There is so much of it, he won't miss it anyway. Until he checks his books—and he'll never do that again."

"True for you. Unless in hell. Where she's going. Now have you a sling ready?"

"There's a bit of canvas on deck that I can make do."

"Go to it then."

It took them the better part of two hours to get the stuff on deck and down the ladder. Half of it went into the *Daniel* dory, half into the *Gaunt Woman's* own boat, which they had used to come aboard. The dawn was still far off when they pulled away. They rowed directly to the wharf. When Patrick pulled his

boat alongside, he called Margaret's name. She came
out of the darkness and stood above them.

"All quiet?"

"Yes, Patrick."

"We've done it, Maggie. Now to hide it. We're not
sure of ourselves in the river. Will you come with us?
Isn't there a cave or a ledge you used to play in?
Where the side-stream comes in? Your father says
you know one."

"Yes. Help me down." She stood in the bow of the
boat and led them up the river a quarter of a mile,
then into a slower run of water that came in at a
sharp angle. "We used to swim here," she said. "But
it's not light enough to see."

"Use the light." Patrick handed his torch to her
and she flashed its beam over the water. For a time,
the beam stayed close at hand and lighted the base of
the cliff; then it suddenly shot deep into a beach
gouged out of the rock. There was considerable ice in
the pool, but the heavy-laden boats broke through. In
half an hour, they had the explosives stowed away,
high and dry, out of sight.

CHAPTER VIII

AT BREAK OF DAY, a wild shouting below the village brought Patrick stumbling out of his bed. He ran to the window and looked out over the harbor. The *Daniel* lay at her anchorage. Her dories, crowded with men, were running toward the *Gaunt Woman*. The German crew had arrived. A dory-load had already climbed the ladder and the men were prancing about on her deck, pointing up to the new spars and shouting with joy. They carried bulging bags and suitcases down into their quarters and then came up again to unload another dory full of bags and boxes. The dory also carried a crate of ducks and chickens, a sheep with its legs tied together and two suckling pigs, ready for the oven. These were gifts from the hospitable Newfoundlanders to the strangers cast upon their shores.

A scowl came to Patrick's face. He drove it away, replaced it with a grin of mock delight and turned his head toward Skalder's window. "Captain Skalder! Ahoy there! Rise and shine!"

Skalder came to the window. He seemed a little

on the bleary side. His big mouth gaped in the splendor of his beard.

Patrick pointed down to the *Daniel*. "There they are! Safe and sound. Good work, eh? Now, if she's brought in some bait—we can both get back to work!"

Skalder clapped his hands in happiness. "Bravo! I'll dress, Captain Bannon. Breakfast aboard my vessel."

They rowed out to her. The returned seamen gave a cheer when they saw their captain. When he came puffing up the ladder, they hailed him with greetings in Danish, greetings so jovial that they made Patrick sick with loathing. Skalder shook hands with each man, called them by name, and, in turn, named them to Patrick. All but one. Despite his burdensome knowledge that he alone was destined to destroy all these men, Patrick was alert, on edge. He quivered behind his genial grin when the men thanked him for the rescue of their vessel and for sending the *Daniel* to carry them from English Village. He smiled blandly and shook their hands and kept saying: "Think nothing of it. Think nothing of it!" until Skalder roared with laughter and told him to belay that talk.

During this gaiety, Patrick kept his eye on the young man who had sullenly balked at Skalder's greeting and now stood staring at the sombre cliffs that shut in the harbor of Trabo. He was a young fellow, hardly more than twenty-one. His cheeks were terribly thin and there were black spaces under his eyes, a discoloration that made him look like a very sick man. Patrick judged that he was also sick within. One glance was enough to show a competent skipper that here was the malcontent. Not a pettifogging sea lawyer, whose rights had been taken from him, but, more likely, a man who had rebelled against Skalder earlier and now hated to be back under his command. A second and a longer glance brought back into Patrick's mind an unforgettable image: the upturned, dead face of the U-boat man he had seen that day on the Grand Bank. That man, sprawled in the boat with his chums, had been killed because he hated Skalder, because he preferred to risk death rather than continued service under him.

"This one," said Patrick to himself, "is another rebel." And he put that sad, gloomy face down as one to be remembered against the crucial hour to come.

Patrick then made another of his audacious plays. It couldn't have been better suited to the present stage of the game if he had given it a long consideration. He waited until Conrad was alone and near at hand and Holger farther removed. He then called their names loudly.

When Conrad stood before him, Patrick whispered: "Say yes to everything."

When Holger joined them and touched his stocking-cap in respectful salute, Patrick took him by the arm in friendly fashion and said: "Stand by, Holger, my friend. I've got something to say about you two."

Skalder, who had been confabbing with his first mate, came aft at Patrick's signal and looked affably at him.

"Captain Skalder," said Patrick, "I've been looking at your fine crew and I must say I never saw a livelier lot of seamen. Very handy men." Skalder bowed and Patrick continued: "But it seems to me that you are short-handed. You've lost one fine man—" here Skalder looked mournfully aloft "—and I find ashore two good fishermen who are willing to make a cruise on the *Daniel.* Well, since Conrad and Holger here are your countrymen and are both damned glad to be among men who can speak their lingo—why! I say: take them on with you when you sail tomorrow. You need them and they'll be much happier here than on the *Daniel.*"

Skalder raised his hands in a polite gesture.

Patrick turned to Conrad. "I'd hate to see you go, Conrad, after being my dory-mate. You've the makings of a good fisherman, but you'd like to go on this vessel, wouldn't you?"

Conrad was a skillful actor. He looked away, glanced up at the new spars, grinned at the German captain and said: "I like to sail with you, Captain

Bannon. I like to see some Gloucester girls sometime. But—yes! I also like to stay here. If Captain Skalder would like to take me."

"My dear boy!" cried Skalder.

Patrick interrupted him by asking Holger to speak. He pretended that he couldn't say a word. Patrick could easily imagine what was going on in that cunning German brain. He smiled at Holger and said encouragingly: "Think of yourself, my friend. Will you be better off aboard this vessel? I think so. You'll like the cruise back to the Indies, eh? It will be good for your sick belly. Much better than fishing through the ice with us."

Holger nodded his head at that. "I will go, Captain, if Conrad will go. If you do not need me. And Captain Skalder says so."

Skalder was obviously delighted at this turn of events. The measure of his satisfaction proved certain things to Patrick. First, that he had been concerned with the job of keeping Holger aboard his own vessel, which had to be done, one way or another. Second, it was plain that he had been worrying, had been suspicious in a sort of routine way; and, last, he was now free of that worry. Patrick ended the business by saying he would fix up the papers in the morning. He told Conrad and Holger to go ashore, settle their accounts, and move their gear.

When the Germans had gone back to their tasks,

Conrad took the chance to argue loudly with Patrick about the transfer. He then said in a low voice: "You are the biggest devil of a man I ever see, Captain Bannon." His eyes shone with fond admiration.

"You haven't seen anything yet, my friend," said Patrick out of the corner of his mouth. "Get to work. You see that chap standing there by the forge? The sick-looking one?"

"The one who does no work."

"Yes. Make friends with him. Take it easy. He's our man. He can live. The others—" Patrick winked a dreadful wink.

Later in the day, something happened that wasn't in the cards. It threw Patrick off his stride. Skalder and some of the men were aloft, bending on new sails and roaring and yelling like good ones. The mate of the *Gaunt Woman* was straddled on the main cross-trees. Some sort of argument was going forward. Somebody didn't like the set of things. The mate, a red-jowled, middle-aged man, was every bit as good a seaman as the master and an eloquent man when stirred by a question concerning the vessel's welfare.

Patrick was putting in some loafing time on the *Gaunt Woman's* deck, there being nothing to do on the *Daniel* except wait for the tardy herring boats to come in with the bait. He was smoking his pipe and enjoying the day, which was bright with sun and white-winged birds against the cliffs. Happening to take a lazy look landward, he spied a figure moving against the sky. It was Margaret walking on the path that ran along the edge of the cliff. She looked more beautiful than ever in that rare setting. She had again doffed her sea-going rig and had a 'longshore dress on. Her head shone copper-colored against a space of blue sky. She was so high up that he couldn't see her face clearly, but he enjoyed the sight of her as she went at a leisurely pace toward the brink of the rock that rose over the sea.

Once she stopped and seemed to be looking down at the *Gaunt Woman*. Patrick waved to her. She made no answer. She took a few more steps, then stopped abruptly and lifted her hand to shield her eyes from the sun. She ran forward and peered again over the westward waters, which were shut off from the *Gaunt Woman* by the harbor cliffs.

Patrick thought that she had seen something far down the Straight Shore. A great stretch of the Atlantic was visible to her from that high place. He looked down the Trabo channel to the open sea, although that area was out of her sight, being too far under the cliff.

He saw something, too. A Canadian corvette was turning into the passage. Two seamen were standing on her deck. Another man was covering the barrel of a gun forward. She seemed to be in fair shape, but Patrick could tell, without settling on any one detail, that she had been knocked about a bit. He was startled by her sudden appearance. He was about to give her a hail when he noticed that things had changed aloft. If he had needed anything to confirm his knowledge of the *Gaunt Woman* and her crew, that change was enough. It was a silence, an absolute, breathless end to the roaring and swearing. Skalder and his men were gazing with fearful eyes at the little warship. Skalder himself hung against the sky, one hand on a topping-lift, the other held up stiffly where it had been caught in a gesture. His bright beard blew in the wind. His big mouth stayed open.

The mate was the first man to get back his wits. He viciously struck at the man next to him on the crosstrees. Both of them sang out: "Ahoy! Hello, the corvette! Hello!"

At that, Skalder laughed and cried out to the Newfoundlanders working on his deck. "Corvette, boys!" and then he added: "Send the Navy some rum, eh? Ask him to send a boat alongside."

The Newfoundlanders, who were proud of their corvettes, began shouting to the lads on her deck. One of the sailors cut them short with a down-wave of his hand. He cried: "That the *Gaunt Woman* there?"

"Aye! 'tis she!"

"Stand by then. Captain's coming aboard."

Skalder carried this shock off well. He never flinched. He sent a smile down to Patrick and cried:

"A nice visitor, eh? You must help me do the honors, Captain Bannon."

"Willingly, sir. Hot water from the galley and a bottle. A bit of grog won't harm him. He's been having a time of it."

Patrick, advancing to join Skalder, took the opportunity to look again at Margaret. She was still in her place, standing tall and lithe against the brilliant sky. Her back was turned toward him. Both her hands now shielded her eyes from the nooning sun.

Patrick walked over to the ladder with Skalder. The corvette's boat came away from her side. He saw the captain, a lanky, tow-headed kid, putting his best cap on. Patrick looked again at the girl against the sky. She was now running back along the path. Once she stumbled, flung up her arms and jumped over a boulder in her path. He gazed a moment in perplexity at that flying figure, then another sudden change aboard the *Gaunt Woman* struck him into attention. The Trabo men, who had built the corvette and knew every plank in her, were talking loudly with the corvette's crew and promising them all sorts of good things, especially out of their barrel of rum. But half of the *Gaunt Woman's* crew had vanished from the cluttered deck. The mate had gone into the cabin. Nine or ten men had gone below.

Before the corvette captain's head appeared over the bulwarks, the mate came out again, putting on a clean jacket, one that had bright brass buttons. And the men, who had gone below so swiftly, came on deck again in two's and three's and began loafing about.

Patrick understood what had happened. They had armed themselves. They were ready to take the corvette by surprise if the captain's visit turned out to be anything more than a routine call. And they could do it. Twenty-one men. Twenty-two, including Skalder. Twenty-three, including Holger, who was still somewhere about the vessel, pretending to make himself useful to the shipwrights. Patrick's hackle rose. He began to tingle again. He was in a tough spot and, as usual, it made him hot. This looked like a chance to let the Canadians take over. If he sprang the trap now, merely gave the approaching officer a wink, the job would be out of his hands.

He figured it out rapidly as he stepped forward with his outstretched hand to meet the captain. He did the sum coldly and took a calm, slow look at it. This weary kid and a few others down on that tiny deck. And here—on the *Gaunt Woman*—bombs, grenades, automatic guns under jackets and men fighting against the hangman. In an instant they would do—God knows what! A shambles on the corvette, the *Daniel* cracked open, himself shot down. Trabo smashed up, too! And the *Gaunt Woman* away. All lost. Nothing gained.

He refused to surrender a quarry that he consid-

ered his own. He smiled and said: "Hello, Captain!
My name's Bannon, master of the *Daniel Webster*."

"Cameron is my name."

The kid held out his hand. He had plenty of good
stuff in him. Cape Breton stuff. Patrick knew his kind
and liked it well. Tough as halibut and faithful to
the last kick of their hearts. There was a deep line
between his pale blue eyes; other lines showed at the
corners of his mouth in a hookish pattern. He was a
wise one. Tired, yet very much on the job. Not suspicious; nevertheless, not the man to be careless in
his duty. He turned and held out his hand to Skalder
and again gave his thin, sweet smile.

Skalder took the hand with his usual careful cour-
tesy and bowed his big body. "Happy to see you
aboard, Captain Cameron. I am the master of this
vessel. *Den Magre Kvinde*. Or, as Captain Bannon
says, the *Gaunt Woman*."

The corvette captain told his story quickly enough.
He said he had made a call at English Village, where
he had been told about the *Woman's* crew going up
the shore in the *Daniel*. He had come into Trabo to
ask the master of the *Gaunt Woman* about the U-boat
that had shelled him.

Patrick watched Skalder's spirits subtly rise while
the corvette captain was speaking; he saw how Skalder took a better grip on himself when it came his
turn to talk. More than that, Skalder had managed

to send out some secret signal to his men. Those that had casually followed him aft, now lounged away. Patrick saw them admiring the corvette or picking up their tools again.

The three captains went into the cabin. While Skalder indignantly related his fancy tale of the bombardment and how he had sent his crew off the ship, he made drinks of hot rum and handed them around. At the end of the story, the kid smacked his lips over the rum, drank again and said: "Halifax will be glad to see you and your vessel, Captain. We're needing a bit of grog now and then, you know." He waved his glass toward the sea. "The war's been going badly. Very badly. That is, up to about ten days ago. Things suddenly slowed up then. Before that, I give my word —it was hell. There was a pack of them running loose, firing at everything in sight. They got into the middle of one convoy off Cape Race and before they finished there were four fine vessels gone and a corvette done for. I lost a chum." His hand shook with anger. "I picked up forty men two days later on rafts. Saved most of them. Five kids—seamen from the London docks—died from wounds and cold in my cabin."

"Terrible!" cried Skalder. He poured his drink down and asked: "You say things slowed up for a while, Captain Cameron?"

"Yes," said Patrick, "I was wondering what you meant by that, Captain. No sinkings?"

Captain Cameron nodded. "All last week not a torpedo fired. I myself went out with two convoys. Over a hundred vessels, all told. Well on their way to England by now."

"Thank God!" cried Skalder.

"We think we've figured it out," said Captain Cameron. "The Yankees caught one of them off Quereau Bank and poured onto her like a commando. U-boat didn't know what the devil hit them. Well, she didn't have a shot left in her locker. Not even a round left for her guns. It seemed to us that something has gone wrong with their way of doing things on this side. Some of us are pretty sure that they're getting stolen oil from boats working in our waters. But torpedoes—that's a different matter."

Skalder drained his glass and cried: "That was good work by the Yankees!" He made a perfunctory offer of his papers. The kid let them slip slowly through his fingers after a hard look here and there. He then did his duty. Whether or not he had caught Skalder in some too perfect play, it was impossible to tell. His keen face remained impassive, even amiable and a little less tired because of the hot drink. He asked: "You are sailing tomorrow, Captain Skalder?"

"Yes, Captain. With the help of God. I am ready to go."

The corvette captain pondered things for a while.

He suddenly held out his hand and shook Skalder's cordially. "I may be able to save you some trouble, Captain. I've a job to do outside tonight. Some very queer talk comes to our ears. But unless something holds me up, I'm to start for Halifax tomorrow myself. My engines are coming out for overhaul, for which I am grateful. So I'll give you an escort all the way down and save you from boarding parties."

Patrick, wishing to avoid the betraying look that might come into Skalder's face, emptied his glass and smacked over it loudly.

Skalder did well, although he must have been hard hit. He bowed again to the Captain. "You are kind, sir." He gave a sigh of relief. "I must admit I was worried about that voyage. Now I shall be all right."

The kid nodded solemnly. "And another thing. What I said about saving you trouble. Be good enough to open all your hatches in the morning and break out enough of your cargo so that I can inspect the best part of it. I think that may save you opening them for my chums outside of Halifax. Is that agreeable, sir?"

"Agreeable, Captain! You are too good. But promise me one thing, please. Will you have dinner with us tomorrow noon? Here? Our cook is a good one and I can promise you a roast young pig—Danish style. And a bottle of good wine from South America." He smiled at Patrick and added: "Captain Bannon will honor us, too, I know."

"Willingly," said Patrick.

Captain Cameron saluted and said: "Thank you. I'll be in before noon. I wish to pay my respects to Captain MacLean." He spoke to Patrick. "Can you tell me how he is getting along? He did a brave thing, you know, and I may have some news for him about it."

Patrick replied: "His daughter came from Gloucester to nurse him. He seems to be getting about a bit. What is the news that you may have?—if it's all right for me to ask."

"Certainly, Captain Bannon." The kid's eyes lighted up with pleasure of handing on a good word. "In Halifax the news is that the King will honor that man."

"The King!" exclaimed Patrick.

"Nobody else!" replied Captain Cameron. "His Majesty has been in these waters and he learns, sooner or later, what is done in them. Especially by heroes."

At that, he saluted again.

"Until tomorrow!" cried Skalder. And in that jovial phrase, Patrick knew, Skalder pronounced the death sentence of the corvette. But in his own heart Patrick heard a hideous laughter. He poured a drink and sat down to it.

CHAPTER IX

ON COMING OUT on deck, Patrick
saw Skalder, half-way up the mainmast, stop and look
down toward the wharf. There was a great hullaba-
loo going on there. Men and boys were running up
and down. He heard Margaret calling to the dorymen
on the *Daniel* and they, in turn, were shouting to the
corvette captain. Some exciting news had changed
hands. The corvette picked up speed and ripped down
the tickle, swung around the headland, and dashed
into the outer channel. Patrick's men kept roaring
some phrase to him. He rowed to the wharf.

He cried out to her: "What did you see outside? I
saw you running."

"A submarine!"

"Are you sure?" He climbed onto the wharf and
ran to her side.

"As sure as I'm standing here, Patrick. There's no
doubt about it. In the channel beyond Widow's Rock.
At first on the surface, then just her periscope showing as it came closer in. Then she turned out to sea.
Going faster."

The dorymen tumbled onto the wharf and joined

the villagers who were scrambling up that path. Patrick and Margaret followed.

He asked: "You saw the corvette, too?"

"Not until I came down from the cliff."

"The U-boat was trailing the corvette."

"That may be, but I think—perhaps it's something else."

They were now high over the bowl-like harbor and could hear the excited cries of the children who were looking out to sea.

"What then, Maggie?"

"That ship there—the *Gaunt Woman*—is the life of the pack. That's what you said in the beginning and you've proved it. This U-boat hanging off the shore is another proof of it. She's looking for the *Gaunt Woman*. She wants more news than she's getting by radio." She stopped there by the grove of stunted evergreens and whispered: "It's all over, isn't it, Patrick? You told the captain of the corvette what she is?"

"No!"

She stared at him in pain and wonderment. "Patrick! Have you gone mad with this thirst for vengeance? You didn't tell the captain? Why, Patrick? Oh, why didn't you?"

"Because I couldn't!" He stopped her angry questions by saying: "Get on a bit, girl. So we can watch this hunt." She murmured some word under breath and he roared in sudden anger: "You win just the same! The corvette's coming back tomorrow to inspect her and things will blow just the same. I'll get word to the corvette somehow. Good God! don't you know what that kid was up against? Standing alone on her deck? With that gang of pirates ready to blow his ship out of water? Why, Maggie, they armed themselves the minute he came aboard." He touched her shoulder gently as she paced sullenly by his side. "Have no fear. Bannon is out of the picture. The *Gaunt Woman* will be finished off tomorrow. I lose my chance. But as long as you're satisfied—who cares?"

She looked at his bitter face in dismay, then smiled and said: "It's better so, Patrick. I want you to live. I want my father to end his days in peace."

They looked in silence over the sea. They could see the corvette speeding down the channel. She swung around Widow's Rock and ran out in the course that the U-boat had taken. Patrick could see the men spring to their depth-charge stations aft. The vessel was half a mile farther out when the first charge went over. A little later, the channel burst upward there in a white fountain. The villagers and dorymen cheered. Ten minutes later another charge exploded. The corvette darted to and fro, seeking the trail. Once she turned and raced through the boiling places where the charges had burst; then she floated idly.

"They're listening!" said Patrick. "But they're in

a hundred fathoms now." He turned to her and asked: "Have you told this to Conrad? I don't see him. He must know. From now on, things will move fast."

"No, I didn't tell him. I didn't see him. But I told Holger."

"Holger! For God's sake—why?"

"Because I wanted Skalder to know at once."

"You're thinking a little too fast for me, Maggie. But it's right, it's right."

"I saw Holger leaving the tavern with his sea-bag. I ran up to him, took him by the arm and cried: 'A U-boat off shore! A great, big one!'"

"What did he do?"

"He almost laughed in my face because he thinks we're such fools. He patted me on the shoulder and said everything would be all right. He told me to tell you and then he ran up the path to take a look for himself. I ran after him and told him to get the corvette. I told him that the *Gaunt Woman* would be shelled again, that the *Daniel* would be sunk. He said I should tell you. He shook me off and ran up the path." She pointed. "There he is! Alone. Look!"

Patrick saw him. Holger stood by himself, his dark face turned toward the sea.

The corvette sped farther out and slowly vanished in the sunlight. He turned to Margaret and they started back toward the village. Some of the children kept watch on the cliff until dark. They came down then and at the usual hour of nine o'clock the village went to sleep, window by window.

Skalder remained at the tavern and put on a mighty show of calm. Holger and Conrad remained there, too. Patrick had paid them some money and they had chosen to spend it on a few more good meals and another night in the soft beds of the tavern. Skalder drank a good deal of his rum at the supper table and gradually grew tense with an inner excitement that he could hardly repress. He pretended that he thought the corvette had a chance of killing the U-boat; then he said that maybe the chase would be long and he expressed his fears that the corvette would not return in time to take him out the next day. He complimented Margaret many times on her watchfulness.

Patrick made an elaborate effort to calm Skalder. Later, remembering this, he laughed at his own guile because, as a matter of fact, Skalder actually was hoping that the corvette would come in. He intended to bag it on his hook; for it was obvious to him that the U-boat must be in a bad way to come so far from the rendezvous and certainly would not go far off without achieving her object. And that was a talk with him.

Patrick set a watch over the *Gaunt Woman*. He had reason to believe that she could slip out and make sail without too much trouble. Her new masts and all her spars were up. Her crew was capable of doing the rest of the work at sea. So Patrick sent Margaret to a hiding-place on the cliff. And, as soon as supper was over, Conrad started off to take some things off the *Daniel*. Halfway down the path, he turned off and climbed back into the woods behind Margaret's house. There he could watch the harbor and the tavern. Holger, meanwhile, had simply vanished, a spy's trick of which he was a master.

Patrick waited until a few minutes before ten o'clock. He then said to Skalder: "I'll say good night, Captain. I have a little business to tend to aboard ship." He winked and added: "Write a little something in the log, you know."

Skalder roared at this filthy joke and bade him good night. Patrick went directly to Margaret's window, crouched there a while, then crawled around the house and joined Conrad.

Conrad whispered: "Plenty doing, Captain."

"Tell it."

"Two boats leave the *Gaunt Woman* and go down the channel. They swing out there first"—he pointed to the river mouth—"so your people do not see. Then go down tickle and out to sea."

"What else?"

"One boat come to wharf. Three men with big burdens come up. Go through woods to keep off tavern. Holger—he waits here for them and leads them to cliff. Where she is."

Patrick took Conrad by the arm. "You kept your knife?"

The Dane struck his hand against his belt. "I will take care of Holger, Captain. He should be killed now. They are too many for us."

Patrick replied: "No, Conrad! Go up there and follow him. See what he is doing. Just lay low along the path until you see him. If he finds you, jump him and drive your knife into his belly. Drag him off the path and then—listen carefully, Conrad!—come back and stand right here."

"Yes, Captain."

"Bear this in mind, Conrad. No fair play. Don't challenge him. Don't give him a chance. You're a Dane. He's a German. Kill him. Stab him in the back, if you can. Above all, don't fight with him unless you have to. Our game is up if they learn we're wise to them."

"Yes, Captain."

"I'm going after him myself. There are two paths he can take. Otherwise, he'd break his neck. You take the one that leads to the left of the woods. Between the two split rocks. I'll take the one that goes to the right. If he catches me, I'll kill him. If not, I'll come back and come after you on your path."

"A question, Captain?"

"Go ahead."

"What does the captain think they are doing?"

"I know damn well what they're doing. They're mining the outside channel. They've got charts of these waters as good as ours. They know there's only one channel for a ship like the corvette. They're putting mines down to be exploded from the shore. They'll knock the corvette off when she comes in tomorrow. Or they'll hang."

Conrad saluted and hurried off. Patrick climbed the path and stole into the grove of evergreens, where he waited a while to see if he had been followed. He went on toward the edge of the cliff. He found Margaret lying in the lee of a black outcropping of stone. She whispered to him: "The moon broke through for a few minutes. I saw the *Gaunt Woman's* boats go down the channel and stop this side of Widow's Rock. I couldn't see what they were doing. Then the dark came on again."

"They're mining the channel. Against the corvette—or anything else that might come along. Anything more, Maggie?"

"I'm not sure whether it was a light flashing or the moon striking on a patch of ice. But there was something over there. Where the old path goes down to the water."

She pointed toward the place where he had sent Conrad. It was black night now. The clouds rolled heavily westward. The moon sent down no light at all. Patrick could see nothing except the straight line of the cliffs and, here and there, a jagged hummock, where the wind whistled and howled. Far below, he saw the narrow beach and the white spread of breakers falling.

He bade her stand by and then ran back through the woods. He bent low as he turned into the first path and went crouching along, stopping now and then to look behind him. It took him almost half an hour to reach the edge of the cliff. There was no one there. He crawled forward on the rock until he could look down the steep side. He searched all that wilderness for a light and the sea for signs of the boats. There was more light on the water now, but it revealed nothing.

He retraced his steps a hundred yards, then plunged directly through the woods until he reached the farther path which Conrad had taken. He hadn't taken twenty steps along this new path before he saw two things: first, the gleam of a lantern near the edge of the cliff; second, a man's face staring from the darkness just ahead. The man was lying at the side of the path. There was a fixed character to his posture that made Patrick think that he was listening for footsteps.

Patrick sank to the ground. He took out his heavy revolver; then put it back and drew his knife, a long, curved tool of the halibut fisheries. He had been going slowly, taking care not to make the slightest noise. He was sure he hadn't been seen. He hugged the ground and waited for the watching man to move. He didn't. The darkness increased until none of the moonlight came through the murk, even on the sea where it had fitfully gleamed. The face itself grew indistinct, but the staring eyes seemed to be brighter. Once they vanished momentarily, as if the man had passed his hand over them or the wind had blown his hair. Patrick crawled back a few feet and off the path. His boots sank into a pool of water. He backed all the way into this gouged-out bowl and hid there.

Meanwhile, the lantern beyond had stayed out or had been shaded. Now it gleamed again. A yellow ray slanted seaward, making the air glitter. Patrick heard a man's shout far under the cliff. He lifted his head and saw the dark forms of men bending in the arc of the lantern's glow. They were hard at work on some job that required tools. He saw one of them lift a hammer and strike several times. He saw a reddish glint, a thick red hoop of light, and he knew that the men were handling coils of cable.

He slid forward again, swung farther to the right, and then came back toward the path. The buttons of his soaked reefer scraped on the stony surface. He unbuttoned the jacket and went forward until he was lying in the path itself. He was now behind the prone watcher, could even make out the sprawling set of his boots. The stillness of the man warned Patrick that something strange was awaiting him. He turned over this new uneasiness in his mind. He tried to figure out what it meant. It did not take long. He realized that the man was not watching, was not waiting.

He said: "That man is dead."

He crawled forward on his hands and knees, came nearer and nearer until, at last, he could almost reach out and touch that immobile body. He did so. His hand touched a jacket wet with blood. He turned on his torch. It was Conrad.

A light flashed from the cliff. Its beam searched the crooked path. Patrick shrank down and waited until the light went out.

"Good-bye to you," whispered Patrick. "Good-bye, Conrad."

He crawled away again and cautiously drew near the workers on the cliff. He advanced about twenty yards and again raised his head, just in time to see two men go over the brink, arm in arm. They bore great spools of cable on their backs.

One man remained. He tinkered busily at a contraption in front of him, a square black box that was set in a scooped-out hollow in the rock. This box appeared to be a sort of switchboard, mounted on an electric battery. Patrick could see a series of brass keys shining in its panel. He lay there, until a flash of the lantern revealed the man's face.

It was the face of Holger. The lips were twisted back off the teeth; eyes staring. He held the lantern close to the battery, then struck the plungers down and lifted them again. He rose and stepped into the darkness outside the lantern's glow. He came back, grunting under the weight of a thick slab of stone. He laid this over the hollow that held the battery. He then put out the light and stood by the edge of the cliff.

Patrick cocked his revolver and crept forward. He swung to the right until he came to a deep cleft in the solid rock. He followed its widening course until he could look out over the water. A weak stream of light now came down from the masses of clouds. It was enough to see a man by, if you knew where he was standing. The line of breakers was a full thousand feet away at that point. The face of the cliff was not so steep there and a rib of rock bulged out of the escarpment. From time to time, Patrick saw Holger bend down and pluck his fingers against a cable that ran out of the box and down the side of the cliff.

Less than an hour later, Patrick saw a brief blue beam of light shoot upward from the beach in a signal to Holger. He made no acknowledgment. A little later, Patrick made out a dark mass moving westward over the water. He judged that these were the *Gaunt Woman's* boats. He couldn't see them plainly. The sea was phospherescent, and the wake behind that moving shape glowed. It curled, this way and that, and then abruptly swung in a half-circle. At that point, another signal came from a red, shielded lamp in one of the boats. Patrick looked toward Holger. He was taking a sight of the signal with some instrument held to his eye. The boats then turned up the channel toward the entrance to the harbor. The job was done and a trap set.

CHAPTER X

PATRICK WAITED. Several minutes passed. Suddenly he heard the Nazi spy cry out. Patrick looked at him. He was standing up, peering over the water. Patrick followed that gaze. Miles away, far beyond the reef of Widow's Rock, a strong beam began to blink rapidly. Patrick tried to read the signals, which were coming over in dots and dashes. It was a jumble, a code. The U-boat was telling some story, a secret story to Germans ashore. Without knowing the code, Patrick knew what the message must be: "Where is the *Gaunt Woman*? When shall we meet?"

He grunted. "The corvette missed that one."

Patrick moved to the attack. He walked on tiptoe to the path where Conrad lay and then he went, bending low, directly toward Holger. He could see him covering the slab with twigs and bits of stone. Holger was close to the edge of the cliff. Patrick couldn't risk an encounter there. So he waited until the German came padding up the path. When he was alongside, Patrick lifted the revolver and gaffed him at the base of the skull. The German grunted. His knees buckled.

The lantern tumbled from his hand. He sagged and pitched forward.

Patrick held the muzzle of the gun against Holger's forehead and said: "Say one word, you bastard, make one move before I tell you to—and I'll finish you off."

The German struggled for his breath. He stared upward.

Patrick said: "It's Bannon, you." A curse in German came from the man. Patrick leaned down again and whispered: "Keep that trap of yours shut, you bloody spy, or I'll bang a bullet through it." He spat in anger and disgust. "This is Bannon, do you hear?" He put his lips close to Holger's ears. "I want you to know, you dumb fool, that I was wise to you ever since Conrad and I took the dead men aboard the *Daniel*. Do you hear that? Speak!"

The broken lips whispered: "Ja!"

"Good! You speak German now? No more Danish? You swine!" Patrick took him by the right leg and dragged him to the place where he had been working. He flung him down, and then set him up against the slab of stone. The German's head wobbled. Now and then he groaned.

Patrick crouched close to him and he thrust the muzzle of the revolver under the German's jacket; "Now answer me in English. Do you know what that thing is against your ribs?"

The spy groaned.

"It's my father's gun," said Patrick. "Make one move, refuse to answer one little question—and you'll get it. Understand? Answer me!"

"Yes!" The lids lifted off his dark, crazy eyes. An intense gleam shot out of them, then the lids dropped again. A skein of blood arranged itself on his forehead.

Patrick said: "Do you want to live? Answer me!"

Six or seven words came out. German words.

Patrick slapped him hard on the jaw. "I'll give you one more chance. Speak again in German and I'll gaff you for good."

The spy whispered: "I wish to live."

Patrick began to search the German's pockets and took all the papers he found. There was a large automatic pistol and a smaller one in a holster under the right arm. In another pocket, he found a claspknife. It was bloody. In the trousers pocket, he came on a wallet, thick with money. He flung it down.

"Now listen to me. I'm going to tell you a few things to show you what fools you and Skalder are— were, I mean. Do you know Skalder's dead?"

The German shuddered.

"Yes," said Patrick, "the Canadians shot him down like a mad dog an hour ago. That corvette captain fooled you, too. He landed men at dusk. Had twenty below decks." Patrick growled. "Skalder talked a little first, then tried one of your Nazi tricks. So they killed him. They cut his beard off afterward and hanged him to the yardarm of his own ship. Do you hear me? You know I wouldn't lie to you, don't you? Answer me! Or I'll break every rib in your body."

"Yes." The shuddering of the body made the voice tremble.

"I made a fool out of Skalder. I slipped the Canadian skipper a note right in Skalder's cabin." He laughed hardly. "Now, I'm going to ask you questions. Answer them the right way and maybe I'll save your life. Maybe. I know enough now. You can't fool me. The first word of a lie—just one little word—and I pull the trigger. Get it? Nod your head, if you do."

The head nodded.

"That's right," said Patrick. "Listen! I want you to ask me one question. Any one. To prove to you there's no use trying to kid me. The only thing that'll save you is the truth. Now ask me something. Ask me something about that hell-ship. About the *Gaunt Woman.*"

The spy's lips tried to move. His eyes showed their hate once more, then closed.

"No? Well, I'll tell you something. I'll tell you what's under the deck of the *Gaunt Woman.* Torpedoes, mines, depth charges. The Canadians and Captain MacLean are taking them out now. O.K.? True, isn't it? Speak!"

"True!"

"That's one thing. Now I'll show you how much more I know. Guess who was the first one into the hold of the *Gaunt Woman?* Come on, pig!"

"Who?"

"Bannon, by God!"

Holger's eyes stared. "How?" said the lips.

Patrick laughed. "Skalder screamed in rage when we told him. I went aboard the first night I took her into Trabo. I opened the main hatch and went below. I found the fake bulkhead of empty barrels, you fat-head!"

The whole body shuddered again.

"Just one thing more, baby-killer. Who followed me out of the tavern that night and saw me safely into my girl's room?"

"I!"

"You! Know who that girl is? Eh?

"Who?"

"A nurse who's been overseas helping the English and hates you worse than I do. Like it?"

The German groaned.

"One thing more about that. She was asleep. And stayed asleep. I just went out the other window and down onto the *Gaunt Woman*. I'll bet that sits pretty in your crop."

Patrick gave the spy a poke in the ribs with the revolver. "I should think you would give up. She begged me to kill you, but I wanted you right where

I've got you. And the *Gaunt Woman* right where I've got her." He paused, stood on his tiptoes and looked out over the water. The low horn of the moon pierced a film of cloud and illuminated the waves. He could make nothing out. He crouched again.

Holger's head sagged and he groaned again. Patrick said: "You're not as badly off as that. Sit up! Now, tell me about Conrad. He isn't able to talk about much yet. You stabbed him with that, didn't you?" He picked up the bloody knife and held it before the spy's face. "Left him for dead back there, didn't you?"

The head jerked in assent.

Patrick said: "How does it feel to tackle a man instead of a kid? Pretty risky, eh? Now you answer these questions. The three dead men Conrad and I found on that boat were Germans?"

"Yes!"

"You made a pretty show of grieving over them, as if they were good Danes. But you know they were hands off a U-boat? Speak!"

"Yes."

"So did we. Your Danish was too good for a common sailor. That's what gave you all away for sure."

The spy spat. "Executed."

"Skalder told me they were shot from his deck while they were trying to escape. That they'd been taken off a U-boat for a rest because they were nearly

crazy. O.K.! Now, listen! The *Gaunt Woman* is the
mother-ship, isn't she? She's been taking on supplies
from a big submarine and handing them out later?"

"Yes."

"That was an easy one. Now, you were sent to
Gloucester to make a cruise here, one way or another,
and get in touch with her? That's an easy one, too.
Nod your head!"

The spy nodded.

"There were four U-boats working with the
Woman. And she's supposed to meet them on the
peak of the Grand Bank. Where we first saw her?
Right?"

The spy made no answer. Patrick lifted the revolver. "Speak up, scum! I know the answer but I want
to find out if you can tell the truth. Go on!"

Patrick pressed the muzzle of the pistol against the
spy's forehead. "I found a chart hidden in the *Gaunt
Woman's* cabin. Another in the hold. They give all
the positions for the meetings. Those past and those
to come. You're not telling me anything, but you'd
better speak. The U-boats are on the Grand Bank
this minute waiting for her." He clicked the hammer
back. "I'm going to kill you now."

The spy whispered: "No! Wait!"

"It's true, isn't it? What I said?"

The spy nodded.

"This thing here"—Patrick pointed to the ma-

chine under the slab—"we know about that. Skalder
gave it away, trying to save his fat belly from the
bullets. It made no difference. I saw your boats go
down the channel with the mines and floats. I saw
you and the others set this thing up. You were going
to blow up the corvette. Well, you won't. You and I
will explode those mines presently. Just to get them
out of the way. But I'm going to tie you up for a
while. Understand?"

"Yes."

"Or will you give me a German officer's word of
honor that you'll stay right here and keep your mouth
shut?"

"I will."

Patrick smashed him hard on the jaw. "That for
German honor! Lie there and think it over."

He turned up the wick of the lantern and searched
the ground until he came upon some discarded
lengths of wire. He bound the spy's hands and ankles,
gagged him, and pulled him to one side.

He hurried up the path and joined Margaret, who
was lying at her post overlooking the open sea.

She said: "I saw a vessel signalling beyond Widow's."

"Can you see her now?"

"I thought I did a moment ago. I'm not sure. She
seemed to be coming up the channel. Where I saw

the U-boat first. The moon is beginning to show things up."

He lay down beside her and told her what had happened.

"Conrad?" she whispered.

"Poor Conrad."

"Did he say who did it?"

"He was gone. I touched his back. Wet with blood. Then the light flashed. I had to jump."

She stayed silent a moment and then asked: "What are you going to do to the German, Patrick?"

"I'd like to kill him."

"It's time for that maybe."

"Just time. But there's something else to be done first. Come with me."

He took her to the place where the spy lay. He lifted the slab off the battery. "For the corvette— or anything else—that enters the channel. This board makes the contact."

She stood in silence, gazing at the plungers on the panel.

Patrick lifted the lantern, took out the spy's papers, and gave them to her. He handed her the thick wallet. He whispered: "If he moves or speaks without my telling him to—I'm going to shoot him. Back now to your post. Keep an eye peeled. Skalder must be anxious. But I'm going to put one thing more

over on him. The *Gaunt Woman* will sail tonight
and the *Daniel* will sail after her."

"Then you will have your way, Patrick, after all."
She spoke without bitterness, yet she turned from
him, took a stride or two away until she stood at the
brink of the cliff. There she crossed her arms upon
her breast and gazed moodily, almost sullenly, into
the dark over the sea.

Patrick made no answer. He had now struck the
first blow in his war. He knew it would be only one of
many blows, that the beaten man, lying there on the
cliff, had cunning allies already seeking him out. Seeking her, too.

"You are in danger here, Maggie. You must go."

She seemed not have heard him. He saw her toss
her head into the wind and lift her hand to brush
back the fall of her hair. A great sea burst against
the rocks below and its burden of foam, flying upward in a gleaming swath, brightened the gloom, so
that he saw her clearly for a moment—boots, jacket
and upraised head—against the glare. She seemed
resolute and strong in that seamanlike pose, yet, while
he gazed, another image of her, an image of a long-
legged child in skirt and blouse standing on that
very rock, changed his own mood from sternness to
a yearning tenderness. He stepped forward and, saying no word, put his arm around her. She would not
turn her face to him. She blindly thrust her hand

against his to push him from her. Yet, when he
touched her cheek with his free hand, she yielded
swiftly, flung her hands up to his shoulders, and
whispered a passionate word, a word lost to him in
the uproar of sea and land. He held her closer until
her trembling ceased.

"There is no time, Patrick," she whispered. "No
time ever! There never was. There never will be."

"There is time. Nothing will happen yet a while,
Maggie. I know what they are doing. Come this
way." He drew her back from the cliff and then
down into the shelter of a great boulder athwart the
path. "Here we can watch the path and the sea. Be at
ease, darling."

He pressed his lips against the cold sheen of her
cheek. At this new sign of his hunger for her, coming
even in the midst of their danger, she slowly turned
the cheek until her lips touched his mouth. After
a time, she spoke again in his embrace. "Do not forget
what I said, Patrick. You are having your way. And
my father—he is having his way. I am going, too."

"Not on the *Daniel,* Maggie! The dories—they'll
be taken aboard tonight full of that stuff off the
Gaunt Woman. No, you must stay ashore until I
come back."

She stirred impatiently in his arms. Her eyes
gleamed in the dark. "Until you come back? You
may never come back to Trabo, Patrick! You must

know that now. And there is nothing for me on shore if you don't come back. And bring him with you."

"But the *Daniel*, Maggie! The *Daniel* with the explosive aboard—why! it's no place for a girl. I can't—"

"A girl! I'm not a girl tonight, Patrick. I'm a nurse and I want a nurse's place. I have my duty and I know what it is. It doesn't lie where I am safe. Never! It's where men are fighting and dying. I must do my duty by my father. I cannot leave him. Nor you. Nor your men. I belong to them as they belong to me. No, I will not leave you. No matter what you say."

He kept back his answer. He rose to his knees and looked down the path. He looked at Holger, a dim, sprawled shape beyond the path. Patrick was aware that the next blow of the conflict was not far off, that even then it was in the making, on sea or on land. He would have need of her. Yet his crowded heart, rejoicing in the return of his old happiness, strove desperately against the justness of her plea. Her own bravery—here and under fire in England—spoke loudly for her; and it was undeniable that her father might well have even greater need of her aboard the *Daniel*, for he was far from recovered of his wound. And there might be other men wounded or maimed in the coming encounters. Only her skill could save such casualties from suffering at sea, even death for lack of care. He groaned within at the thought of an explosion aboard his schooner. If she stayed ashore, there would then be nothing but a medicine chest and his own crude hands to tend to wounds. He was fit enough to cut a hook out of a man's hand, or to set a leg that had been broken by a sea, but for the wounds of war his doctoring was no good, might even be dangerous.

She whispered to him then: "You are thinking a long time, Patrick Bannon. What is it that you are thinking, Patrick dear?"

He rose to his feet and stretched out his hand to bring her up from the earth. "I'm thinking, Maggie, that you are right. It was I who brought you into this. You and your father. If it was a matter of my own business—my vessel or my fishing—I'd take you both out of it. Aye! if I had to put you in irons. But since it's our country that is concerned—well, you may do your duty." He took her hands and held them to his lips. "Yes, Maggie, when the *Daniel* goes after the *Gaunt Woman*—your place is aboard with us. We will come back together or—" he closed his lips.

"Say it, Patrick. I want to hear it."

He shook his head. "No need of saying, Maggie darling. You know in your heart what I mean."

CHAPTER XI

HE TOOK HER back to her station where she could look down upon the channel and catch the signal of the U-boat when it came again. He gave her the electric torch and said: "Flash a short one, if you see it. Flash two when it passes the *Widow*. That's where the mines are. In the channel. Lie down so that you can't be seen against the sky. We have a little time yet. But if anybody comes—beat it. You're a gone goose, if you don't."

She lay down on the cliff. Patrick stood by her for a few minutes and then went back to his place. He dragged Holger closer to the battery and sat him up with his back toward the place where Margaret kept watch.

"You cold?" asked Patrick.

"Yes, Captain Bannon."

"You'll be warm enough in a minute. I'm going to take you down to the tavern."

"No."

"Why not?"

"The Canadians."

"I'm running this show."

"They will kill me. You made a promise."

"What in hell's name do you want me to do? Put you on the U-boat?"

"Yes. You made a promise. It is empty and must go back to Germany."

"You're crazy! Besides, the sub isn't in sight. It signalled and put out again."

"They are sending a boat ashore. I ordered it. By the *Gaunt Woman's* radio. Keep your promise."

"An important guy you are somewhere."

"Yes. Very."

"Not here. Just a Nazi dope, that's all."

A single short beam shot out from the place where Margaret watched. Patrick saw it.

"There's something else," said the spy.

"What?"

"You are not a rich man."

"You're a liar. I have eighteen hundred dollars in the Gloucester bank."

"Five thousand, Captain Bannon. I have it."

"Where?"

The spy kept his silence.

Patrick said: "I know where the money is. Skalder told me when I got through hammering him."

"No!"

"It's in your boot, Nazi, and nowhere else."

Patrick laughed at the spy's tell-tale glance. He struck

his revolver against the right boot, where the eyes had briefly rested. "That one!"

The spy shuddered. He cursed the name of Skalder.

Patrick laughed again. "Bannon knows everything! Get that into your thick head. I even know your name and rank. You've no secrets from me."

Margaret's light flashed briefly again. Patrick looked down to the sea. A dark mass was creeping into the channel. Its wake, a curl of phosphorescence, had already washed against Widow's Rock. The moon was far down, but, while he gazed, the wind came up stronger from the northwest and rolled away a barrier of clouds. He stared at the moving thing on the water until he saw the glint of greenish metal under a pouring sea, the same glint that he had seen on the Grand Bank days before.

He knelt and unwound the wires on the spy's wrists. He said to him: "How do I know then that your cutthroat boys aren't coming up the cliff this minute? I don't trust you. I think I'll kill you now. You make me nervous." And, indeed, his own hands trembled more than the spy's.

"The time."

Patrick pulled out his watch and held it close to the lantern. It said one o'clock. "A few minutes past twelve. Why?"

"You are safe. They will not come yet. Take the money and let me go down to the beach."

"I'll think of it. But first you must do something for me."

"Yes." His eyes opened a little and his breath came quicker. Patrick could plainly see that the spy had worked up a measure of hope. "What is it, Captain Bannon?"

"You must not harm the corvette. I like that kid."

"I promise."

"You must explode the mines. I won't touch that detonating rig of yours. It looks phony to me. Move over!"

The spy hitched his body closer to the battery.

Patrick stood up again. "I'll first make sure there's nothing in the channel. The herring-boats are on their way home." He looked down and could see the U-boat. Its tower was high out of the water. A lantern gleamed on its forward deck. Then, on the far edge of the cliff, Margaret's double signal flashed.

"All clear!" said Patrick to the spy. "None of your funny business. Each key contacts a mine. Right?"

"That is right."

"The mines are all in the water?" Again he put the anxious note into his tone. "I don't want to be blowing up boats or my own schooner."

"All in the channel. But I wish to look." He tried to heave himself to his feet.

Patrick tapped him on the skull with his gun. "Make another move like that and I'll split your head open. Come on, now."

The spy's hand rested on the upper key. He looked up at Patrick and brushed his left hand over his eyes. "Channel is clear?"

"Didn't I just say so? Let her go. I'll tell you if it works."

The spy pushed down the key.

Patrick, gazing down, trembled with a deep joy. The explosion took place directly aft of the U-boat. The water sprang up in the form of a gigantic sunflower and stayed poised there momentarily. A shaft of blue flame came slanting out of the center of the spout and then an enormous fountain of spray and flame vaulted upward. The sound of the explosion came in a single loud note like a thunder peal over hills. The U-boat's stern rose out of the sea. Her forward platform went dashing down and then the whole vessel plunged forward in jerky motion. Patrick saw the lantern float an instant, a speck of gold in a black welter.

"Pretty good mine!" he said. "You've deepened the channel a fathom or two, I'll bet. Go ahead now!"

The spy pushed the middle key.

The sub had now rocked forward two or three lengths. It rolled, then pitched. The second mine exploded directly beneath her. The blow tossed her stern clear. The shaft of blue flame cut right through her hull amidship. Patrick saw her break in two. A flame of another color—yellowish black—rolled away from her and covered the breakers.

"Let her go, you!"

The spy jerked the last key.

The last mine exploded with free force. No part of the U-boat had gone that far. Once again the flower-shaped spout, black at its base and foamy at its spreading top, shot skyward. A cone-shaped object roared heavily out of the new welter and burst into flames. The surface of the water grew placid, then began to burn like a meadow in autumn.

Patrick dragged Holger to his feet and slapped him so hard that his head turned seaward. "Good work! I'm giving you a little taste of hell on earth before you go to the real one. Look!" He pointed down to the fiery sea. "How many U-boats were going to meet the *Gaunt Woman*?"

The spy stared. Patrick, looking at him in the light of the moon and lantern, saw the mouth wrenched in agony. "How many? Speak up!"

"Three." The word came listlessly. His arms fell to his side and his fingers scratched at his trousers. His lips lifted from his teeth and he began to curse

in German. He uttered low-voiced, musical words
that seemed like a hymn said by rote.

Patrick took two steps away. "Three, eh? Oh, no!
Two now, you swine, maybe just one. Because my
friends on Quereau Bank took one. And I'm going
to get the last one just as I got that one down there.
By your own hand, you idiot, you did the job. Look
here!" He held up his watch. "Past one o'clock!"

"One o'clock!" The spy swung his body around,
leaned forward on his hobbled feet, and flung his
hands to the sky. His wretched face, drawn white,
seemed like a mask dangled on a cord; for the gloom
hid his body. "Wolfgang!" He screamed the name
out. "I have killed you!"

Patrick lifted his revolver. "Absolutely! And I
hope he was your own lousy brother!" He stepped
back another pace. "I'm going to turn you in now
and let the Navy hang you."

The spy lunged forward, howling his hate. He
swayed, twisted his body to the right, and raised his
hand.

Patrick saw something flash behind the spy's
head; then the upraised hand jerked and the flashing object hurtled through the darkness and struck
Patrick between the eyes with a force that blinded
him. It was a jagged stone, pounds in weight. A knife-
like edge split his forehead. The impact knocked his
head back so hard that he could not keep his bal-

ance. He tottered and began to fall. Blood spurted. He felt its hot stream rush over his closed lids. He fought to keep his boots straddled, but the shock ran back into his brain so swiftly, numbed it so suddenly, that he barely had time to pull his gun close to his chest before he pitched forward and fell upon his face. In the moment of his fall, he forced his eyelids up against the flow of blood. He saw the hated face above him and the hand stretching toward his throat.

Patrick opened his mouth and sucked the air into his lungs. He blew blood and sand off his lips, flung up his right leg, and rolled over on his back. He twisted his head to the left and saw the German come lurching down, saw him trip on his bound feet and struggle forward on his knees for the next attack. He heard a hiss of sharply taken breath and a curse from Holger as he fumbled for the stone.

Free for the second of time that he needed, Patrick rolled over again, then sat up and turned toward the German. The hand rose high again and again the stone flashed against the sky.

Patrick fired. The first shot shattered the face, the second rammed into the spy's skull like a high-swung hammer. Patrick broke the gun open. He thrust his hand into his pocket, and took out two big cartridges. He pushed them into the empty chambers and went sideways into the shelter of the dark.

He lay there, gun in hand, and wiped the blood from his face. Nothing stirred. Hundreds of gulls flew screaming over his head in their flight from a cloud of smoke that floated up from the water. He waited there until the birds had soared off, their white wings gleaming. He listened until he was sure no foreign noise was mingling with the noises of the night and the sea and he rose to his feet and walked to the edge of the cliff. The fire on the sea had gone out.

The torch flashed twice from the place where Margaret watched. Nothing moved on the sea. He ran up the path and entered the woods. There he heard her calling his name. He ran toward her. She grasped his arm and led him inland to the summit that overlooked the harbor. She pointed to the anchorage. The *Daniel* lay there, dark and asleep. The cliffs and the roar of water in the tickle had shut off the sound of the explosions from her. But on the deck of the *Gaunt Woman* he saw men running with lanterns. The skylight above the master's quarters glowed. He saw other men coming and going in the light of the opening doors. He heard the shouts of a gang up forward, where an electric light played on her windlass. They were rigging the capstan, were making ready to weigh anchor.

"The *Gaunt Woman!*" Margaret shouted the words into a gust of rainy wind.

He touched her on the cheek, stepped forward and watched in silence. The bustle below could mean nothing but hurried flight. More lights swung and jumped on her deck and in the rigging. Even at that distance, he thought he could hear a loud, familiar voice shouting orders. Something flashed in the rigging of her foremast. The *Gaunt Woman* was making sail. Her lower topsails dropped down, then the uppers rose.

At this sight, exultation roused his heart. Skalder, warned by his boatmen of *Conrad's* attack on Holger, was now on that deck, making ready for the run to the open sea.

Margaret shook his arm, shook it hard as if she had found him in a dream and his vessel foundering beneath him. "She is escaping!" Again she repeated the vessel's name. "Patrick, the *Gaunt Woman!*"

He replied: "I've just killed him. Holger. I made him kill the U-boat first. You saw it go?"

"The *Gaunt Woman!*" she repeated urgently.

"Escaping?" He laughed and reached out an arm and hugged her. "She's not escaping, Maggie. She's going to her death. And to the death of others. In my own backyard." He took another step nearer the brink. "Let me take a look at her. Ah, there goes a jib. That new suit of hers gives her a shine."

The beam of a large electric torch shot down from a hand working on the jib-boom. The beam slid to and fro, turned backward once, as if the light had picked up a floating object that was suspicious.

Patrick turned to her. "Wait and watch. Have no fear about the *Gaunt Woman*, Maggie darling. Wait!"

She grasped his arm and turned the light onto his forehead. "You're wounded!"

"I'm bleeding a little. It's nothing. Leave it for now, Maggie."

"I'll bandage it—"

"No! I'll have no bandage there. For them to shoot at. Let it go, I say."

"I've the right thing here, Patrick." She unbuttoned her jacket and ripped at the gray shirt beneath.

She bound up his forehead, moistened a handkerchief with her lips and dabbed at his eyes. "You may go now."

He ran back into the path where the dead spy lay, intending to take the body down to the men of Trabo. He bent over as he ran, not daring, even then, to show himself against the sky, now glittering with stars that trailed in cloudless space after the setting moon. The off-shore wind had piped up and had cleared the sky for him, had cleared, too, the open sea where he must now go to amass his final triumph. His exultation grew.

In grim playfulness, he thumped one hand on the

battery as he jumped by it toward the hidden body. He took four long strides over the space of crumbled stone and knelt down. He stared in a quick agony at the empty hiding-place. The spy's body was gone.

"But he was dead!" whispered Patrick.

His astonishment slowed him up. He realized that living men, enemies, must have been there in the few minutes that he had been gone. Both mind and body grew weak. Only his sure instinct, operating without warning or knowledge, jerked him back from that place. He moved only a few inches, six at most, but the hot, red stream of bullets, blasting from the shadows beyond, missed him by that much. He fell over backwards, waited a breath, then rolled onto his side. The air seemed to have been heated by the explosion, hundreds of them, all melding into one uproar. The bullets plowed and spattered among the rocks behind him. Some flew singing into the sky. The gulls vaulted in stricken silence.

Patrick lifted his revolver but waited until the blazing stream from the automatic gun left off, waited until its echoes had waned under the stars. He gave a deep groan of make-believe anguish and he cursed; then he shut his lips.

An exclamation, nothing more than a grunt of triumph, answered him. The head and shoulders of the careless gunner appeared, a vague outline against a pyramid of gray stone. A glint of metal showed in dead center. Patrick fired one shot above that metallic shine. A scream burst out of the shadows. Boots thrashed and stumbled in the drift of pebbles and earth. The German gunner lurched forward and began to fall. Patrick saw his face twist and turn. The body wrestled with itself, tumbled over a boulder and straightened out at Patrick's feet.

Patrick gathered his feet under him for a jump away. At that instant, an arm swung over his right shoulder and jerked his head back. The choking thrust of a hand on his throat stifled his outcry. His eyes bulged. He let his neck yield in order to free his throat of pressure. He won a little leeway, opened his mouth and sank his teeth into the flesh of the hand. But the other hand, a fist, came down on the back of his neck. Straining to get his legs straddled, he swung around and grappled his enemy.

It was Skalder. Patrick glimpsed the red beard, the white teeth gleaming in a grin, and the eyes glaring. Patrick wrenched his gun-hand free, bent backward against the strength of the arms that crushed him, and struck at Skalder's face. The gun barrel bit into the German's forehead. Patrick roared with joy and lifted his gun again. He pulled the trigger, but at that moment he felt himself lifted into the air. The shot went wild, and the revolver fell from his hand.

Skalder, fighting in silence, struck at Patrick's right

arm, then caught the wrist in his enormous fingers
and began to twist. An exquisite pain ran up the
arm, numbing as it went. Patrick, unable to escape
from the arm that lay straining on his back, bent his
hips away and brought up his knee with savage force.
He rammed it into the big belly. Instantly he struck
out with his free fist. He felt the impact of the
knuckles against the bearded jaw. He heard a grunt.
He struck again. This time the head was not there.
The fist flailed him. He jerked back his head in one
last, terrible strain and broke loose.

Skalder was too big to be brought down that way.

Patrick opened his mouth and shouted: "Help!
Captain Skalder—help! The Germans!"

The great bulk advanced in the dark, then paused.
Some sort of foreign curse came from his lips.
Patrick pulled his knife out of his belt and held it
behind him.

"You call Skalder? You young devil, you call me?"
Patrick saw the white cuff fall over Skalder's wrist
when he reached down and took up the revolver.

Patrick groaned. "You! You, Captain?"

"Yes! Yes! What have you to say?" He lifted the
gun. Patrick heard its hammer go back.

"Good God, man! They're after your vessel!"
Patrick took a short step forward. "Don't shoot, Cap-
tain. It's Bannon. They've killed Holger and Conrad.
They just tried to kill me!" He took another step

forward. He could see the revolver plainly now and the bloody, bearded mask of a face behind it. He let his voice break in its last appeal. "I sent for you. I sent the girl for you."

Skalder cursed and said: "You lie, you devil! You will be killed now!"

"Captain Skalder!" Patrick lifted his voice into a scream. "I never told a lie in my life! Never! Don't —for God's sake!—don't shoot. Let me speak!"

At that moment, the dazzling bull's-eye of a torch struck full into the German's staring eyes. Margaret spoke coolly from the darkness. "Why, Captain Skalder! I've been looking—"

Patrick lunged under the beam. He knocked the gun away with his left hand and swept the long knife up in a flashing blow. The blade plunged under Skalder's ribs. He howled and flung up his hands. Patrick jerked the knife back and struck again, this time even harder. The blade drove in up to the hilt and kicked the heart. Skalder toppled.

Margaret held the light on the distorted, dying face. The big teeth tore at the lips and the lips spattered blood and curses. Patrick held the revolver against the forehead.

"Look away, Maggie dear. We've no time and we must be sure."

He fired. The whole great body shook.

She switched off the light and they crouched together in the shelter of the great boulder. They gazed into the wilderness. Only the frightened gulls cried high above them.

He put his arm around her. Her body was trembling. "It's all right, Maggie darling. We're in the clear now." She groped for his hand and held it against her. He whispered again. "You saved the Bannon boy. He had me."

She made no reply. Her face gleamed dead white. He pressed his lips against her cheek. "The Mac-Lean!"

She spoke then. "Now it is over. Yes, now we are safe, Patrick. The corvette can stop the *Gaunt Woman*. Fire her. Attack her. Blow her up!"

"No!"

"Dear God!" She moaned in his embrace. "What now, Patrick? It is over. Over! You yourself said so. The corvette can do the rest. The *Gaunt Woman* will not sail without him." She turned her pale face toward Skalder's huge body, sprawled in the cold starlight. "She can be taken."

He held her by the arm and led her to the path. "That is what I am going to do now, Margaret. Board her! Storm her!"

She ran by his side and pleaded with him. "You must wait for the corvette, Patrick. You haven't the men. Or the guns. You said so yesterday when the corvette was in."

He made no answer. He took her hand and they hurried down the path until they came near Conrad's body.

Patrick said: "I'll take him down now. It's a long way from home he'll be buried."

Halfway to his knees, he whispered: "Watch out now, Maggie darling. Skalder's men will be looking for him now." He stretched out his hands toward the body, then jumped away and dragged her off the path.

"Patrick!"

He put his hand over her mouth and took the revolver out of his pocket and cocked it. He whispered: "I'm a fool to take this path. Wait!"

He began a search of the shadows cast by rock and bush. He swept the wilderness from the left to the right, pausing at every glint, staring long at the changing shadows under the stunted trees. At last, he whispered: "Did you touch him?"

"I? No! I came into the path farther up."

He returned to his silent watching.

She whispered: "Has that body been moved, too? Has it, Patrick?"

"No!"

"What then?"

"Turned over. He's face down now. It was his face
I first saw when I found him. Staring at me."

Her hand came to rest on his arm. "Then Skalder
saw him. He came this way."

"Skalder and his gunner both." He laid his fingers
on her hand and comforted her with a gentle pat.
"Let me think a bit, Maggie. They're so damned
stupid that I can figure them out. Once I set my
mind to it. Wait."

After a time, he said: "They knew somebody
would come for him. Sooner or later. A man's not a
man to them. He's bait."

"A booby trap, Patrick. They put bombs into the
pockets of the dead and dying at Dunkerque."

"And yet, Maggie, there's a chance of something
else here. Conrad himself—God help us! I'm going
to take a look at him. Get back behind the rocks,
Maggie darling."

"No!"

"Do what I say!"

"No! You get back, Patrick." She took his hand
off her arm and crept forward an inch.

He seized her roughly around the waist and
dragged her back. "Will you do what you're told,
Miss? This is my show. Don't you start giving me
orders."

She struck his arm down. "The big show's yours,

Patrick. The *Gaunt Woman.* Live for that. Don't take a chance on a bomb here. It would cost us the ship." She moved forward again. "Shall I go?"

"No! We'll go down and come back at daylight."

"But Conrad—he may be alive, Patrick. You said you barely touched him." She looked at him. "Let me go, Patrick dear. Shall I go now?"

"Yes."

"Then you go back. Back behind the rock. And wait until—" She glided toward the body. Patrick crawled into the shelter of a rock and knelt there, bowed over his useless hands, his useless weapon. He looked up once at the climbing stars and at a red planet low in the West; then turned his eyes to the dark earth and listened to the breakers sluicing up and down under the crannies and caverns of Trabo. The passage of the seconds, doled out in his heart like hours, left him so numbed that he knew nothing of her return until her hand touched his face.

"He's alive!"

The fresh gale of her words blew him back to life.

"Alive! Conrad?"

"Yes! He moved again when I touched him. He's been bleeding and—"

He ran from her and took up the body of his dory-mate. He whispered: "Conrad!" and then said to her: "Will he live, Maggie?"

"I can't tell, Patrick. The knife went deep. But sometimes a deep knife wound doesn't bleed so much. It's his head—they hit him with a gun. Or a club."

Patrick, straining under his burden, went down the path. She went before him, flashing the torch now and then to light his way.

The village lay asleep, undisturbed by the thunderous noises of the explosions as it had been undisturbed through all the centuries by the thunder on its beaches. Patrick halted at the head of the lane, where they could see the harbor. He laid the Dane's body down.

There was little sign of life in the anchorage now, even less than when he had looked down from the heights. The *Daniel Webster* lay in her berth, her riding light dim above. One light burned on the deck of the *Gaunt Woman* and a yellow glow came from the skylight over Skalder's quarters. Yet, even at that distance, she gave out her sinister meaning; for he could see her headsails gleaming and he knew that her dark bulwarks were lined with armed men, waiting for their captain or getting ready to make up a landing party. He thought of his schooner. She lay only a quarter of a mile away from the *Gaunt Woman*. He knew she would be the first victim of an attack if the *Gaunt Woman* had been informed that he had become her open enemy. He hoped that it might not be so. Yet there was no help for it. There was a good chance that, hastening in fear toward the open sea, the Germans might ignore her. He had to take that chance. And he had to get his men ashore.

He turned to Margaret and said: "I'll put Conrad in his room. Go to old Ben. Tell him that there is trouble and that I want all the men to come to the tavern. Tell him to keep their families quiet and their houses dark. And that they should bring every gun in the village. Guns and knives. And clubs."

She ran down the path to old MacDonald's house. Patrick went into the tavern and stretched Conrad out on his bed. He then hastened to Margaret's house and awakened her father, who was lying fully dressed on his bed. The captain listened without a word. When Patrick had done, he asked the same question that his daughter had asked: "You've done well, Patrick. And what now?"

Patrick replied: "The *Gaunt Woman* must be stormed now. I'm sailing her out to the Grand Bank tonight. And you're coming with me."

"You're damned right I am." He took his pistol out of a drawer and followed Patrick down the stairs.

A man came toward them in the darkness. Patrick called out: "Is that you, Ben MacDonald?"

The old man, wrapped in a long coat, came forward. "Here I be, b'y. Yes, Skipper Patrick." He held an old Colt pistol in his right hand and in his left a club of thornwood. "The others are not far behind me. Jonathan is bringing the *Daniel's* people ashore. Not one to stay aboard her, Skipper Patrick. That is what the bold girl says to me."

"That's right, Skipper Ben. We'll wait for them before I tell you what's to be done."

Three younger men came through the garden. Two carried rifles and the third came empty-handed.

"I'll take these men," said Patrick. "Hold the others until I came down, Captain. Set a watch over the *Gaunt Woman*."

He led the three men back up the cliff and came down again with the bodies of the three Germans. All the men of Trabo were lined up. Some held un-lighted lanterns, others gun and clubs. His dorymen, having come last of all, stood in a little rank by themselves. They kept a perfect silence. Patrick said no word for a time; then he switched on his torch and let its light play on the dead face of Holger.

A sigh ran among his dorymen.

"Conrad's up there. At death's door!" Patrick pointed to the lighted chamber, where Margaret had gone to dress the Dane's wounds. "Knifed by this one!" He shifted the light to the face of the spy. "Stabbed in the back and clubbed by Holger!"

The Newfoundlanders groaned.

Patrick said: "Why? Because Conrad is a true

Dane and a true man, who risked his life for his country. And for yours and for mine." He paused until they became quiet. "Holger! A hand on my vessel. Said he was a Dane and so accepted until Conrad and I found him to be a German spy. A foul spy! Working with the U-boats and with the *Gaunt Woman*—a German vessel!"

The dorymen growled and edged forward. The starlight glittered on the blades of long curved knives. Their stern and gloomy faces became clearly visible.

Patrick spoke again. "Who killed Holger? I did. He was laying a mine-trap for the corvette, but I tricked him into blowing up the U-boat that Maggie MacLean saw today." Patrick took a step sideways and let the light fall on the face of the second man, the gunner. "From the *Gaunt Woman*. He let drive at me with that there." He pointed to the stubby automatic rifle. "I had to shoot him through the heart."

"Merciful God, lad!" cried a Newfoundlander.

Patrick swung toward him. "There's hotter work than that waiting for those of you who'd like a taste of it." He then took another step to the right and pointed his torch straight down into the face of dead Skalder. "Skalder! Take a look at him! The skipper of the *Gaunt Woman*. That great and charming man. I killed him, too. He jumped me the moment I shot the gunner. He had me. Had my own gun on me.

But for that girl—I'd be lying there. Not Skalder. She flashed this light into his face and I ran this"—he held up his bloody knife—"into his ribs. Then I shot him."

He shut off his light and stood in the starlight facing them. "The *Gaunt Woman* is a German vessel. Conrad and I boarded her and found that to be so. She's loaded with torpedoes and mines and depth charges. She has a secret radio shack in her. She has been the tender of the U-boat pack. She is the murderer of women and children and men and ships.

"We've got to take her now. Capture her and sail her out to the Grand Bank tonight. And tomorrow we'll blow her up. Her and the last of her foul companions." He walked toward old Ben and the Newfoundlanders. "Any man who will strike a blow for King and Country—let him step forward!" His voice rose: "There's great danger of death, but honor and glory for them that come along. And revenge! Revenge for babies killed in their sleep. For a hundred ships!"

Captain MacLean stepped forward. Solemn, speechless faces turned to the one-armed veteran, pistol in hand. The rank moved up. Old Ben hobbled forward. He rapped the earth with his stick. "Jonathan! Bob! Luke! James! Take another step, lads," He spoke to Patrick: "Square-rigger men. All of them. I taught them, Skipper Patrick, and they be the best on the Straight Shore. They'll be crew for the *Woman*!"

The Gloucestermen waited, staring at the young captain.

He threw his words at them. "A game against us all! Against all free men and free livelihood! This is the freemen's war. Against slaves. They are murderers! She—the *Gaunt Woman*—is the bitch at whose dugs they must feed or starve. They will come to her. Without her, the pack is lost. Weaponless and lost! One I've taken already. Our men on Quereau Bank have taken another. There's a third to be killed—if not more—and we must do it. I know where she's going. Where and when they must meet."

He flung his hand up. "I can order no man to join this boarding party. Those who must stay—let them stay! Those who can stand by ship and country—let them raise their right hands!"

Not a hand went up. Their gazes never shifted from his shining eyes.

Patrick's hand dropped slowly. A sigh shot from his lips.

At this sigh, their voices burst out in one terrible cry. It was an oath. Oath of an old Yankee feud.

Patrick flung back his head and laughed.

Captain MacLean asked: "Patrick, there are how many left on the *Woman*?"

"Twenty, I reckon."

After a pause, the captain said: "There are thirty men here."

One of the Gloucestermen snorted. "Twenty Heinies? To hell with them!"

"What's the matter with you, Joe?" asked Patrick. "Keep your shirt on, will you?"

The Gloucesterman grumbled and spat. "You ain't sending thirty white men to take care of them yellow-bellies, Cap'n?"

"Why not?" cried Patrick, stepping forward. "Look here, Joe—"

"Ten's enough, Cap'n. That's why not!"

Patrick waited until they were silent and then he said: "There'll not be twenty on the *Gaunt Woman* when we storm her. The first fight will be right here. Now then"—he paused again and swiftly turned his head toward the sea—"here it is!"

A boy came running toward them. "They be coming ashore! Two boats."

Patrick said: "It will be the mate and eight or nine men. They are looking for Skalder. They will come here first." He called to the Trabo men: "Break out some ropes. Net twine. Wires. Anything! Lively now. We've got twenty minutes to work in."

He then spoke to Captain MacLean. "Put men with rifles there"—he pointed to the garden wall —"and there under the window of the tavern. I'll go up to Skalder's room and light the lamp. When they come, I'll stick my head out and tell them the captain wants to see them, that there's trouble on the cliff. Then I'll come down and face the mate. The moment I speak your name—flash the light on. If the mate as much as bats an eye, Captain—you'll know what to do." He walked across the little green into the shadow of the taller trees. "Men without rifles will lie here. At the sound of a shot—jump them! They are to be taken alive if possible. I'll tell you why. There's a rebel amongst them. Of that I'm sure. And if he's in this party, he'll be a help to us."

The Trabo men came running back with coils of rope and balls of net twine. One carried a net over his shoulder. Patrick flashed his light at the great tree that stood a little removed from the village green. He said: "Put those bodies there. Side by side at the foot of the tree. We'll give those babies a jolt that will stop them in their tracks."

CHAPTER XII

PATRICK WENT UP to Skalder's room, lighted the lamp and sat at the window, staring down at the ambush. The men had hidden themselves; the bodies were only shadows under the waving boughs. The light of the oil lamp fell upon the earth below in a square. In a little while, he heard the crunch of boots and voices; then a pause came in the marching step, a single word was uttered, and the silence returned. Patrick turned his back to the window and began talking. He laughed at the end of a sentence, twisted around in the chair and thrust his head out of the window. "Here they are!" he said loudly.

A man was standing in the dim fall of lamplight. Patrick cried out: "Is that you, Mister Mate?"

"Yes."

"Captain Skalder was about to send for you. He wants you to come up. There's trouble on the cliff. A man has been killed." He turned his head back into the room and then spoke to the mate once more. "Wait there. We'll come down. Bring your men around."

Patrick walked down the stairs and pushed open the door. The mate stood there, staring at him. His men stood behind him. The man Patrick wanted stood directly behind the mate.

"It's about time you showed up," said Patrick. "The Germans have sent a landing-party ashore and they have killed my man Conrad."

The mate spoke. "Where is Captain Skalder? Why doesn't he come down? Stand aside!"

"I'll tell you what you do, Mister Mate," said Patrick. "You keep a civil tongue in your head. And I'll tell you and your men something more. You're armed. You have automatic rifles under your jackets. I advise you to take it easy. There's plenty of queer business going on here tonight. I don't understand it and I don't like it."

"Why will Captain Skalder not come down? Stand aside, Captain Bannon!"

"Captain Skalder can't come down. However, Captain MacLean—"

The electric torch flashed and filled the air with a dazzling light.

Patrick lifted his hand. "There's your Captain Skalder! Look!"

Mate and men turned their blinking eyes to the foot of the great tree. Skalder's horrible mask glared up at them. Patrick said: "Take it easy now! Don't move! The man that moves will die in his tracks!"

The mate yelled an order and pulled back his jacket. A brace of bullets caught him in the belly before he could touch his fingers to the metal. While his hands were still clutching at the bright air, his rank of men went down under the roaring attack of the Gloucestermen. Hard fists cracked against their jaws; long knives glittered before their eyes. Two or three of them began to shriek for mercy. One, who had a little slang, kept shouting: "Lay off now! Lay off now!"

Patrick bent over the dying mate. His fingers were closed on the stock of an automatic gun in a holster under his jacket. Patrick struck the fingers away and unbuckled the belt. The dying man was trying to say something. Patrick knelt and listened. The whisper ceased.

He buckled the gun around his waist and then began disarming the others. As he removed each gun, he pulled the prisoners to their feet, looked into their faces, and passed on. When he came to the man he had picked out as a rebel against Skalder, he said: "They knifed your friend Conrad."

The man's dark eyes stared in fear. He was trembling. He ran his tongue over his bruised lips and, at last, whispered: "I know. Yes, Captain."

Patrick smiled. "You have nothing to be afraid of. Your name is Drasch—Heinrich Drasch, isn't it? Conrad told me."

"Yes, Captain."

"Have no fear, Heinrich. Take it easy."

Patrick spoke to a Trabo man. "Go up and get some rum out of Skalder's room. Give this man a mug of it." He told the others to light their lanterns. He then handed out the German guns to the unarmed men. He said to Captain MacLean: "We'll put these men into the tavern cellar. All except that one there. I'm going to work on him. Then the ship is next. It's going to be tougher than this, unless—"

"Storm the bitch. Up over her chains on all sides at once."

"She's lying deep enough for that. But this man may do us some good. He's the radio man. Or one of them. Leave the lights on. I'm going to give him a chance to speak his piece. Unless I miss my guess, he hated Skalder worse than I did. And he's yellow to boot."

Captain MacLean led the prisoners away.

Patrick signed to his men to stand back. He said to Heinrich: "You've an electric torch hanging at your belt. You're a signalman?"

"Yes, Captain."

"Conrad said you were the radio operator."

"Yes, Captain."

"Step this way." Patrick led him nearer to the tree."

"That's Holger who knifed Conrad. That's a gunner who tried to kill me. According to the military law, they were spies and should be hanged." He waited a little. "The others will hang in the morning. Maybe not you."

The German seemed not to be listening. His eyes were fixed on Skalder's face. The Trabo man came forward and gave a mug of rum to Patrick. Patrick handed ito the German, who drank it in one gulp. Yet, as he drank, he never removed his eyes from the face of his dead commander. He let the mug fall to the ground. "Who killed him?"

"I did."

Patrick watched the lips frame a curse.

"Why do you hate him so, Heinrich? He is dead."

The toneless reply was even more than Patrick had hoped for.

"He killed my brother. Shot him down on deck. No trial. No mercy. My brother was sick. Sick and crazy."

"I saw him, Heinrich."

"Yes, Captain."

"I found him dead on the deck of your ship when I first boarded it. Shot between the eyes."

The German groaned.

Patrick laid a hand on his shoulder. "That one there—he told me the dead man was his own son. Killed by the Germans when the U-boat stopped the ship. I, at least, gave your brother a Christian burial.

I gave him an honest prayer when we slid him over."

The flat voice began again. "We have not been home in a year. First a long cruise on the U-boat, then a rest on his vessel. Rest! There was no rest. Who could say when it would blow up? Then back to a U-boat. I said to them when your schooner came: 'No! Let us kill this Skalder and give up the ship. Let us be men. Let us sleep again.' But they were afraid of him. But I would kill him. I would kill him this very night when he came aboard. Now he is dead. And all must hang!"

Patrick lifted up the torch that hung at the German's belt. "There's no escape for any man aboard the *Gaunt Woman*. We're going to storm her now. But there is an escape for you. You will be a prisoner of war. On one condition. There is something for you to do. Go in there and think it over." He called a Trabo man and ordered him to take the German up to Skalder's room and stay there with him.

Partick followed up the stairs. He hurried down the hallway to Conrad's room and tapped on the door. Captain MacLean opened it and whispered: "Come in, lad."

The Dane lay naked on the bed, his throat and head already bandaged. His eyes, darkened by pain and grief, stared upward. Margaret's aunt stood at the bedside, holding a basin of bloody water. Margaret herself, without looking up, skilfully passed the bandage round and round Conrad's back.

Patrick looked at the captain. To his unspoken question, the captain shook his head sadly.

"Has he spoken, Captain?"

Margaret answered. "He whispered your name, Patrick. He's lost much blood. I'd give him some of yours if I could. But he must do without it. His heart is not—it troubles me."

She turned from the bed and washed her hands. She laid her fingers on Conrad's wrist and held up her watch. In silence, they gazed at her calm face while she counted his pulse; and they sighed together when her look of grave concern grew deeper.

Patrick said: "I was afraid I'd killed him by letting him lie up there, Maggie."

She shook her head. "It's not the knife wound so much. His skull—they battered it with stones when he fell." She bent over Conrad again and, after a little while of watching, she calmly said: "Aunt Julia, I shan't need you any longer tonight. I'll come downstairs soon."

When the old lady went out, Margaret turned to Patrick and said: "She liked him so much. I'll tell her in the morning."

Patrick took a step nearer to the bed and looked

down into the eyes of his dead dorymate. Even the darkness had gone from them. They were empty.

Captain MacLean said: "God rest Conrad's soul!"

Patrick took up his cap. "I'll be on my way, Maggie."

She stood between him and the Dane's body. "You're going to take the *Gaunt Woman* now?"

He nodded.

"And my father?"

"He's to stay ashore until it's done."

She laid her hand over her trembling mouth; then let it fall against his arm. "I may not see you again, Patrick. Do as well as you can for yourself."

"I will, Maggie."

She pressed her lips against his cheek and turned back to the dead man.

The two captains went out of the tavern. Presently the attack on the *Gaunt Woman* got under way. The night was dark. The easterly wind was rising. It blew black clouds before it and these shut off the faint starlight. Patrick made a display of lanterns on the wharf. Now and then he hailed the *Gaunt Woman*. No answer came. All her lights were out. He sent three dories, full of armed men, along the upper shore with orders to row into the river current, then pass beyond and come down on her port side. Each boat was to put its men into the chains and wait until the shooting began.

As soon as the dories had vanished, he took a lantern and stepped into another dory. Two Gloucestermen, armed with the German guns, lay in the bow. Two Trabo men sat at the oars. Patrick stood in the stern-sheets. He unlimbered his gun and laid it at his feet. He turned to Captain MacLean and said: "When I signal, come aboard. Bring that German with you and be ready to sail. When you go to get him—tell Margaret to go aboard the *Daniel*. I have agreed to that."

Patrick waited a few more minutes and then set out toward the *Gaunt Woman*. He talked loudly to his men. And they, obeying his orders, laughed and answered him as loudly. He made a trumpet of his hands and cried: "Ahoy, *Gaunt Woman*! Show a light there!"

The dark ship made no answer.

The men rested on their oars, then pushed forward a few strokes. He hailed her again and added to it a jovial curse on all Danish blockheads. He could now make her out dimly. Her decks were hidden in darkness.

Once more he shouted: "Ahoy, the *Gaunt Woman*! Is Captain Skalder aboard! This is Captain Bannon. Show a light there, you squarehead lubbers!" He flashed his own torch directly at her quarterdeck.

A man aboard her sang out: "Keep that boat off!"

Patrick swore loudly. "What's the matter with you people? Where's your captain?"

"Keep that boat off!"

"Keep off be damned!" Patrick shouted. "Show a light there, you fathead! Let me speak to your captain. It's Bannon, I tell you." He bent his head and whispered: "Give her a couple of short ones, boys." To the men forward, he said: "Jim, if they turn a light on us—fire at the light. You, Darby, sweep her rail fore and aft—then into her waist." He picked up his own gun.

The first Trabo man whispered: "Ask him be we going to get our wages, Skipper Patrick."

Patrick trumpeted with his hands again. "Hey, you! You've been making sail. You going to skip off without paying these men their wages? Tell that captain of yours to speak to me or I'll come aboard and arrest him! Where is he?"

"Keep that boat off," said another voice. "Captain is ashore."

The dory moved a little nearer. It seemed to Patrick that he could hear the talk of disputing men. Yet he could see nothing. He shouted again: "Captain Skadler's not in his room. You say he's ashore. Where is he then? What sort of funny business is this? Show a light, you blockhead!" He bent down to the oarsmen and whispered: "Let drive when he speaks again."

An electric torch splashed a whirling ray of light upward and then began to search for the dory. Both guns forward opened up. Patrick yelled to the oarsmen. The dory jumped. He held his own gun ready. A man on the poop-deck opened fire. Patrick saw the stream of bullets kick up under the oars. He pressed the trigger and held his fire on the flaming gun above. The oarsman nearest to him yelled in agony and let fall his oars. The dory was alongside by that time. He heard a howl of men on the *Gaunt Woman's* port side. He dropped his gun into the dory and leaped for the chains. He laid hold of the royal back-stay, pulled himself over the bulwarks and jumped down on the deck.

The two gunners from his dory came roaring after him. The big torch rolled on the deck. Its beam showed him his Gloucestermen locked in hand-to-hand struggles. A gun spattered from the cross-trees. He struck one of his gunners on the arm and yelled: "Give him a burst! On the trees!"

Both of his men opened fire on the man aloft. One gun stopped and the Gloucesterman who held it gave a cry of "Hey!" and toppled over. The second gun turned the trick. Something clattered at Patrick's feet and then a screaming man came hurtling down. Patrick heard a loud cracking sound. The German rolled against his boots. He kicked at the body and swiftly jumped aside.

The firing ceased; then a silence came, perfect except for the muttered curses in German of men being strangled where they lay. Patrick picked up the light and passed it over the deck. "Bring them here, men! Count heads! Lively now! Or they'll blow her up under us."

The dorymen dragged the living and the dead forward. One of the Germans was missing, but they soon found him on the poop-deck, where the opening bursts had caught him. Three others were dead. There were six prisoners. The dorymen bound them tight and stretched them out alongside the dead. They lined up then to count their own wounds. Darby, the Gloucesterman who had come with Patrick, lay dead against the bulwarks. One bullet from the gun aloft had killed him. The oarsman in Patrick's dory had an arm broken. Others were wounded and they bled, but they were able and willing to stand up.

"All hands!" Patrick flashed the light up and down the ranks. "Here's Darby dead, boys, and we may thank God that it was a lone man they killed and not one of you with a brood. I've lost the best mastheadman that ever rode a stay. But he died happy, I'll swear to that."

He stepped away from Darby's body. "And now we're taking this vessel to the Grand Bank for her last job of work. A job that's for us and not against us. Let the square-rigger men step forward!" The

Newfoundlanders and three of the Gloucestermen came out of the ranks. "The headsails are on her. They'll swing her around and take her out of here. Once outside, we'll crowd it on her."

CHAPTER XIII

PATRICK SENT his wounded men back to the schooner with the first gang of the *Daniel*. He gave them orders to make sail and clear out of the harbor. He said to Caleb: "You keep the vessel, Caleb, and don't let my topsails out of your sight. Tomorrow night—come alongside at my signal. Send Captain MacLean and that German aboard us here." He stepped closer to Caleb and said in a low tone: "If Maggie MacLean is there—take her along. There's plenty for her to do. And there may be more hurt before the night's out."

Patrick said nothing to the prisoner when he came aboard of what had happened on the *Gaunt Woman*, knowing that Heinrich could tell easily enough what had been the fate of those Germans who resisted the Gloucestermen. He gave him the freedom of the ship; then took him along while the crew brought the anchor to the cathead and lashed it there.

The easterly wind was blowing even stronger now and the first crack of dawn was showing beyond the hills of Trabo. They kept the headsails sheeted back and the ship swung heavily around until the main staysail and spanker put her under way sluggishly.

The *Daniel* glided by and sailed down the tickle. The Trabo men, on their own hook, hoisted the upper topsails. At this, she picked up and ran easily before the wind, went faster when the lower topsails came down. Once clear of the tickle, Patrick brought her around on the port tack and began to crowd it on her. She went contrary for a few miles, but she soon settled down and sailed for the open sea at about ten knots.

There was a good supper of roast mutton ready in the galley and all hands took their turn. Patrick broke out a few bottles of rum from Skalder's locker and made toddy. He took a jug of it into Skalder's quarters and sent for the German prisoner. Captain MacLean, who had made a close search of the vessel, joined them there.

Patrick said: "The helmsman has a course for the peak of the Grand Bank. There's shoal water there—thirty fathoms and less—and I intend to heave to or anchor in it at midnight tomorrow. This vessel will be blown up at that hour." He turned to the German and asked: "Is that perfectly clear to you?"

"I hate this ship!"

"So do I. Your brother died on her. Right out there. And she has killed hundreds of other men. Well, she'll kill no more. But it makes no difference to us whether you hate this vessel or not. You know that Americans are brutes, don't you?"

"You are a red devil of a man. So Conrad said. Now I know."

"Yes. We would rather fight than talk. As for me, I prefer to kill people who stand in my way. I told you tonight that you were to have no fear. Isn't that so?"

"Yes."

"You understand that you have to do something in return for your life?"

"What is it? Tell me."

"If you don't do this," said Patrick evenly, "I will cut your throat."

The German's hands, laid out before him on the table, shook.

"What is it, Captain? Tell me."

"Are you a man of honor, Heinrich?"

"No! I have lost my honor long ago. By what I did for that monster."

"Then we'll forget that. You will, at least, make a promise and keep it? If you do, I promise you that you'll be taken to the United States and kept there as a prisoner of war."

"What is it?"

Patrick took some sheets of paper out of his pocket. He said: "Captain MacLean here is invalided home from his command. He can handle explosives and he knows radio. He's been using codes on warships and he can't be fooled. If you try any funny business, he will find it out. I will then cut your throat. As I said before."

"What is that paper?" asked the German.

"It has a message on it. A message in Skalder's handwriting to you. To be sent over the radio."

The German glanced at it. "I never sent it."

"No. Because I killed the swine before he could get it aboard." Patrick opened a drawer in the table and took out a thin notebook, bound in blue leather. "You know what this is, Heinrich?"

"His code-book."

Patrick pushed the sheet of paper toward him. On it was written a long, chatty sentence about the price of herring and the whereabouts of certain boats. "Tell me what it means, Heinrich."

The German glanced at it again. "I have sent this many times. It tells the U-boats we will be at position R-184 at twelve o'clock tomorrow night. That is Saturday."

"Position R-184. I find that on the chart below. It's the shoal water of the Grand Bank peak."

"Where we abandoned ship. Yes."

"You say all U-boats. How many are there?"

"Five to begin, Captain. One was sunk by a destroyer. By gunfire. One submerged off Cape Race under attack and could not blow her tanks. She is dead. Three left."

"Have you heard from them lately?"

"Signals from three. They ask where is *Gaunt Woman.*"

"I'm going to tell you something that you don't know. The Navy caught up with one of them. She had no torpedoes. No shells for her guns. She was taken into Halifax."

"Who was she?"

"I don't know yet. One more thing—you picked up signals from a boat a few hours ago?"

"Yes. Asking us to come out."

"She came in."

"Yes, Captain. To take a man on—the dead one. Holger."

Patrick grinned and tapped the German's knuckles with a pencil tip. "She was blown up tonight."

The German shuddered again. Captain MacLean pushed a full mug toward him. He drank greedily. He looked from one to the other in terror. "Who did that?"

"Holger did. I made him blow her up with the mines your people laid to destroy the little corvette. It was a pleasure to do it."

"What is there for me to do, Captain?"

"Listen! Captain MacLean can send this message, but the U-boat men know you. You talk with them when you send a message, don't you?"

"I send a few words—yes. For my friends."

Patrick rose. "We'll go below. And you will send this message." He picked up the code-book. "You will send this and one phrase from the book. Is it agreed?"

"I agree, Captain."

"The words to be added are 'herring boats still out.' Which means, as you know, 'acknowledge at once.' That's right, isn't it?"

"Yes."

They went down the main hatchway and through the secret door. No great change had taken place below. The vast hold was still as well supplied as on that first night in Trabo. The torpedoes had not been disturbed, but there was a gap in the first rack of mines. It was from there they had taken three mines out to destroy the corvette.

Captain MacLean led the way to the sliding door in the after part of the steel cage. He pushed the door to the left and it slid smoothly into the bulkhead. He sat down at the operator's table and put on the head-phones. He searched the air a while, then shook his head and made way for the German, who took one look at Patrick's face and began sending out a call signal. He followed it with the message. Captain MacLean, listening to the key, wrote down the words as they went over.

At the end, he nodded to Patrick, who handed him

the code-book and said: "Stay here with him. Have him send again in half an hour. Unless the sub acknowledges it. I'm going to turn in."

He paused and looked at the prisoner, who was scowling at a glassed-in list of stations above his board. "Let him sleep in that bunk." He pointed to one in the far corner of the room.

He climbed the ladder. The daybreak came, half green, half gold, while he stood on the quarterdeck under the towering pile of the *Gaunt Woman's* new sails. He remembered then, while he listened to the anxious calls of the sailors aloft, how he had told Skalder of his desire to make a long voyage on such a vessel, to see her in full dress on southern seas. A feeling of sadness came over him that it could never be, that it would not be long before he would blast her into a cinder, turn all her stout, rolling beauty into a cloud of gas, a rivulet of molten iron to lie forever on the Grand Bank shoal. He drove these thoughts away by a memory of the dream he had dreamed of her; then her decks had been bloody under a bloody flag. But it had turned out otherwise. The blood had been German blood, not the blood of freemen; and her flag of evil would never again be hoisted to a German wind.

He climbed to the poop-deck and exchanged a few words with the helmsman, who was finding the ves-

sel hard to steer and thought it would be even harder
if she had to go onto the starboard tack. Patrick told
him that there was no hurry and that he was free to
take off some sail, if that would help her.

The helmsman lifted his left arm. The sunlight
speeding on the far horizon to the south-east had
briefly washed against a thing so white that a glint
came sharply away, like a signal off a glass.

Patrick peered at the flash. It came again and
again. He waited until he had finished his slow study
and then said: "Ice. And a big one, too, by the looks
of her." A little later, the great berg began to lift her
columns and gleaming towers against the blue. Farther to the southeast, other islands and headlands of
ice began to shoot their signals across the Grand
Bank.

Leaving word that he should be called if the wind
changed, or the vessel was challenged, he went down
into the mate's quarters and threw off his jacket. He
began to ransack the mate's locker, thinking there
might be papers of some value to the Navy there. He
came upon a log-book, marked with symbols like
those he had seen on the charts below. He was trying
to make some sense of the words when Captain Mac-
Lean came in, his face happy with relief and confi-
dence.

He said: "It's all right, Patrick. The U-boat came

in and took the message. Went off for a minute and then acknowledged it. She'll be there for the party." He laughed and rubbed his hand grimly against his empty sleeve. "That Hun's frightened to death. He kept begging me to tell him what you were going to do with him. I said I didn't know what would happen to him if things went wrong."

Patrick replied: "He'll behave. We can bank on that yellow streak of his. Just the same, you'd better post a man in the cage."

"I've done it, Patrick. He's to be killed if he starts sending without asking me."

"Right." Captain MacLean went out and Patrick fell asleep. He remained there undisturbed while the *Gaunt Woman* sailed down the bleak shore of the peninsula, past the headlands and the forests that bordered the sea. The easterly wind blew steadily. The sunrise came in full. A cloud of gulls flew silently along her steady wake. Now and then a man sang out and pointed to the East and to the South, where sails gleamed in the fresh light. The Gloucestermen stared at the distant hulls. Time after time, they shook their heads; then, at last, the welcome cry came down from aloft. Far to the West, her topsails sparkling, the *Daniel* sailed on the same course.

Toward noon, when Patrick came on deck again, the sky had become overcast. Snow began to fall. At first, the flakes came in a light whirl out of the East.

The wind hauled a little into the North and the flakes began to pour straight down. The snowfall quickly shut out the immense bergs that lay in the East and South. Patrick steered for them just the same, because he calculated that the ice was moving into the very waters where he must take the *Gaunt Woman*.

The change in wind and course left the vessel running before the wind and she began to behave badly. The helmsman couldn't keep her on the course, but he soon found out that, left alone, she would get back on it by herself. When the first gang went to dinner—this time on roast suckling pig—Patrick took the wheel. He soon noticed a subtle change in the snowfall. The flakes began to harden and now and then a squall came tearing from the northeast. The sea then became calmer and he judged that the vessel had settled into a lane between the two icebergs that formed the vanguard of that stately procession.

An hour later, when he and Captain MacLean came from the galley, a freakish blow lifted up the snow on the weather hand and he saw that his judgment had been right. The sea set up a louder roaring where it crashed on the reefs and ledges that extended from the bergs. He had time only for one sweep of the western berg's mountainous pinnacles and cliffs; then the snow once more poured down and hid that gray continent of ice.

The *Gaunt Woman* steered slowly onward. She

drew near the berg on her lee side, a vague, phantom shape against the sky, even more majestic in size and shape than the other. It was like a piece cut off the Straight Shore of Avalon itself. It was a wall that rose two hundred fathoms out of the breakers, a wall so even and white that it caught all the meagre light from the snowy sun and, from time to time, sent it flashing in a stream upward. The sea, at this point, lay calm as a pond. Its color changed from brightness to a leaden hue.

The vessel was leaving the lee berg behind when an even stronger flare shot outward from the vast porcelain wall and struck against the water. In that instant, a vessel appeared between the *Gaunt Woman* and the gleaming battlements.

Patrick barely had time to touch Captain Mac-Lean's arm before three or four quick voices sang out: "A sail! A sail!"

"Against the ice," said Patrick. "The *Daniel*."

"Jib and foresail," said Captain MacLean. "Same course as ours."

Patrick watched his big schooner for a while. "It's all right. She sees us. There's no need of a signal yet."

Patrick looked again over the loud waters where the *Daniel* had briefly shown herself, then he said: "I'm sorry now I didn't send the wounded ashore and leave Maggie with them."

"She'll be in no danger, Patrick. Take your mind off her, lad."

"But I don't like the character of this wind, Captain. It's jumping around too much. If it holds for the *Daniel* to get away—all will be well." He took a long look aloft and said: "The danger is here. Below."

"Yes," replied Captain MacLean. "I'm going down now. I'll need a little time to work in. It won't be hard, Patrick. But with this"—he glanced wryly down at his empty sleeve—"I'll be wanting your help for a little while."

"Go down first and send the prisoner to me. I don't want him to figure out what we're going to do. Not exactly."

"He thinks he knows. He thinks we're going to storm the U-boat. If she ties up to us."

"Let him think so. But I've had enough of storming. I'll lose no more men in this affair, if I can help it. Still, I'll not have him see us at work on the mines. He's got a big hatred in him. And something worse— cowardice. Like the rest of them when the knife is at their own throats. If he even knew what was piling up below decks—he'd go out of his head. Send him up and I'll stow him away with the men off watch."

Presently the German came along the deck, his eyes bright with his surmising and his tongue ready to clack. Patrick shut him off rudely and led him into the forecastle, where three of the dorymen lay dozing. "There's nothing more for you to do just now, Hein-rich," he said. "Stay here until I come for you. And keep your mouth shut."

Patrick went below and joined Captain MacLean in the *Gaunt Woman's* arsenal. They swiftly set about the business of turning the vessel into a gigantic time-bomb.

"This is our baby, Patrick." Captain MacLean put his hand on the largest of all the mines. There were six of that size, each resting on a steel cradle and made more secure by steel standards clamped to the cradles and then screwed to the timbers.

"The best thing to do," said Patrick, "is to make sure that this one will go. Then do the same with the smaller mines. And with the depth charges. That will give us three set-ups. To hell with the torpedoes. They'll go all right."

"I was thinking of that," replied the captain. "We'll take off this one's horns—two horns—just as we did before. Then we'll take some of the stuff out of a depth charge and stuff it into a piece of pipe. I've found some lead pipe in that cage that'll serve. Then I can lead the pipe back into the depth charge and put one of these horn-tips on it. We'll rig up a time-bomb so that it lies near the tip. Then she'll go all right. This one alone will split the shoal."

"Go ahead," said Patrick. "We'll set the bombs

for midnight sharp. If the U-boat doesn't show up, we can turn them ahead. Or turn them off. Or just let them go. Whatever we choose."

"That's the story. Then we rig up another on that big baby and we're all set. They'll both blow at the same time."

"That's two. One more in the small mines and we can't miss."

"Can't miss anyway," replied Captain MacLean. "Here goes!"

He went to work on the depth charges and casually banged away with hammer and chisel as if he were knocking in a barrel-head. When he had breached the can, he put a bucket under it and then bade Patrick turn it in the cradle. The explosive poured out in a smooth stream of dun-colored grains. When the bucket was full, Patrick let the charge roll back into its place. In half an hour, the pipes were stuffed and capped with the lead tips from the horns. Captain MacLean breached another charge and then led the pipes into the openings. Patrick built supports for the pipes out of the scaffolding that ran between the rows of mines. They then went to the work-bench and knocked together three wooden boxes. They lashed one of these into place near the stuffed pipes. They bolted the second against the big mine and laid the third in a space between the rows of smaller mines.

Patrick broke out the time-bombs. Each cylinder

had a small clock sunk into its top. Captain Mac-
Lean, who knew these devices all too well, could
hardly help giving them a glare and a curse for his
gone arm. He showed Patrick the winding keys and
the setting levers. Patrick wound up each clock and
listened to the clicking that began. He pulled the setting levers around to the hour of midnight and then
placed the bombs in the places made ready for them.

He stepped back and gazed with satisfaction at the
engine they had made.

Captain MacLean said: "It's done now, lad, and
you may stop sweating over it. I've only one thing to
say over: the *Daniel* must be handy. She must pick
us up on the fly. At twenty minutes before midnight.
Because this stuff will make a hole in the sea big
enough to pull us down."

"I have that much in mind, Captain. Now I want
to talk with her."

They went back on deck. Darkness was closing in
on the vessel rapidly. Patrick had some hours of sailing before he could profitably sound for the shoal
bottom, but he had no wish to have the *Daniel* be
close to him at all until the moment came to abandon
the *Gaunt Woman* and escape destruction. He waited
until the snow grew thin and the darkness increased;
then he took the big torch to the poop-deck and sent
a signal to leeward, where the *Daniel* had been sailing. It was ten minutes before he caught her answer-

ing blink. He sent his message, telling her to proceed
to the peak of the Grand Bank and there sound for
the shoal. He told her to keep her lights out and not
to approach until she saw the light sending the last
signal from the fleeing dories. The *Daniel* acknowledged and sent "good luck."

CHAPTER XIV

AFTER SUPPER, he called all hands, armed them with the German guns, and sent look-outs aloft and out onto her sprit. He took the wheel with Captain MacLean and another man standing by. They settled down for the last leg of the run to the rendezvous. Twice he sent the captain to the radio shack with the German and they listened for a signal. None came. Those were cautious, anxious men on the boat now coming, above water or below, to the meeting place, and they would not be sending a signal that was not absolutely required. She kept her silence beyond the night-covered sea, yet Patrick had no fear that she would escape. He knew her frantic needs, knew that she cruised weaponless and alone, her crew harassed by the lack of signals from the U-boats that had been destroyed. He now needed only a sign, merely the brief gleam of a light, to bring the moment of destruction to hand. And the moment of his freedom for which he longed.

It was close to ten o'clock that the sign came in a way that it had come before. He was peering into the gloom, marked only by the whitecaps that the steady breeze was picking up. The sea had turned into a peculiar color, a glassy hue like that of a mirror in darkness. There was no moon, yet a sort of luminosity ran below the surface. This was a thing he had often seen when the Greenland ice was coming down. It was said among Gloucestermen that the rapid melting of the bergs and their gradual deposits of earth sometimes created this phosphorescence under sea. It often made the sea brilliant as opals, a brilliance that showed itself only when a keel drove through it. Otherwise it remained a dull sheen.

Now the *Gaunt Woman's* wake gleamed and sparkled. But it was not the only wake.

"Look there, Patrick!" Captain MacLean pointed to another shining lane that lay across their course.

Patrick saw it clearly. A vessel had crossed his bow only a little while before. He could see that it hadn't been a large vessel; for her wake was much narrower than the *Gaunt Woman's*.

"What say, Patrick?" Captain MacLean, closest to the helmsman, made a gesture toward the new wake.

Patrick nodded and they brought the vessel into the wind a little. She slid across the dark patch and ran along the tell-tale wake that curved in sparkling fire towards the peak of the Grand Bank. Patrick watched the seas roll into that gleaming swath and watched it fade away under the brilliant rush piling before the *Gaunt Woman's* bow. He couldn't quite make out the vessel that was leaving the wake. He stared, conscious that with every fathom she sent rolling under her he was nearing a time of conflict, a time when he would make good all that he had sworn. Or suffer a terrible defeat.

A half hour of silent watching passed. No change came in the darkness and the *Gaunt Woman's* heavy gait remained unaltered. But the vessel beyond came into dim view. He saw the thing that was leaving the wake. It was an object not much larger than a dory. Yet it sailed firmly onward, sometimes going altogether out of sight when it ran into a sea, sometimes rising so high that he could catch a shadowy hint of a superstructure. In the end, his seamanship gave him the sign, told him the story. Again he saw the sheen of metal under pouring water, just as he had seen it days before in those very waters.

He said to Captain MacLean: "The U-boat. Slowing up. We'll do without that mainsail now."

"Headsails are enough, Skipper Patrick," said the Newfoundlander at the wheel. "We'll be heading her into the wind soon."

"Headsails let it be then."

Captain MacLean went down to the quarterdeck and the waiting men jumped to their tasks. Soon the vessel began to lose way. Yet she behaved well.

Patrick stepped to the wheel and sent the helmsman to make the first sounding. Soon the word came back: fifty fathom.

"We'll wait a while," said Patrick. "Rig up that working-light over the main hatch and let her burn. Send that German punk up here. See that he carries his signal lamp."

A doryman came aft with their prisoner. Patrick said to him: "Stand by. We're abandoning ship presently and I want you to come along. You want to come along?"

"Yes, Captain."

"Then watch yourself. Do what you're told. Don't get cocky—or I'll split you in two."

"Thirty fathom!" The call came passing down the deck, now full lighted by the electric lamp.

Patrick caught Captain MacLean by the arm and whispered: "Pass the word along that that's the U-boat ahead. At twenty-five fathom we'll put her head to the wind and let her anchor go. Peel their eyes for them, Captain. This is it. My belly is beginning to churn."

The German spoke from the darkness. "What are you doing, Captain, please?"

Patrick flung a word at him. "You speak when you're spoken to. I'm going to abandon ship. We'll drop her hook now and clear off. That's all you need to know."

A man in the lee chains called out: "Twenty-four! Twenty-four!"

Patrick put the helm up hard. The vessel pulled up into the wind, then steadied herself and ran even more slowly ahead. Patrick heard a shout forward and the clanking of her anchor chains.

Captain MacLean came running up from the quarterdeck. "She's down, Patrick!"

"She'll hold. Did you look at the lead?"

"Aye, we're spank on it. This is it."

In a short time, the vessel lost all headway. The strong current seized her. The anchor took hold and the *Gaunt Woman* came to rest.

Patrick went down to the quarterdeck, the German at his heels. Patrick took a turn or two from mizzen to main and back again, striving to keep his calm for the last dreadful minutes. The men were jumpy. He heard one of them curse. He spoke to them, ordered them to break open the main hatch and to rig up the crane. The *Gaunt Woman's* boat and the *Daniel's* dory, which had been taken aboard at Trabo, were let down on the weather side; for he knew that the submarine would tie up on the lee. He had no doubt that he would see her in time. It would be unnatural if she failed to make a signal before she joined the *Gaunt Woman*.

He called the German to his side. He also called

Captain MacLean and said: "Break out that gun of yours, Captain." The captain did so.

Patrick turned to the German. "See that gun? The instant you make a wrong signal—it's going to cut you in pieces. Understand?"

The German, his teeth pressed on his lip, could only nod.

"There's a U-boat sailing out there," said Patrick. "If she doesn't come alongside in the usual manner— you're going to die. If she does come alongside— you're coming with us. A prisoner of war, as I promised. Go ahead! Signal!"

"I don't care if you take her."

Patrick roared in anger and swung his own gun up. "You shut your trap!" He rammed the muzzle against the German's ribs and repeated his order. "Go on! Signal!"

"Kill him, Patrick," said Captain MacLean. "I can signal her all right."

The German began sending. It was only a short message. When it was done, he held the torch down, then repeated it. No answer came out of the dark.

"The weather side, Patrick," said Captain Mac-Lean.

They crossed the deck and again the short signal flashed. At once, a beam of orange-colored light shot across the waves. It sent three or four letters; then went out.

"She will come now," said the German. "To the lee side."

Patrick looked at his watch. It said 11 :20.

"What will you give her to get around, Captain?" he asked. "Ten minutes?"

"Aye! ten. She's not far off."

"Ten more to take on the hawsers and to get settled."

"Lines and hawsers are ready."

"That's well." Patrick shouted: "All hands! All hands! This way, boys! Lively now!"

The Newfoundlanders and the Gloucestermen, who had been gathered on the quarterdeck, came forward. Patrick said: "That sub is coming alongside. The prisoner is going to hail her. No one else say a word. If they hail you—just yell and laugh. The moment you get the hawsers down to them—cut and run for the boats. This ship blows up at midnight sharp. We'll have ten minutes rowing before the *Daniel* picks us up. Now watch yourselves!"

Captain MacLean sang out: "Here she be!"

The U-boat, with her decks submerged and tower clear, appeared directly aft. She was running at slow speed and rising higher and higher out of the water. Patrick saw a small beam play within the tower. It shone briefly on a man's hand; then the tower filled with the orange-colored light. She approached on the lee side and soon came so close that he could see the water shedding off her forward gratings.

"If she starts her Diesels—she's in the bag."

Patrick had no sooner said the words when the engines were clutched in. He heard a whistling rush of air. Her seamen clambered down her ladder and seized the lines tossed to them by the Gloucestermen. The seamen heaved on the lines, then laid hold of the hawsers in silence and without looking up.

A man shouted from the tower.

Patrick lifted his hand and shouted in reply. He turned to the German and said: "Now tell him the captain is coming aboard in a few minutes. Tell him there are five men in irons and that we want six men to bear a hand with the torpedoes." He pushed the muzzle of his gun against the German's side. The German cupped his hands and shouted the message. The officer in the tower asked an angry question. The prisoner, baffled and afraid, turned to Patrick.

"Repeat it," said Patrick. "Tell him the captain will be over the side in a minute or two. Then come with me."

The German obeyed. Patrick took out his watch and said to Captain MacLean: "Twenty minutes to go. Are they in the boats?"

"All over."

"Let's go then." He prodded the German again

and said: "Walk ahead of us, you. And take it easy."

Patrick and Captain MacLean walked slowly behind the German. They were halfway across the quarterdeck when a man, dressed in oil clothing, appeared on the lee bulwarks, his hand on a stay. It was a German from the U-boat. He had a pistol strapped to his waist. Patrick never was able to figure out how the man had reached the chains so easily, unless the sub had rigged up a crane to handle the torpedoes and had put the man aboard from it as a routine precaution.

Patrick whispered to the captain: "I'll take him. Go to the boats!"

The German prisoner had come to a stiff stop. His hands went up in a gesture of dismay. The man on the bulwarks greeted him casually, then turned and shouted a word to the officers below.

It was the last word he ever spoke. He jumped down to the deck, stumbled and fell forward. He laughed and stretched out his hand to push himself up. Patrick stamped on the fingers with his left boot and kicked the man's ribs in with the other. He lifted his gun and smashed at the German's skull. Then Patrick swung him up to his shoulder, carried him to the weather side, and flung him into the water.

Captain MacLean and Heinrich were already in

the dory. The other boat was rowing away. Patrick let himself down into the bow and it sprang away. He turned on his torch and looked at his watch. "Sixteen minutes to go! Put your backs into it!"

Keeping the *Gaunt Woman* between them and the U-boat, the dory sped into the darkness where the *Daniel* was hovering. Patrick let the dory run until it came up with the other boat. He then lifted his torch and began to call the *Daniel*. Twice he sent her name flickering across the waves before a Newfoundlander in the other boat sang out: "Light to port!" That boat swung sharply off and the dory followed.

Patrick signalled again. This time he also saw the answering light. "Hit it hard!" The men at the oars groaned and forged ahead of the other boat. While they ran together, Patrick shouted: "You're rowing for your lives! Board her on the lee side. Let the boat go. Don't bother with it. Row! For God's sake, hit it!"

Patrick knew that his shouts and any noise the men made at their oars could no longer be heard by the men on the sub or the *Woman*. His men began to swear. They groaned when the blades struck deep into the furrows and they groaned again when they sent them sweeping through. Patrick turned and stared at the lighted deck of the *Gaunt Woman*. Nothing moved there yet. He looked down at the swaying, bending bodies of the oarsmen and cried out: "What the hell are you fooling around for? Sweat it!"

They roared back at him and lifted the dory until it flew.

A lantern swung back and forth in the darkness ahead.

"Here she comes, the darling! Now watch it, boys!"

The *Daniel* came swooping in her circle. The oarsmen spent their last ounce in a drive to run alongside her. Patrick grasped a hand held out over her rail and came aboard with the painter in his hands. He jumped aft and found Captain MacLean with one boot on the dory's gunwale. He took his hand, pulled and then lifted him clear and swung him inboard. The other boat spilled its men over the lee rail. They sprawled forward, breathing heavily and half-sobbing in their anger and haste. Some of them stretched out their hands and took hold of the lifelines that had been rigged fore and aft and across her deck.

Patrick waved his hand to the grim faces that stared at him. "Drive her! Crowd it on her!"

He struck Caleb, the helmsman, on the shoulder and cried: "All set aboard her! She blows up any minute now!"

He saw Margaret, straddled on the deck, her hair

dank with spray, her face white with a terrible fear. He said nothing to her, only touched her wet, cold cheek in passing.

Patrick pulled out his watch. It lacked five minutes to twelve. He looked again at the *Gaunt Woman*. Her working-light shone bright as ever and showed him clearly the hull of the U-boat lying against her, while other lights were moving and flashing. In that last glimpse, he saw the gleam of the wet hawsers still in place. He roared with joy and struck his hands together amidst a whirl of spray; for he had feared that, in their impatience and haste, the U-boat men might have gone aboard, despite the signal from the man they had sent up.

Suddenly another squall sprang up and came striking in over the *Daniel's* bow. Caleb yelled in agony as he put the helm hard over, but the vessel failed to answer the rudder and began to fall off heavily. A sea leaped over her forecastle and came thundering down. Patrick saw his men seize the lifelines. Two of them, staring in fascination at the German vessels, climbed into the shrouds and clung there. For what seemed an eternity, the *Daniel* labored under the burden of water; then she shook it off and shot forward again.

Patrick ran to Margaret, where she stood by her father's side.

"You must go below! Both of you!"

Her father shook his head and cried: "Better take it here, Patrick, if it comes. What time is left?"

Patrick, staggering on the deck, managed to turn on his torch and held the watch under it. "Four minutes and a few seconds!"

"Merciful God!" The captain's mouth twisted in pain over his prayer.

Margaret stared down at the wide face of the silver watch. A drop of spray splashed on the crystal, obscuring with its film the slow circling of the minute hand. She sighed deeply and touched the glass with her finger to clear it. The vessel lurched in her slow flight and shipped another sea. The water poured against their boots. She put her hand on his rigid arm. Others came near and stared, some at the watch, some at Patrick's tortured face which told the real time more accurately. He breathed heavily, gave up all pretense to calm. The hand that held the watch trembled.

Caleb called out again. Now his voice showed the strain. His words were piercing thin and high and they came cutting through the hissing and roar of the water. "Are we in the clear yet, Patrick? Are we—in the name of God?"

"Drive her, Caleb, drive her! Every foot counts now."

A Newfoundlander cried out: "How much time be left, Skipper Patrick?"

Patrick stared at the dial. The second hand swung up the circle: 40, 50, 60. He replied: "We're in the last minute now! Watch yourselves! It's going to hit us hard. Stay aboard the vessel. She'll swim it out!"

The watch hand swung down into its last circuit. Mark by mark, it jerked out the last breath of time before the hour of midnight, the hour of the time-bombs. The whispers and the questions ceased. Each man stood silent in his place, moving only to meet the heaving of the deck.

At the half-minute, Patrick sucked in his breath. Once again a drop of moisture fell on the crystal and spattered there. This time the drop came from his forehead, where the sweat poured.

He spoke in a low, hoarse voice. "Five seconds more!"

The repeated words went rattling through the throng until they came to Caleb, braced against the kicking wheel. He cried out a word to the vessel, urging her on.

Margaret placed her hand on her father's shoulder.

The breeze came stronger and the schooner fled. The squall raced off, raced and hit the *Gaunt Woman* momentarily in a flurry of spray and snow.

Caleb sang out: "How much more, Patrick?"

Patrick didn't answer. The second hand reached the end: 50, 55, 60. He slowly pushed the watch back into his pocket and raised his head. He stared out over the sea towards the *Gaunt Woman*. The other heads turned with his. For that moment, the sea stayed as it had been, dark and ribbed with foam. The *Gaunt Woman's* light, serene and gentle, remained unchanged.

The night then vanished in a spread of silvery fire. A pillar of fire ran up into the sky, exploded and fell in a molten flow. The sea shook. The *Daniel* shied in her pace and fell off under the impact of the first blasts. Her deck trembled violently; then it suddenly seemed to fall away beneath their feet. The schooner struggled to regain her buoyancy, but the sledge-hammer blow of the explosion knocked her over until she was almost hove down.

Patrick stretched out his hand to the useless wheel. A black sea struck them. A frothy avalanche poured upon the black water, ran so deep that he saw men vanish under it. He saw Margaret's face, a white mask suspended over the glitter. She made no outcry; only kept her luminous eyes steadily fixed upon his face. He jerked his head upward, held it for a moment above the flood. In that glare beyond, the *Gaunt Woman's* masts stood clear and black and motionless. Her new yards gleamed against a wall of flame and against that same fiery screen the U-boat rode, poised on high like a toy.

The sea shook again. The air split under the thrust

of new explosions, one after another until the whole world bellowed. He saw a globe of red fire rush up into the silvery night. When it burst, a bloody dye poured from it and hundreds of burning things rocketed down into the sea and outward to the horizon.

The onrushing tidal wave struck Patrick's face. He jerked his head upward, held it for a moment more above the flood. A man's whirling body struck against his belly. He thrust an arm down and grasped the empty sleeve of a jacket. He groaned and seized the head by its hair and held on until he could force his leg to one side. A searching hand laid hold of it and clung.

The *Daniel* began to rise. Inch by inch, she fought her way against the tons of water. At last, she emerged and the seas poured off her in a cataract. The uproar waned beyond. A wave, tipped with tongues of fire, began to roll from the churning water.

The sea itself then seemed to burst. Three huge spouts of steaming water ran skyward and the air between the spouts caught fire so that a new wall of flame was raised. This time the explosions took place within the shattered hull of the U-boat. She blew apart. Shafts of yellow and blue light struck through the fragments of the vessel. Their heat consumed the fragments of the *Gaunt Woman* before they could fall. Clouds of vapor, tinged with flames of scarlet, rushed back and forth and thin rivulets of burning liquid gushed up like lava.

The blows of the last explosions ran through the sea with such force that the *Daniel* lurched again. The fire-tipped wave, increasing in height as other blasts forced it upward, sprang after the fleeing schooner with a speed greater than the wind's. A hot cyclone ran before the wave. It bore strange, choking odors, spewed up from the sulphuric acid of the U-boat batteries. The hot wind consumed the air on the face of the water. The *Daniel's* crowded sails cracked, filled again, and once more sent her driving along her course. The burning wave fell behind. A pall of black smoke flowed over the spot where the *Gaunt Woman* and the last of her pack had perished. Soon the smoke began to move off before the wind. In a little while, there was nothing visible except one small yellow flame, burning like a campfire on a plain at night.

Patrick, straddled on the clearing decks, lifted Captain MacLean to his feet. He looked from face to face, saw Margaret's, saw the weary faces of all his men. He lifted his clenched hands in a gesture of malediction. "So perish the enemies of free men!"

The others neither stirred nor spoke. They stood in their places, suiting their rhythmic sway to the sway of the vessel. They stared spellbound at the little fire.

They turned their heads slowly and stared at the livid mask of his face.

A man spoke the name of the vanquished vessel. "The *Gaunt Woman*!"

A Newfoundlander cried: "She be gone to hell, Skipper Patrick, where she do belong."

"Aye!" whispered Patrick. "And may God have mercy on their souls!"

He turned to Caleb and said: "Trabo!"

"Trabo, Cap'n?"

"Trabo for herring. If the herring boats are in."

Caleb stared at his young skipper for a moment; then he let his mouth open and the gale of his laughter swept among them. He put the helm down hard and shouted: "Trabo! Trabo he wants! Trabo for bait!"

The Gloucestermen on the shrouds, stretched like crucified men against the lightening sky, repeated the laughter and shouted down to Patrick.

He looked up solemnly. "Aye! Trabo! Why not? I'm not forgetting there's old Mister Dolan back home at Gloucester waiting for his thirty thousand pounds of halibut. 'Twon't take long. After the ice gets by."

Captain MacLean stretched out his hand and laid it gently on Patrick's shoulder. "No," he said in a tender tone, " 'twon't take long, lad. But you go below and stretch out for a time. We'll take her to Trabo."

Patrick went below. He went slowly, step after step, down the companionway. He watched Margaret bending over a wounded Newfoundlander stretched in his own bunk. Her arms, bared to the elbow, moved back and forth, up and down, as she renewed the bandage on his shoulder. Patrick heard her murmur comforting words and he saw the man's lips move stiffly in a question.

She replied: "No, Jonathan, no! You'll be fishing again in a week. But now you must sleep." She lifted his head and held a glass to his lips.

Patrick leaned against the bulkhead. He relished in his heart this retirement from the clamoring sea and the laughter of his men, exultant in their victory. Hitherto his hatred of the *Gaunt Woman* had filled him almost to the brim, leaving too little room for all things else. Now the *Gaunt Woman* blew, a cloud of gas, across the Grand Bank, as he himself had foretold in the hardihood of his hate. And Skalder—well! he would say a decent prayer over that man and give him a Christian's grave, no matter what he had been in life.

Those images departed and others, the images of peace, took their place. He became happier and happier, merely by standing there and watching the bend and unbending of her arms and shoulders under the folds of her blouse. He looked away from her, looked almost drowsily at the lamp again. He blinked childishly at its yellow flame and at the kettle, noisy on the stove. He gazed at his father's picture beyond the lamp and smiled solemnly at the sea-wise face behind the glass. Patrick said to the picture: "Did I not do well against our old enemy?" The serene eyes sent him the signal: "Well done, my son!"

She turned then and saw him waiting for her. He took a step toward her and she took one toward him, so that they met in the downward flow of lamplight. He placed his hands on her shoulders, held her at arm's length to search her eyes. All the dark of anger and the dark of fear had gone from them and they were gray again, gray and peaceful as the sea under a summer rain. When he saw this change in her, he drew her in silence toward him and she, also keeping their silence, came close to him. He raised his hand to brush away the wet strand of hair that gleamed upon her forehead. He kissed her forehead and she lifted her hand and held it fondly against his flat, unshaven cheek.

He whispered: "I have given orders for Trabo, Maggie."

"Trabo!" She reported the name in a dreamlike way. "Trabo!" And: "It is over now, Patrick. Now, indeed, is it all over."

A man on deck shouted: "That's well, lad! Ah, that's well!" A louder voice aloft replied cheerily.

Patrick said: "Indeed, it is all over, Maggie. The

job is done. Mine and yours—and we are saved. By you."

"By you, Patrick!"

Now the schooner, settled in her new course, struck lightly into the seas. He smiled at the new pace and said: "They're crowding it on her. It won't be long before we see the hills again and then—I'll have to leave you there, Maggie darling, with all your patients while I fill old Dolan's pens for him. It won't take long, if the herring-boats are in at Trabo."

She stirred in his arms. He heard her sigh. "No, not long, Patrick. There's time now."

"And when I come back to Trabo, you'll come aboard the *Daniel*—won't you, Maggie? You and your great father. And we'll sail back to Gloucester to get old Dolan's blessing and his permission to stand before a priest. You want that, Maggie MacLean, don't you?"

"I do."

"With all your heart?"

"With all my heart."

"You'll be a Navy wife—after a little while!"

"I am willing to be, Patrick. Ready to wait and watch as my mother watched before me."

A sombre look came over his dark face. "Yes, wait and watch. Until the greater victory is won and there's peace again in the world and on the Grand Banks. And even then—even then, Maggie, there'll always be waiting and watching for my wife. Waiting for the *Daniel* to come home through the ice of winter and the bergs of spring—"

She lifted her lips to his mouth and whispered again: "With all my heart, Patrick Bannon. I know! I know the *Daniel* must always go to sea and there must always be a Bannon to take her there. And safely home again."

A sea sprang over the weather rail and struck with a bellow against the skylight. The *Daniel* soared upward in triumphant strength and flung off the burden.